MADAME DU BARRY

Marie Jeanne Bécu was but the illegitimate daughter of a humble cook yet, by the time she was 23, she had become Madame du Barry and the official mistress of King Louis XV of France. This is the dream-like story of a woman who, by virtue of her exceptional and seductive beauty, her enchanting wit and her unfailing good nature, came to govern the monarch.

Yet her life at court had its setbacks for Madame du Barry incurred the jealousy of Madame du Pompadour and many others who constantly sought to usurp her. Then, when Louis XV died, her power dissipated and it was not long before she was obliged to retire to the beautiful mansion of Luciennes which the King had built for her. Even so, there was worse to come for in 1789 the French Revolution cast its long shadow and her very life was in danger.

In her own inimitable and masterly fashion, Jean Plaidy relates the moving story of this remarkable beauty and wit who dazzled king and commoner alike.

Jean Plaidy also wrote

The Norman Trilogy
THE BASTARD KING
THE LION OF JUSTICE
THE PASSIONATE ENEMIES

The Plantagenet Saga
PLANTAGENET PRELUDE
THE REVOLT OF THE EAGLETS
THE HEART OF THE LION
THE PRINCE OF DARKNESS
THE BATTLE OF THE QUEENS
THE QUEEN FROM PROVENCE
EDWARD LONGSHANKS
THE FOLLIES OF THE KING
THE VOW OF THE HERON
PASSAGE TO PONTEFRACT
THE STAR OF LANCASTER
EPITAPH FOR THREE WOMEN
RED ROSE OF ANJOU
THE SUN IN SPLENDOUR

The Tudor Novels
UNEASY LIES THE HEAD
KATHARINE, THE VIRGIN WIDOW ⎫ Also available in one volume:
THE SHADOW OF THE POMEGRANATE ⎬ KATHARINE OF ARAGON
THE KING'S SECRET MATTER ⎭
MURDER MOST ROYAL (Anne Boleyn and Catherine Howard)
ST THOMAS'S EVE (Sir Thomas More)
THE SIXTH WIFE (Katharine Parr)
THE THISTLE AND THE ROSE (Margaret Tudor and James IV)
MARY, QUEEN OF FRANCE (Queen of Louis XII)
THE SPANISH BRIDEGROOM (Philip II and his first three wives)
GAY LORD ROBERT (Elizabeth and Leicester)

The Mary Queen of Scots Series
ROYAL ROAD TO FOTHERINGAY
THE CAPTIVE QUEEN OF SCOTS

The Stuart Saga
THE MURDER IN THE TOWER (Robert Carr and the Countess of Essex)
THE WANDERING PRINCE ⎫
A HEALTH UNTO HIS MAJESTY ⎬ Also available in one volume:
HERE LIES OUR SOVEREIGN LORD ⎭ CHARLES II
THE THREE CROWNS ⎫
(William of Orange) ⎪
THE HAUNTED SISTERS ⎬ Also available in one volume:
(Mary and Anne) ⎪ THE LAST OF THE STUARTS
THE QUEEN'S FAVOURITES ⎭
(Sarah Churchill and Abigail Hill)

The Georgian Saga
THE PRINCESS OF CELLE (Sophia Dorothea and George I)
QUEEN IN WAITING ⎫
CAROLINE THE QUEEN ⎬ Caroline of Ansbach
THE PRINCE AND THE QUAKERESS (George III and Hannah Lightfoot)
THE THIRD GEORGE
PERDITA'S PRINCE (Perdita Robinson)
SWEET LASS OF RICHMOND HILL (Mrs Fitzherbert)
INDISCRETIONS OF THE QUEEN (Caroline of Brunswick)
(continued on page 256)

JEAN PLAIDY

Madame du Barry

ROBERT HALE · LONDON

ISBN 0 7090 5329 0

Robert Hale Limited
Clerkenwell House
Clerkenwell Green
London EC1R 0HT

Printed and bound in Great Britain by
Mackays, Chatham, Kent

CONTENTS

CHAPTER		PAGE
1	*Coucher* at Versailles	7
2	The Duc de Choiseul	30
3	Jeanne Bécu	50
4	Supper at Versailles	78
5	Consternation at Court	100
6	The Marriage	111
7	Apartments in Versailles	130
8	To Be or Not To Be—Presented	151
9	*Maîtresse en Titre*	173
10	The Dauphine at Versailles	184
11	The Defeat of Choiseul	195
12	Enemies at Chanteloup and Versailles	202
13	The Passing of Louis	216
14	The Pont-aux-dames and Saint Vrain	223
15	Louveciennes	230
16	The Place de la Révolution	240

WORKS CONSULTED

Memoirs of Madame du Barry	Pidansat de Mairobert. Edited with an Introduction by Eveline Cruickshanks.
The Life and Times of Madame du Barry	Robert B. Douglas.
Louis the Fifteenth and His Times	Pierre Gaxotte. Translated from the French by J. Lewis May.
Memoirs of Madame du Barri	
The Du Barry	Karl Von Schumacher. Translated by Dorothy M. Richardson.
The Real Louis the Fifteenth, 2 Vols.	Lieut.-Colonel Andrew C. P. Haggard, D.S.O.
The King's Pleasure	Iain D. B. Pilkington.
The National History of France— The Eighteenth Century	Casimir Stryienski. Translated by H. N. Dickinson. Edited by Fr. Funck-Brentano. With an Introduction by J. E. C. Bodley.
The History of France	M. Guizot. Translated by Robert Black, M.A.
Portraits of the Eighteenth Century	C. A. Sainte-Beuve. Translated by Katharine P. Wormeley.
Women of the Revolutionary Era	Lieut.-Colonel Andrew C. P. Haggard, D.S.O.
Personal Characteristics from French History	Baron Ferdinand Rothschild, M.P.
Versailles	Ian Dunlop. With a foreword by Sir Arthur Bryant.
Louis XV—The Monarchy in Decline	G. P. Gooch, C.H., D.Litt., F.B.A.

1

COUCHER AT VERSAILLES

IT was the hour of the *coucher* in the Palace of Versailles. The brilliant candelabra suspended from the ceiling lightened the deep purple and brocade of the hangings; everything was in its place, for there must be no faltering, no hitch; such would be unthinkable in the formal atmosphere of the Court. There, laid out in readiness was the bedgown, made of white Lyons silk, and delicately embroidered; there was the robe of lace and brocade with slippers to match; while the nightcap and handkerchief were lying on a purple velvet cushion.

The King was silent, and naturally the gentlemen of the bedchamber must reflect his mood. One of them—the Duc de Choiseul—ventured to address him.

"Did the King enjoy the day's hunt?" he asked, etiquette at this important ceremony demanding that the King should be referred to in the third person.

The King grunted an affirmative, although he looked as though he would never enjoy anything again.

As the white Lyons silk was slipped over his shoulders courtier exchanged glance with courtier. There was no doubt about it; His Most Christian Majesty was growing more and more melancholy with the passing of each day.

Should they make a light joke, a witty quip such as the King had once delighted in? Better not. Since the death of Madame de Pompadour he had changed. Gone were those days when he had held little supper-parties in the *petits*

7

appartements and there had been such rivalry to acquire an invitation. Those had been the days when he had commanded that his table should be laid with gold plate and such oddities as the basket of fresh eggs on which was perched a life-sized hen fashioned in gold and enamel, and had himself sat affably among his guests, for in the *petits appartements* Louis *le Bien-Aimé* had been a different man from the somewhat reserved monarch who appeared on ceremonial occasions.

It had been necessary of course to be a friend of Madame de Pompadour to obtain admission, for she it was who had ruled the King, and Louis, being by nature an indolent man —except in the hunting of wild animals and women, at which sports he had been as indefatigable as most of his forebears—was content that this should be so.

And after the suppers, during which the talk would be of the hunt and *amours*, there might be a theatrical show in which Madame de Pompadour would excel. In the old days Louis had often invited his Queen to attend a performance and she—that meek and long-suffering woman who had had to learn that at the dazzling Court of Versailles a King's cherished mistress took precedence over the wife whom reasons of State had forced him to marry—had accepted invitations now and then and graced the occasion with her presence.

But now the Queen was dead, the Dauphin was dead; and Madame de Pompadour herself was dead. Her body had been taken in solemn procession from Notre-Dame de Versailles to Paris; the wind had howled, the rain had fallen heavily and, as Louis had stood at the window of his *cabinet intime* and had looked out on the procession, his grief was as stormy as the weather, sobs shaking his body, and tears falling down his cheeks.

Monsieur Le Bel, the chief of his *valets de chambre*, liked to recall the King's emotion at that time. Le Bel should know, for it was said of him that he shared the King's secrets as did no other man of the Court. It was Le Bel who had led many a young girl up the private staircase after the solemn ceremony of the *coucher*, when Louis had been wont to leave the state bed in the state apartment—which was in any case very cold in winter—for a smaller and more cosy chamber.

Louis, said Le Bel, had suddenly wiped the tears from his eyes, controlled his sobs, and it was as though he had made up his mind that he must become accustomed to a life which was not ruled by the Marquise de Pompadour.

"The poor Marquise is having bad weather for the journey to Paris," said Louis almost conversationally; and Le Bel had rejoiced. His Majesty would recover from his grief.

But melancholy persisted. At Louis' age it was not easy to change. Every man who dreamed of the power which would come to him through the King was determined that the place of La Pompadour must be filled; and it must be filled with a woman who would not forget the friends who had helped her to acquire the most important and powerful role at the Court of France.

The Duc de Richelieu, partly to amuse the King, partly to anger Choiseul, began to talk of that exquisite creature— the Comtesse d'Esparbès.

A faint flicker of interest gleamed in Louis' eyes, but it was momentary and even before Choiseul could cut short Richelieu's praise of the Comtesse with eulogies of his own sister—whom he had recently married to the Duc de Gramont, that old, debauched but extremely wealthy noble-man—Louis was yawning and his eyes had turned languidly to his nightcap lying on the velvet cushion.

Indeed there was a change. Could it be that he still yearned for Pompadour, the woman who had been *maîtresse en titre* for eighteen years? It was impossible. The entire Court knew that for several years before her death she had borne the title in name only.

The King was growing old—that was apparent to every man in attendance at the *coucher*, including Choiseul who, on this occasion, had the honour of holding the candle as the King was lighted to his bed, and Richelieu who jealously watched him. They were all thinking that a new mistress must be provided for the King; and that if she were sufficiently skilled, beautiful and malleable in the hands of her promoters, what great good she could bring to them.

Meanwhile Louis XV of France was lighted to his solitary bed.

"My youth is past," murmured the King to himself when he was alone, "and it is not the fact that I can no longer compete with myself as a younger man which makes me melancholy, but that I should feel this lassitude which makes me think I almost do not care."

The eyes of age did not see as had the eyes of youth. Nothing held the same enchantment, whether it was a beautiful painting, a beautiful building, or a beautiful woman. Once this room had delighted him, for he had designed it himself. The state bed of Great-grandfather Louis XIV had not pleased him, and he had often retired (after the *coucher*, of course, and always remembering to be back in the state bed for the *lever*) to the Cabinet du Conseil, and a comfortable warmer bed and a pleasant companion. Thus he had decided that he would build a bedroom of his own. A beautiful room it was to be, decorated by the sculptor Verberckt, and he would have his own apartments surrounding this bedroom; and this he had done, and thus had been created the *petits appartements*, the construction of which had made the reputations of such artists as Verberckt, Rousseau and Le Brun.

As a young King of seventeen, adulation following him wherever he went, he had first become aware of the beauty of stone.

Versailles! The creation of that fabulous great-grand-father, the days of whose glory were still spoken of with awe!

Now lying in his bed he could recall but hazily the last time he had seen his great-grandfather. It was like a picture seem from a distance, its colours blurred. There was the state bed with the old man in it, his face serene yet lined with pain; a priest was kneeling at the balustrade before the foot of the bed, which kept people from coming too near. There had seemed to be many women weeping in the room; he could recall their air of solemnity, the faint sickly smell of death.

It was August, and the windows were open, and from below them rose the music of hautboys and drums.

Madame de Ventadour, his governess, had come to him and told him that his great-grandfather wished to see him, and the manner in which she took his hand was different. And he—he was aware of a great excitement, of a sense of great events about to occur. Had he really felt that, or had he imagined it afterwards? Could he, so young, so ignorant, have realised that, although he was five-and-a-half years old, he was soon to be the King of France?

He thought of the man in bed—the great King come to the end of his life, now unable to leave his bed because of the gangrene in his leg. This was the King who had once enchanted the Court by his performance in the ballet, the handsomest King of France, the creator of Versailles, all its beauties and all its follies . . . *le Roi Soleil.*

Madame de Ventadour had lifted him on to the bed at the request of the dying King, and the old man had taken the dimpled hand of the boy who was to be King, while a tender sorrow came into his eyes.

"You are going to be a great King, little Louis," he said. "Do not be too ready to go to war—as I have been. You must not follow my example in that—nor must you fritter away the nation's wealth in building as I have done. Look after the people instead, my child. Relieve their suffering.

That is what you must do. My beloved child, I give you my blessing."

It was a solemn moment. Was it for me? wondered fifty-eight-year-old Louis. Did I understand that one King was passing on his crown to another, or did I merely wait patiently for the embrace to end because I did not like the touch, the feel of the aged?

For young people did not like the touch, the feel of the aged—unless of course they were old enough to realise what advantages could accompany them.

The touch of a King can cure repulsion as it does King's Evil, thought the King, smiling grimly into the dimness of his bedchamber.

Memory persisted. He had not followed his great-grandfather's advice, for the love of fine buildings was in his blood as it appeared to be in that of all the Bourbons. That was one of the reasons why he missed La Pompadour so sadly. What joy it had been to plan together the châteaux they would build. He thought of the result of those enchanting hours of exchanging ideas, of planning and replanning. There was the delicious Petit Château at Choisy and the two Châteaux of Saint Hubert and La Muette; there were those charming hunting places at Fausse Repose and Saclay; and there was that little gem yet to outshine all gems: Petit Trianon.

Certainly he had not followed his great-grandfather's advice.

With this strange mood upon him he thought with remorse of that extravagance. He had bought the Château de Crécy-Couvé for La Pompadour. He began to calculate; that must have been nearly twenty years ago; he remembered how 700,000 livres had been spent on that place. Shortly after he had built the Hermitage at Versailles; then there were the Hermitages of Fontainebleau and Compiègne besides La Celle St. Cloud. Even then his extravagant mistress was not satisfied and she must have Château de Bellevue. But why blame Pompadour? It was he who had loved these master-pieces in stone, even as had his great-grandfather. He had squandered the nation's wealth on this hobby, in spite of the warning of Louis XIV; and because, while he lavished such vast expenditure on these stone goddesses, poverty had overtaken his suffering subjects, the name of Well-Beloved, which they had given him when he had been a young and charming boy from whom they hoped for so much, had become a mockery.

Images flashed in and out of his mind. There was that day when he had discovered a pamphlet on the floor of his bed-chamber, and had read:

"Louis, if we once loved you it was because we had not discovered all your vices."

Such words sent a shiver down his spine, but only momen-tarily; he felt so safe, so secure in the gilded splendour of Versailles.

He remembered too that note which had been posted on the walls of the Louvre. The words seemed branded on his brain even now.

"*Crains notre désespoir; la noblesse a des Guises,
Paris des Ravaillacs, le clergé des Cléments.*"

This had been a reminder of how the Guises had once risen against the Crown, of the assassins of Henri Trois and Henri Quatre.

He had not thought a great deal of these words at the time, though he knew there was discontent in Paris. He had heard that women had gathered in crowds at the Pont de la Tournelle crying: "We are dying of hunger. Give us bread." He knew that a man had climbed on to the Queen's coach and had thrown a piece of black bread into her lap, crying out that this unwholesome stuff was what they were asked to pay such a high price for. Distressing, it had seemed, but it did not prevent a pleasure-loving monarch from planning alterations to his palaces, from laying out new and more exquisite gardens.

Then had occurred the *affaire* Damiens.

He had been leaving Versailles for Paris and had come down from the *petits appartements* by way of le Petit Escalier du Roi to the Cour des Cerfs; he made a habit of using this little staircase which was a short cut and much quicker than coming down by way of the Escalier de la Reine. He had crossed the Salle des Gardes to the Cour Royale, where his coach was waiting for him and, as he emerged into the courtyard, Damiens had rushed at him and stabbed him with a hunting knife.

It had happened so quickly that those about him were not immediately aware of what had happened. It was only when he gasped out that he had been stabbed and pointed at the escaping Damiens, that the would-be assassin had been caught.

He had believed at first that the dagger had been poisoned though Lasmartes, his huntsman, examining the wound, declared that in four days they would bring home a fine deer from the woods together. He did not then believe Lasmartes, thinking that the good fellow sought to comfort him. But Lasmartes was not far wrong; the wound was soon healed and he was well again.

But the people of Paris did not care for his well-being as they had once cared. When he had been seriously ill at Metz, thirteen years before, the nation had been plunged into sorrow; then he had been Louis le Bien-Aimé. Since then he had taken Jeanne Antoinette Poisson and made her la Marquise de Pompadour; he had allowed her to rule him and the country, as the people thought, to the disaster of both. And the price of bread had risen beyond the means of many of his suffering people.

Damiens had paid a high price for what he had done.

This out-of-work lackey from Artois was weak in the head, but that had not saved him. He was condemned to a horrible death even as had been the murderer of Henri Quatre. Hanged, drawn and quartered! It was a hideous spectacle and one which filled the people with disgust and horror. Louis had heard that his executioners took an hour and a quarter to kill Damiens, and that the man watched the grim preparations for his end for half an hour on the scaffold before the ghastly operation began.

When Ravaillac had died—suffering even greater torment than Damiens—the people had cheered and called abuse and delighted in his sufferings. He was deranged, even as Damiens was, but he had killed the greatest King that France had known, the beloved of the people; and Damiens—he had merely attempted to kill a King who was fast becoming unpopular.

So the people did not applaud the execution of Damiens; moreover times had changed, and these Parisians were more cultured than those of the preceding century. There had been however one woman who, seeking to curry favour with the King, watched the foul and barbarous ceremony intently throughout.

Louis shuddered even now to think of that woman. "The disgusting creature!" he said now, as he had then.

That was a time he would never forget; a scene to return to a man when he was lonely at night.

The growing unpopularity, the state of the treasury, and a dissatisfied people who starved in the streets and no longer called "*Vive le Roi*" when the royal coach clattered by; all these things made the times uneasy, and they would grow more so. People no longer had the same reverence for royalty.

"But I am growing old," said the King into his pillows, "and it will last my time."

.   .   .   .   .

Still sleep would not come; and rather than consider the state of the treasury, or the feelings of the people, it was better to turn his mind to pleasanter subjects. Love! He would think of love. He tried to look back over the years and saw a procession of women; there were so many whose faces he could not remember.

He thought of the rivalry which had existed between the Chantilly and Rambouillet factions; and how each side had sought to win his favours by providing him with a mistress who would look after their interests.

Louis knew of their machinations; he smiled now to recall them; he enjoyed their manœuvres; essentially a lazy man he liked his mistresses to be found for him.

It was at Rambouillet that he met the Comtesse de Mailly; and that was a pleasant interlude. She was so demure, so devoted, and behaved more like a nun than a King's mistress. But of course one eventually grew a little weary of such modesty and devotion; Great-grandfather Louis had found the same qualities in little Louise de la Vallière; and the same eventual ennui; it was not such modest women who could continue to delight the Kings of France; and he had turned from the little Mailly to her sister, Madame de Vinti-mille, who was different. Ah yes, ambitious and something of a virago; the people had hated *her*. He remembered the day she was buried and how the news was brought to him that the people had shouted insults after her funeral cortège. And the little Mailly, fearing he might be suffering on account of her rival's death, had come to comfort him.

He had a fancy for that family. Had not Great-grand-father felt a similar affection for a family of girls—the beautiful Mancinis! There was yet another sister, Marie-Anne, the delightful widow of the Marquis de la Tournelle. She had charmed him more than any woman he had known up to that time. She had been a fire-brand, a woman who knew her own mind. One of the first things she had insisted on was that her sister should be dismissed from the Court!

He laughed now at the thought of her. He could remember her clearly because there was the Nattier portrait to remind him. She was vivacious and her blue eyes sparkled with enthusiasm when she talked excitedly of what she wanted.

He had allowed himself to fall under her influence perhaps because he knew that the course she insisted on his following was designed by Richelieu and Noailles. He had made her Duchesse de Châteauroux, but she was in time replaced by the all-powerful Marquise de Pompadour.

If he had allowed La Châteauroux to beckon him along the road she wished him to go, he had allowed La Pompadour to take his hand and lead him her way. He had given her honours, titles, riches, all that she asked; even that great honour of the *tabouret* had been hers—the highest honour of the Court which enabled her to sit down at the Grand Couvert and all Court ceremonies. Never had this honour been bestowed on a commoner before, and the noblemen and women of the Court were aghast.

Louis had snapped his fingers at them. He was ready to brave them all for the sake of his mistress; he wanted them to know that if they wished for honours at his Court they must first pay homage to his mistress. The Dauphin had been furious, they had quarrelled, and their relationship had never been on a really friendly footing since; it was only because the Dauphin was so sensible of his duty that in public they appeared to be on the best of terms.

"He would have made a better King than I!" sighed Louis. Alas, now he was dead and the heir to the throne of France was that shuffling boy, *gauche*, quite unattractive, happier in the company of builders and locksmiths than in that of his equals.

"What will become of *him* when I am gone?" Louis asked of the darkness. "What will become of France?"

But he was supposed to be brooding pleasantly on his loves of the past.

There had been the *Parc aux Cerfs*—that establishment which he knew was spoken of in shocked tones in the streets of the capital.

But what was the *Parc aux Cerfs*? Merely a house in the quiet environs of Versailles, a house in which Le Bel installed those young women who he thought could restore his master's jaded appetite and rouse him from his interminable boredom.

In the King's eyes there was nothing shocking about that. The girls came willingly enough, and it was not true to say he kept a harem there; there would be two—or three—perhaps four or five or even six. And these charming girls considered themselves honoured and indeed fortunate, for when they left the *Parc aux Cerfs* they were given dowries which were handsome enough to make them very desirable *parties*.

The *Parc aux Cerfs* had existed in the time of Madame de Pompadour, with her approval; she had ceased to share his bed at that time, and the relationship between them was one of great friendship—and all the stronger for that. He had needed her friendship; he had found it comforting to mount the stairs to her apartments, to know that she was always there. He did not expect her to provide the entertainments which awaited him at the *Parc aux Cerfs*; that was for the young women who had their youth and beauty to offer him; he had always realised that La Pompadour had had more than that.

He had closed the *Parc aux Cerfs* three years before, for after the death of La Pompadour and the Dauphin he declared that he had little taste for such activities.

Was this really the case, or was it because he was growing old and was losing his zest for the pleasures of life?

So thoughts of love brought him back to his melancholy

observations on the loss of his youth; and now from thoughts of the women whom he had loved he turned to his family. Yet he could only think of his family with mild distaste, for there was not one of them for whom he had any real affection.

"Royal marriages!" he grumbled. "Matters of convenience. It is not our Queens whom we love. Poor Queens, forced into marriage even as we are. What chances have they of pleasing us when they are in competition with the exquisite Châteauroux and dazzling Pompadour and their like?"

His Queen had tried to please him. Well she might. She, the daughter of the dethroned King of Poland, to marry with the King of France! Marie herself once told him how she had first heard the news.

"We were living precariously," she said. "We had nothing. It was all charity for us since my father lost his throne. Philip Weber, a Councillor of the Elector Palatine, allowed us to use his house at Wissembourg; and here we lived uncertain how long we should be able to stay. My father tried to live as a King, and he had a few faithful friends who made our little Court, but he could never forget that he had been dispossessed of his kingdom. He was very sad, and as we loved him dearly we also were sad. And one day he summoned us all to his presence and made us kneel at once to give thanks to God. When I rose from my knees I ran to embrace him, for there was always great tenderness between us. I said: 'Father, so your throne is restored to you.' And he answered: 'No, my child. There is better news even than that. You are to be Queen of France.'"

Poor Marie! Was it such good fortune?

In the first place she had been six years older than he was, and six years was a great deal when a bridegroom was fifteen. Those about him had chosen her because they believed that

she who had been brought up in simplicity would not interfere with their schemes. They wanted a Queen in whom
they could arouse a sense of inferiority. Madame de Prie was
in whole-hearted support of the marriage, and Madame de
Prie was in complete command of the Duc de Bourbon who
had been made Prime Minister because he was a member
of the royal family. There had been, of course, many who
opposed the match, who could not understand why it had
been made.

A *mésalliance*, it was called in some quarters. He was the
first King, said others, to marry a simple *demoiselle*.

Oh, those pamphleteers! How they exulted in a situation
which gave them scope for their satirical verses! They had
lampooned the Queen, Madame de Prie and the Duc de
Bourbon. As for himself—their charming fifteen-year-old
King—he could do no wrong in those days; they said he
was in the hands of the schemers—their little King, Louis
the Well-Beloved. Now, of course, it was a different matter.

He remembered how he had waited in trembling apprehension to meet his Queen, for rumour had it that she was
deformed and hideous, that her feet and hands were webbed,
that she suffered from scrofula, that she was epileptic, that
she was a monster. It had been such a relief to meet the
somewhat raw-boned plain young woman that, in those first
weeks of marriage, he had thought her beautiful.

Considering her, now that she was so recently dead and
he so much older and perhaps wiser, he realised that he had
not been unfortunate in his marriage. When he studied La
Tour's portrait of her, he saw a charm in her face which
during her lifetime he had not noticed. She was intelligent
and kind, plain of course, quite unexciting; but she had
borne his children and she had loved him as he had not
been able to love her.

Their first meeting. It was at Moret at a spot which had
from that moment been called Le Carrefour de la Reine,

for he had had a small monument set up there to mark the spot. The weather had been appalling, and he remembered now how the mud had spattered his fine clothes and those of his courtiers. Then he had seen her, and in his overwhelming relief had embraced her with a fervour which astonished all those who looked on, and so won the heart of the trembling Marie that she adored him from that moment.

There had followed the marriage at Fontainebleau and all the Bourbon glitter and Bourbon pomp of dazzling jewels and brilliant raiment. He remembered Marie in purple velvet and ermine and how the proud Princesses of France were a little piqued because they were obliged to hold the train of the little upstart.

What he remembered more clearly than anything was that moment when the Duc de Montemart gave Marie the velvet-covered casket in which were the trinkets which she was to distribute to her household—the traditional *corbeille*.

"It is the first time," Marie had said simply, "that I have ever been able to give presents."

He had warmed towards her then—she was so lacking in affectation, so delighted to be able to bring such good fortune to her family through her marriage. He had not been able to concentrate on the Molière play which had followed, because he was thinking so tenderly of his bride.

She loved her father dearly and on the marriage Louis had given permission for her parents to come to France. They had stayed at the Château de Chambord, and Marie could not express sufficiently her rapture, her gratitude. What pleasure he had derived from watching her joy! If only he could find such pleasure now!

The honeymoon at Fontainebleau had been a great success. Foolish Marie! Had she been a wise woman such as La Pompadour she might have recognised the great opportunity she had then of ruling her husband. But she believed—and her father believed this also—that it was not the fifteen-year-old King whom she must obey, but her benefactor the Duc de Bourbon.

But Cardinal Fleury, who had been Louis' tutor and had great influence with him, was determined that the Duc should go; and when he had achieved his ends—and it should have been obvious to any wise man or woman that he would eventually achieve his ends—the Queen's chance of being the great influence in her husband's life was over.

Louis had tired of her; he was already discovering the enchantments of other ladies of the Court. Poor Marie! She was doomed to become yet another neglected Queen of France.

This very year she had died and that was why, lying in his solitary bed, he was thinking more of her now than he had for many years.

There was his family; and his family should delight a man. Marie had been a fertile woman, but it was a pity her ten children had been mostly girls, although she had given him the Dauphin. But it was better not to think of the Dauphin. The coldness between them had been uncomfortable and now he was dead. He would say it was a great tragedy, and leave it at that. What a King he would have made! And now there in his place was that shuffling, uncouth locksmith —the Dauphin's eldest son, and Louis' grandson, the heir to the throne of France.

What will become of him? What will become of France? Such foolish thoughts these were to come in the dead of night to a King who has ruled badly and who knows that the state of his country's wretchedness is in some measure due to himself. There is only one consolation, if that King is determined to suppress his apprehension: "It will last my lifetime." Perhaps he was not entirely selfish. Perhaps he had not completely subdued his conscience, and this was why he could scarcely bear the shy young heir to the throne to come into his presence.

The Dauphin was born in . . . it must have been 1729. The third royal birth. There were the twins, Louise-Elisabeth and Anne-Henriette first and after them a girl who had died. Then great rejoicing throughout the kingdom: Louis the Well-Beloved has his heir—a fine boy.

And a fine boy the Dauphin had been. It was France's tragedy that Fate had not allowed him to come to the throne. Would he have been able to set the frail ship of State on a straight and successful course once again? Who knew? Sometimes, in the quiet of the night, when the King was at his most perceptive, it seemed to him that there was no way to elude the steady march of events. A people will not suffer indefinitely; and the philosophers and the writers were busy. Oh, how mighty were the weapons wielded by these men who betrayed the existence of the cancers in the diseased body of the kingdom! "Cut them out," the writers were warning. "People of France, replace tyranny with liberty."

He had tossed about so much that his silk nightcap had fallen over one eye, but he felt too indifferent to push it back.

Stupid Louis, he thought; how can you hope to control a kingdom when you cannot control your thoughts?

Where was he? Ah, the family. His big family among which there must be surely one to delight a lonely old man.

The Dauphin should have been that one, but of course in his lifetime they had not appreciated him. He was too reserved, and he resembled his mother in that. He was pious too—continually so, not only, thought Louis wryly, when he was ill and feared he might not be long for this world. No, the Dauphin had been truly religious, and had concerned himself with the welfare of the people; *sérieux*, something of a statesman, it would have been a comfort to have felt he was waiting there to take the throne.

The Dauphin had married twice, first Marie Thérèse Raphaëlle, the Infanta of Spain, who had died soon after the marriage, and then Marie-Josèphe of Saxony, who had proved to be a model wife for this model Dauphin, although at first she had doubtless found him a cold husband.

But there was young Anne-Henriette, the Dauphin's elder sister, to take Marie-Josèphe under her wing and teach her how to understand not only her husband but her new country, so that very soon the discerning were praising the Dauphine no less than the Dauphin.

The Dauphin had been but thirty-seven when he died; and he had known before his death that it could not be long delayed. Suffering from pulmonary tuberculosis he had continued in his State duties to the end, giving as little trouble to those who served him as he possibly could. He had been nursed by his devoted wife who was heartbroken on his death. She was lost, poor Marie-Josèphe, without the husband whom she had adored. Louis had seen the letter she had written to her brother which expressed the sincerity of her grief.

"It is the will of God that I should survive him for whom I would have given my life a thousand times over. I shall spend the rest of my pilgrimage on Earth in preparing myself to join him in Heaven."

Poor Marie-Josèphe, her pilgrimage was a short one; a year later, suffering from the same illness which had killed her husband, she died.

"My son, the Dauphin, and his wife dead within a year of each other," murmured Louis, "and less than two years later my own wife the Queen has died. Ah, Death has been too constantly with us."

Anne-Henriette had died when she was twenty-five. He

had mourned Anne-Henriette deeply; she was the best of all his children. Her sister Louise-Elisabeth he had married to the Duke of Parma and she was lost to him. The little Duc d'Anjou who had been born a year after the Dauphin, had died when he was three years old.

Death . . . death . . . it was a tale of death. Yet some of his children had lived. He grimaced in the darkness. What affection he had ever had for his remaining daughters had been long replaced by contempt. He could scarcely bear to think of them. They increased his boredom, the very thing which he was endeavouring to drive away.

He must think of them as little girls when they had pleased him a great deal more than they could today. Adelaide the eldest, then Victoire, Sophie, Thérèse-Félicité and lastly Louise-Marie.

Thérèse-Félicité had died when a child in the Abbey of Fontevrault. He recalled how conscience-stricken he had been when he had heard of the death of the little Princess. The little girls had not wished to go to Fontevrault; they had wept and pleaded; but, said Fleury, who was then to all intents and purposes ruler of the kingdom, there they must go for the need for economy was urgent and the Princesses, with their households and all the attendant pomp, were a drain on the royal exchequer.

Adelaide was the only one who had not gone. Adelaide was sly. Stupid as she now seemed, she had twenty times as much intelligence as her sisters. She had waylaid him in his *chambre intime*, had flung her arms about his knees and wept pathetically, and when he had lifted her in his arms and asked what ailed her, she had put her hot wet face against his and almost suffocated him with her embrace.

"Dear Papa, I do not wish to go away. I do not wish to leave *you*."

Clever Adelaide! She knew how to wheedle in those days. She was the most handsome of the sisters, and he had been

25

affected. Thus the other four went to Fontevrault and Adelaide remained at Versailles.

Louis lifted his shoulders. Poor children! What had they learned in their convent? Precious little, it appeared, for when they emerged ten or twelve years later they seemed quite stupid compared with all the bright young ladies of the Court.

Adelaide of course had been different. But life had become sour for Adelaide. She had won release from the convent and could not accept life as her sisters did. Poor Victoire and Sophie thought her wonderful, and echoed all she said. Alas, they were foolish imitators of a fool.

Adelaide wished to be a clever woman; she tried to learn everything and succeeded in learning nothing; she wished to be a *femme fatale*, and failed even more wretchedly in this.

Louise perhaps had more spirit. Had she not been hunchbacked she might have made something of her life. She had at least refused to stay on at Court as one of the King's quartette of unmarried daughters, growing yearly further and further from marriage, more and more unattractive, more and more odd. Louise had become a Carmelite.

Did they hate their father? Did they think he had failed in his duty towards them? And had he? Not a husband among the four of them! Surely that showed a distressing *laisser-aller* on his part. Surely it should not have been so difficult to find husbands for the daughters of the King of France.

They haunted the Palace, like three crows; Adelaide in command, Victoire and Sophie nodding as they echoed her words—something of a joke, these three sisters, to be tittered at, to be treated with mock respect by the Court because it was well known that the King had no respect for his daughters.

Yet when they were younger he had been fond of Adelaide, and often he would go down the little staircase which separated her apartments from his, taking her coffee which he had made himself, for he had always liked to do a little cooking.

Even in these days there was a strangeness about these three. No ceremony was necessary in this very heart of the family—for he did not wish it. But Adelaide insisted. When the King came to bring her coffee, she would ring for Victoire, and Victoire in her apartments had orders from Adelaide to ring for Sophie in hers, and Sophie must ring for Louise. They would come trotting in at the arranged intervals while Adelaide sat nodding her head with approval, almost like a mechanical figure, he had thought. They were all like mechanical figures.

"*Mon Dieu!*" sighed the King. "I thought I was waving adieu to boredom and melancholy by these journeys into the past. And I think of my daughters Adelaide, Sophie, Victoire! It would seem I am bidding ennui return. Ah, my dearest Marquise, you should not have left me thus."

A rustle in the room. He was alert suddenly.

"Who is there? Answer!"

He could see a figure at the door; it swayed in its draperies, infinitely graceful. For a moment he thought he had called up the ghost of Pompadour.

"It is I, Sire," said a gentle voice. "May I approach Your Majesty?"

"What do you want?"

She did not answer. She had decided not to wait for permission; she was advancing on tiptoe towards the bed in a childish way as though to say "See how daring I am!"

Reaching the bed she threw herself on her knees and stretched out her arms so that they were spread across the coverlet, and as the draperies fell away from them he recognised from their rounded perfection that they belonged to the Comtesse d'Esparbès. He had admired those arms many

27

times at table; they were said to be the most beautiful at the Court—and the most rapacious. There was scarcely a man, whom *la petite Esparbès* considered handsome or powerful enough, who had not been embraced by them.

"Rise, Madame," said Louis. "I feel sure your present position is a most uncomfortable one."

She leaped to her feet with a little laugh, sat on the bed and adjusted his nightcap which had slipped too far over one eye.

"This," she said, placing the famous arms across her breasts, almost protectively, "is far more comfortable, Sire."

"For you perhaps," he said. "For me less so. You are sitting on my foot."

"A thousand apologies, Sire." She moved closer.

"Who allowed you to enter?"

"Sire, I would rather not say."

"Yet I ask you."

"I take full blame, Sire. . . ." She added saucily: "Or credit, whichever Your Majesty should think fit to award."

Richelieu? he thought. D'Aumont? Certainly not Choiseul. Well, Esparbès was an improvement on some women he could think of.

"Which, Sire," she went on, "shall it be?"

"It is too early yet," said Louis, "to pass judgment."

She clasped her hands ecstatically.

"Tell me what gives you such pleasure?" he said.

"Sire, it is because there is to be a judgment."

Louis laughed wryly. "I am an old man, my dear," he said.

"Sire, there is not a man in your kingdom who could match his youth with your age."

"I was saying," went on Louis with a touch of coldness, "that I am an old man and not easily deceived. A lady of your undoubted talents could match them more happily with one near your own age."

28

"Sire, there is none other who could give me what I crave."

"That's true enough," said the King. "Tell me what it is you crave. What title would you like, my dear?"

She leaped from the bed pouting. "I fear I have not made myself understood, Sire. I will ask leave to retire."

"It is granted."

She moved away from the bed, walking backwards with the utmost formality. Then she stood still looking at him wistfully.

Louis shrugged his shoulders once more. She laughed suddenly. Louis adjusted his nightcap and made room for her in the bed.

2

THE DUC DE CHOISEUL

MADAME D'ESPARBÈS sat gracefully on the chair opposite the Duc de Choiseul, the flounces of her sleeves falling back, as if by chance, to disclose her perfectly rounded arms. The Duc de Choiseul forced his eyes to remain upon them because he knew that was what was expected of him, and one of the reasons why Monsieur de Choiseul had risen to his high position was because he knew how to give people what they expected of him—particularly women.

"It is gracious of you to let me intrude my foolish self upon your precious leisure," simpered the woman.

"It is generous of you to bestow your far from foolish self upon my worthless leisure," answered Choiseul.

"Oh, you are a most grateful man, Monsieur de Choiseul. And a generous one. I have said again and again that besides being grateful and generous you are the *wisest* man in the kingdom."

Choiseul raised his eyebrows. What did she want of him? Clearly she wanted something. The woman was smug, and seemed to be in no doubt whatsoever of getting it, whatever it was. She was more foolish than he had thought. Did she think a night or two in the King's company made of her a Pompadour?

He waited for her to state what she wanted; instead she said: "His Majesty has a more contented look these days. Do you not think so?"

Choiseul lifted his shoulders. "Since his misfortunes there

30

have been times when the royal spirits have been lifted; but, alas, they quickly fall."

"His Majesty is discovering that he is a young man yet," said the Comtesse with a laugh. "He said to me that there is some company which brings him back to spring when he had thought he was entering upon the winter."

"His Majesty is turning poet," murmured Choiseul.

"His Majesty, like yourself, Monsieur le Duc, is grateful to those who please him."

"So grateful I doubt not that it will not be necessary for those who please *him* to make requests of others."

She frowned slightly. "Oh, but there are matters which are so trifling that it would be a breach of etiquette to discuss them with His Majesty."

"Such as, Madame la Comtesse?"

"I am looking for a place in the army for a cousin of mine. A simple matter really."

"Not so simple," said Choiseul, "when the promotion lists have already passed His Majesty's approval."

"Then they can be changed."

"Alas, they have gone too far for that."

"I say they shall be changed."

"At the King's command perhaps."

"Monsieur de Choiseul, you referred a moment ago to the King's bereavement. Were you by any chance recalling the death of La Marquise?"

"Hers among others. The Dauphin, the Dauphine, the Queen—they were all bitter bereavements to His Majesty."

"And you shared deeply the King's sorrow for the bereavement of La Marquise, did you not?"

Choiseul raised his eyebrows once more. "It is fitting that a subject should share his monarch's grief," he said.

"And you, Monsieur le Duc, must have had a greater share in that grief than most of the King's subjects. All knew what great friends you were with the Marquise. It was she

whom you supported, was it not, and you whom she helped
to raise to your high position? You were very good for each
other—you and the Marquise."

Her foot was tapping angrily. She was daring to warn
him. You knew you must make friends with Pompadour, my
little Duke; now you must know that if you will keep your
position you must pay equal tribute to the new favourite.

New favourite indeed! thought Choiseul. Never! An
empty-headed woman who had been the mistress of almost
every man at Court! One swallow did not make a summer;
two nights in the King's bed did not make a Pompadour.

"We worked well together," he mused.

"And ruled the country between you."

Now she was smiling almost coyly. *Mon Dieu!* thought
Choiseul. Is she suggesting that *she* and I should rule the
country together?

He smiled at her slyly. "La Marquise was the cleverest
woman in France." His eyes had come to rest upon her
beautiful arms.

"Why do you stare so?" she asked.

"*You*, Comtesse," he said, "have the most beautiful arms
in France."

She retorted tartly: "Monsieur de Choiseul, you will
consider my cousin's application for a high place in the
army?"

"Alas, as I told you, the lists have already gone before
the King."

"So you mean you will do nothing for my cousin!"

"My dear Comtesse, if it were in my power . . ."

"Your power is great and it is such a small thing that
I ask."

As again she watched that irritating lift of the shoulder,
Madame d'Esparbès lost her temper.

"You will be sorry that you have refused me this small
request, Monsieur le Duc."

"I am sorry to disappoint you now, Comtesse."

"Oh yes, Monsieur de Choiseul, you will be very sorry indeed. Give me a week."

"Willingly will I give it," answered Choiseul, "for at least it is in my power to do that."

She rose and hurried from the room. Choiseul bowed and stood, thoughtfully listening to the swish of her silk petticoats.

After she had gone, he was faintly uneasy. The woman was a fool, but fools before now had ruled Kings.

She was right when she had hinted that he owed his rise to Madame de Pompadour. Cardinal Bernis had lost his place because he did not regard that lady with the seriousness which she thought her due, and because, in other words, he was a short-sighted fool. He, Choiseul, had taken over the ministry of foreign affairs in place of Bernis. He was the wise man who understood that the King's powerful mistress intended to arrange more than the King's pleasures.

When Marshal Belle-Isle had died, it was to Choiseul that the office of minister of war had fallen, and by taking that and passing the important post of foreign affairs to his cousin, the Duc de Praslin, his position was strengthened, and with the aid of Pompadour he had become the most powerful man in the government of the country.

He had been wise enough to know that while La Pompadour supported him and the King continued to support La Pompadour he could keep his position.

Then had his treatment of Madame d'Esparbès been foolish?

He did not think so. He was sure that he would be a match for such a woman at any time. Moreover, although he had remained the friend of Madame de Pompadour, he had in a way remained independent of her. He believed that, even while relying on the support of the King's mistress, he had served his country well.

He snapped his fingers. Madame d'Esparbès would not last three weeks.

Suddenly he burst out laughing.

He said aloud: "Madame d'Esparbès *shall* not last three weeks."

All the same it was necessary to replace her, and quickly, by someone who would be loyal to him, for in his desperate attempt to banish ennui, the King might turn to a woman such as Madame d'Esparbès, might even try to make a Pompadour of her, and then, in the subtle hands of his enemies, who knew what might happen!

Choiseul had his plans. His foreign policy had been far from successful. The Seven Years War and the Peace of Hubertsburg were very bitter in the memory, and he feared that his enemies would be ever ready to remind others and themselves that he had played a prominent part in them.

Looking back he wondered whether France would not have been wise to have kept out of that struggle between Frederick of Prussia and Maria Theresa, the Empress of Austria, for the possession of Silesia, in which England had taken part with other European countries.

He had believed that France's place was beside Austria, and he was planning a match now between the two countries that their friendship might be strengthened in the surest possible way when the Duc de Berry, heir to the throne of France, married little Marie Antoinette, the daughter of Maria Theresa. With Sweden, Poland and Russia, France had fought against Prussia and England; and when a year before the conclusion of hostilities the Russians changed sides, France had begun to wonder what she was gaining out of this war. It was perfectly clear what she was losing. The dreams of a French colonial empire had evaporated, and the English had become supreme in North America and India.

Yet Choiseul had determined not to lose heart. He

planned fresh conquests for France, and that very year he had seized Corsica.

He had great plans; he meant to make France the major power of Europe; he intended to reform the army and navy. He was not going to have these plans spoilt by some foolish woman whom the King fancied for a week or so.

He shrugged aside his fears. The woman had been threatening him. It was quite ridiculous. He considered himself, Étienne, Duc de Choiseul, the most powerful man in France. The King relied upon him; the King approved of his policies. He was a nobleman of illustrious birth, related to the great House of Lorraine; this connection made him especially privileged with Maria Theresa, who had married a Prince of Lorraine. His connections were royal; he was a brilliant statesman. He was charming and popular both with fellow politicians and the people. He had had the foresight to fill the most important posts in the Court and government with those who would serve him well. Recently he had agreed to the expulsion of the Jesuits from France, a move which had assured his popularity in Spain and Portugal.

Indeed he was foolish to feel this twinge of apprehension at the hints of a stupid woman.

While he was meditating, his sister, the Duchesse de Gramont, came to his room. She came without ceremony for they were very close, and there was no one in his life who knew his secrets as did his sister; there was no one whom he trusted as he trusted her.

She was a large woman without any feminine charm; as ambitious as he was, her greatest desire was to set them both above all others in the country and keep them there.

She came swiftly to him, bent over him, took his hand and pressed it hard—a gesture which contained more affection than many a caress.

35

"I was thinking of you at that moment," said the Duke. "Did you guess?"

"Be assured," she answered, "that if you wanted me I would not be far away. What is it?"

"That woman, d'Esparbès has been to see me. She wants promotion for an impecunious relation."

"Poor Étienne! How many people have asked you to provide for their impecunious relations?"

"This was more than a request; it was almost a threat."

"A threat from that little fool! How can she be in a position to threaten *you*?"

"She imagines that she is fast wriggling her amorous little body into that position."

The Duchesse laughed her deep masculine laugh. "Does the little fool imagine herself to be a Pompadour?"

"Do not let us forget that when Madame de Pompadour was first noticed at Court it was said of her: 'Does she imagine herself to be a Maintenon?' Imagination can do a great deal, sister—imagination, plus a King's lust and the machinations of our enemies."

"My dearest brother, you are seriously perturbed?"

"Not . . . seriously. But in politics, my dear—and believe me, the love affairs of Kings, and particularly Kings of France, can quickly become politics—it is advisable to examine every possibility with care."

"Then we must make sure that this little upstart never reaches Pompadour status."

"If only . . ."

She nodded. It was not necessary for him to complete his sentence. They had been so much together that it was sometimes possible to convey their thoughts without a great many words. She knew that he meant, If only we could find a protégée, the perfect little puppet, skilled in the arts of lust and ignorant of politics, someone who would be for ever grateful to the Choiseuls for having established her in that place where almost every woman of the Court longed to be! But where was such a paragon to be found?

When the Duc was alone with his sister he was a different man from the statesman who faced the council chambers or charmed his way about the Court. He was the little boy again, dependent on his big and capable sister.

The bond between these two was stronger than any which bound either of them to another person. There were some who said that the affection between them was unnatural, and certain of his enemies had nicknamed Choiseul "Ptolemy", after Egyptian kings who married their sisters.

In their childhood they had lived on the family's impoverished estates, brooding on the greatness of the family in the past, dreaming of the manner in which they would restore its fortunes. They often talked of the old castle at Stainville where they had spent their impecunious childhood. They would often delight in shuddering over those early days and comparing them with the present. Château Ennui, they called the old home at Stainville, and now that they had places at the glittering Court they were going to fight with all their might to retain them.

The Duchesse had been sent to a convent—what else was there for a daughter of a penniless and highly aristocratic line?—while her brother had gone to Court to make his fortune.

Urbane, charming, a courtier to his finger-tips as well as a man destined to be one of the most astute statesmen of his times, he was not long in making his way; and one of his first acts, when he had the power to perform it, was to bring his sister from her convent to the Court and there arrange a brilliant marriage for her. It was true that her husband was the depraved old Duc de Gramont, but with a powerful brother to support her, there was no need for her to stay with her husband. She had his name and the standing that

37

gave her; her brother would provide the rest. And this he had done most successfully.

A thought had struck them both. They looked at each other and averted their eyes; for they were both a little ashamed of it.

Choiseul had married recently a young lady of great fortune; he was lucky because not only was she extremely wealthy but she was also very pretty. Mademoiselle Crozat-Duchâtel had added to these qualities by falling deeply in love with him, and such a marriage had brought nothing but good to Choiseul for since it had taken place the King had been even more friendly than previously. Louis had a tender feeling for the beautiful lady who had been Mademoiselle Crozat-Duchâtel. But the wife of Choiseul was noted for her virtue as well as her beauty, and she had made it clear that the only man who interested her was her brilliant and fascinating husband.

Now the thought had come to the Duke and his sister: If the Duchesse de Choiseul could be induced to charm the King, what hope would there be for such silly little women as the Comtesse d'Esparbès?

Neither of them mentioned this. It was unnecessary. They both dismissed it immediately. Choiseul for all his ambition was a man of dignity. Only in the most extreme necessity could he consider deliberately becoming a cuckold.

His sister was aware of his feelings. He was right, of course. Such methods were unworthy of the Choiseuls.

There was another alternative. The Duchesse de Gramont was not afraid to voice this.

"I fancy," she said, "that Louis does not dislike me."

Choiseul was astonished. His sister was a big woman, broad, masculine and past forty.

"Well," she said, "Louis is fifty-eight. He is a good deal older than I."

"There are so many young girls fluttering about him."

"Pompadour was no young girl and in what esteem he held her!"

"She captivated him when she was young and beautiful," put in Choiseul.

"He was younger then too. No, what he wants is a woman who can be all things to him . . . not only mistress but companion and adviser. Louis grows old. He wants a woman who can match her wits with his, a woman of intellect."

Choiseul's perception, so sharp in most concerns, was blunted where his sister was concerned. He did not see her as a horse-faced woman, overpowering in her personality, lacking the graces of Madame de Pompadour. To him she was a woman of great attraction—and if she was ageing, well, she was right when she said Louis was no longer young.

"Who knows," went on the Duchesse de Gramont, "there might be a marriage. His great-grandfather married late in life—and Madame de Maintenon of all people! Ah! We will mould him to our way of thinking."

"He grows fearful of death as he comes nearer to it," put in Choiseul eagerly, because his sister was making him see through her eyes a glorious future for the family when they were joined in marriage with royal Bourbon.

"And," put in his sister, "like his great-grandfather he might wish for a regular union which would be acceptable in the eyes of the Court and Heaven."

Choiseul was doubtful. "While such a union would be acceptable in the eyes of Heaven I doubt whether it would in the eyes of the Court, dear sister."

Then they were laughing together. She snapped her fingers. "That for the Court!" she said. "Once this is accomplished the Court will do as it is bid. The Choiseuls will be the ones to call the tune."

"You are truly possessed of genius, sister. I salute the Queen of France."

She put her fingers to her lips. "Not so fast, Étienne, my

39

dear. We must take no chances. This flighty Esparbès is not without attractions. We must not underrate them."

"What do you suggest, my queen?"

"She is indiscreet. Let us ponder her indiscretion. Perhaps we could find some means of bringing it to the notice of the King. An indiscreet mistress can be very tiresome."

Choiseul began to nod slowly. Then he put his arm about his sister and hugged her almost childishly as he used to in the Château Ennui.

They were both thinking that the way ahead could be even more brilliantly successful than ever for the Choiseuls.

The Duc de Choiseul begged an audience with the King and received it.

"What I have to say," he murmured, "is for the ears of Your Majesty alone."

Louis nodded his dismissal to his attendants and they left him alone with the Duke.

"And this important news?" asked the King.

"Sire, it is of such a personal nature that I tremble to utter it."

"I see no sign of this trembling," said the King. He smiled wryly. "Indeed I detect a certain eagerness in your manner, Monsieur le Duc."

"My eagerness is to protect Your Majesty from . . . scandal."

"Ah, that is a dish I have tasted often in my life, so perhaps another sip or two will do me little harm."

"This is scandal with a difference, Sire. Previously we have heard of your gallant adventures and Frenchmen have said: 'He is a little *méchant*, eh, this King of ours, but he is a man. He has his mistresses at Court and out of Court—his little entertainments, his *Parc aux Cerfs*.' And they smile and nod. It is not that sort of scandal."

"Then what is it?" said the King somewhat testily. "Get on and tell me."

"There has been an insult to your Majesty's manhood."

"How so?"

"Lampoons are being written and circulated throughout Paris and Versailles. Your Majesty has lately shown interest in a young and beautiful woman and, Sire, your whole Court has been delighted to see you happy. But this woman whom you honour is unworthy, for it is she who babbles to the world of matters which should be the secrets of the bed-chamber. Sire, this woman has said that in spite of repeated stimuli it is quite impossible to make a lover of the King."

Louis flushed with anger.

"I will not believe such . . . such monstrous lies."

Choiseul drew a paper from his pocket. "May I ask you to cast your eyes upon this, Sire. It will explain, more fully than I can, my concern for your reputation."

He watched Louis' face become purple with rage as he read.

It had been a clever stroke to bribe one of the Comtesse's women so that it was possible to give an accurate account of words which had actually been spoken between the King and his mistress. Here it was—an account of the night's proceedings: the discussions as to when the Comtesse was to be openly proclaimed King's mistress, and then the damaging comment that in spite of repeated aids the King had been too exhausted to play the lover.

Louis screwed up the paper and threw it to the floor. Choiseul picked it up.

"Its fate shall be utter destruction, Sire," he said. "That is neither more nor less than what it and its authors deserve."

"Is a man to be blamed because he grows old?" demanded Louis.

"No, Sire. He could only be blamed for indiscretion."

The angry lines on Louis' face deepened for a second or so before they cleared.

He then laid his hand on Choiseul's shoulder. "You did well to show me this. It is better to be turned round—however unpleasant the operation—in order that one may see what has been going on behind one's back."

Choiseul took the King's hand and kissed it.

"Sire, I am forgiven then. You now understand my trepidation. I dared risk offending your dignity because my own would not stand aside and let that of France be tampered with."

"My good fellow, my gratitude for your honesty forgives you your temerity in broaching this delicate matter. Your advice is sound. Who can ward off the encroaching years and their disabilities? One would need to be immortal. But I am still King of France, and foolish indeed I should be if I ever saw again one who has held my honour so lightly."

"She has committed the unforgivable sin, Sire."

Louis looked appealingly at his minister.

Choiseul continued: "Her father-in-law would receive her at his estates. They are far enough from Versailles and Paris to be quite convenient. Have I Your Majesty's permission to make the arrangements?"

"Do so," said the King.

Choiseul bowed and retired. He was exultant. That little affair had been worked out to the satisfaction of himself and his sister. It had been an excellent idea and, in view of the indiscreet nature of the lady concerned, certain of success.

The only thing that remained now was to banish the Comtesse d'Esparbès to the country, before she understood the reason for her dismissal.

Then the way would be clear for the King's new mistress, for the domination of Louis and France by the brilliant Choiseuls.

.   .   .   .   .

Monsieur Le Bel had turned in at the Pavillon Mazarin to drink a glass of wine when he met Jean du Barry.

Monsieur Le Bel was faintly interested. Du Barry was an optimistic fellow who had often tried to bring to his notice some beautiful young woman whom he wished Le Bel to bring to that of the King.

Le Bel was rather sceptical of du Barry, but he had a liking for the fellow, and his company was always amusing, so it was with pleasure that he realised that they were to drink a glass of wine together.

"Good day to you, Monsieur Le Bel."

Du Barry's bow was dignified yet friendly.

He was in his forties and the marks of the dissipated life he had led were beginning to show themselves. So much the better it would have been for him, thought Le Bel, if he had never left the country. He knew something of du Barry's history, that he came of a good family—of provincial nobility —somewhere in the neighbourhood of Toulouse. In his own setting he must have been a very important person; he consequently wore even now a faint air of surprise, as though he were astonished that Paris did not take him at Toulouse valuation.

He had married and, no doubt feeling himself to be possessed of genius, was not content to remain in the country, so had come to Paris to seek his fortune.

His wife had been a wealthy woman, but it had not taken him long to spend her fortune. He had hopes of taking office under Choiseul, but the minister was not interested in the ambitious young man from the country.

Turning to business he had been more successful, and in supplying goods to the army he had made money; he gambled a great deal; and he lived in splendid style, indulging in debauchery to such an extent that, even in the society in which he mixed, he earned the nickname of Le Roué.

However, he wanted more than success in business, and dreamed of becoming a power at Court. That way might seem at present closed to him, yet he would not accept this as final. He was determined to find a way in, and Le Bel was well aware that he planned to do this.

All those who had witnessed the rise of Madame de Pompadour believed that the way to success at Court could only be reached through the King's mistress. Therefore in the heart of this provincial nobleman was a fixed idea. He would, among the girls of Paris, find the perfect mistress who, while she dominated the King, should be dominated by him, du Barry.

Le Bel laughed inwardly. How strange that in this great city, in Versailles itself, there was scarcely a seeker after power who did not hope to provide the King with a mistress.

These Bourbon Kings from Henri Quatre onwards were as wax in the hands of the women whom they loved. Thus the most important person in the country was the King's mistress-in-chief.

That was life—the life of France, certainly the life of the Bourbons. None could change it, so what could any ambitious man do about it, except seek to provide the King with a mistress who should excel all other mistresses and, in ministering to the pleasure of the King, bring power to her procurer?

It was, however, amusing that this little provincial should imagine that he could, in the streets of Paris, or wherever he picked up his women, find that for which men and women of the Court were searching through high society.

"Good day to you, Comte," answered Le Bel. "I pray you join me in a bottle of wine."

"It will be a pleasure," said du Barry.

He settled himself and asked after affairs at Court, being well aware that there was not a man who could tell him more of that which interested him than Monsieur Le Bel.

"Matters are not what they were," said Le Bel.

"You regret the passing of the *Parc aux Cerfs*, monsieur?"

"His Majesty was a younger man in those days, and I must say that the *Parc* was a continual delight to him. At the *Parc* there could not have been anything like this sad affair of the Comtesse d'Esparbès."

"And what is this?"

Le Bel then told his companion of the indiscretions of the King's mistress.

"It simply could not have happened in the *Parc aux Cerfs*," he reiterated. "There matters were conducted with much more decorum. In the *Parc* Mère Bompart reigned like a Queen. I can assure you that even the King himself was in awe of her. Do you know, Monsieur le Comte, that the cost of that establishment was somewhere in the neighbourhood of 4,000,000 livres a year?"

"It is small wonder that the people murmur."

"Yet I say, better a *Parc aux Cerfs* than a King too full of boredom to rule his people, and everyone endeavouring to provide him with a mistress."

"And since the departure of Madame d'Esparbès for the country whom does the King favour?"

Le Bel laughed. "It is something of a joke. You would never guess whom, my friend, so I will tell you. It is the Duchesse de Gramont."

"What—that old mare!"

"So says the Court, but it is true. Monsieur de Choiseul is such an important man. He advises the King to sign this and that agreement. His power is great, but none of us realised that it was great enough to make His Majesty accept the Gramont."

"It is impossible!" breathed du Barry.

"So we should have said. But the Duc de Richelieu had it from the King himself that she came to his bedchamber unannounced and unexpected and . . . there was no help for

it. Her determination overcame the King's indifference.
They say she plans to marry him."

"My dear friend," said du Barry, "such an arrangement
could only bring disquiet to all. I could introduce the King
to the most enchanting creature in France."

"Alas, there are so many enchanting creatures in France."

"I said the *most* enchanting. Allow me to make the
introduction."

"Some time, perhaps."

"Meanwhile His Majesty is being savaged by that great
mare."

"After the first surprise I doubt not that His Majesty will
know how to protect himself."

"Yet if you could bring to his notice this beautiful creature,
imagine his gratitude! She would not forget you, Monsieur
Le Bel. I swear to that."

"Well then, some time you must let me make the acquaintance of this charming girl."

"Come home with me now."

"Alas, I must return with all speed to Versailles. I had
not realised it was so late."

"It is a promise, Monsieur Le Bel, that you will see my
young lady?"

Le Bel sighed. "Very well. It is a promise."

The two men said their farewells and parted, but not
before du Barry had made a definite date for their next
meeting.

When he left Le Bel he made with all speed to a house
in the Rue des Petits-Champs opposite the Rue des Moulins.

He found that he was breathless; this was due more to
excitement than to the fact that he had been hurrying; he
had not noticed that his fine clothes were splashed with mud
—the filthy mud of Paris with the sulphurous tang. At any
other time he would have been annoyed, and the fact that

it escaped his notice gave a clue to the intensity of his excitement.

As he entered his house he called to a servant: "Is Madame du Barry in her room?"

"Yes, sir," was the answer.

"Then tell her to come to me at once. No . . . no. I will go to her."

He ran up the wide staircase, past the great *salon* in which almost every evening he entertained so lavishly. He went up another flight of stairs and opened a door.

"Jeanne!" he called. "Jeanne!"

She was combing her hair and turned to smile at him. Every time he saw her, after even the shortest space of time, her beauty astonished him; it was so perfect. Her hair was thick and fell in golden curls about her shoulders; her skin was fine and delicate, her eyes a dazzling blue and, because it seemed that Nature had wished to give her that kind of beauty which occurs but rarely, her brows and lashes were of dark brown in an entrancing contrast to her sparkling fairness.

Such a beauty might have been petulant, but this could not be said to be true of little Jeanne Bécu. She was generous, open-hearted, tolerant almost to carelessness.

She was slender and graceful with perfectly formed hands and feet; she could wear clothes like a Duchess—which came of her training in Labille's dress shop. And if, when she opened her mouth, she betrayed a rather closer acquaintance with the *faubourgs* than could have been possible in a young lady of the Court, that could be said to add a touch of piquancy which was a necessity in the midst of such perfection.

"My Jeanne!" cried du Barry, taking her hands and kissing them.

She gave him her friendly smile.

"Now what's been exciting you?" she asked.

"I have just left Monsieur Le Bel."

"Is he as handsome as his name?"

"This is no time for frivolity, my dear. He is the King's principal *valet de chambre* and you are to meet him."

Jeanne dropped a mock curtsy.

Du Barry held up an admonitory finger. "The trouble with you, Jeanne, is that you can never be serious. It'll be your downfall."

"It is better to die of laughing than of some things I've heard of."

"Now listen to me."

"I'm listening. We're excited. We're going to meet the King's *valet de chambre*. And we've to be nice to him . . . very very nice . . . but *serious*."

"What I want for you is not the *valet de chambre*, my dear. He is merely the stepping-stone to the King."

Jeanne put a beautiful hand to her mouth to stop a gust of laughter. Du Barry groaned. Such beautiful hands to be forced to such crude gestures. He took her by the shoulders and shook her angrily.

"I'll get you to the King if I have to drive you there," he said.

"No need to," she told him. "I am ready. Take me to this stepping-stone and I'll take one leap into the Palace."

"Sit down," said du Barry. "Now . . . think of what happened to Madame de Pompadour, and remember that can happen to you. You have to forget Vaucouleurs and all the lackeys and housemaids who were your companions; you must forget all that has happened in your life until this moment. You must forget that when I found you you were a saleswoman in the Maison Labille. That is past and over. Now . . . you may well be going to Court."

There was silence in the room, apart from the ticking of a gilded clock over the fireplace.

Du Barry was aware of it; it seemed to add to the importance of this occasion. He was certain, as he kept his eyes fixed on the beautiful young woman, that this time he could not fail; he saw her opening the way to power and wealth for him; he believed that he was going to achieve that which so many powerful men in France had failed to do.

Jeanne was staring into space, a fixed smile on her lips.

Du Barry said suddenly: "Well, are you excited at this prospect?"

She went on smiling as though she had not heard him; then she said: "You said forget . . . forget it all . . . everything that's happened to me since I was old enough to remember. The funny thing is that when you say forget I can't help but remember. I see it all so clearly. My mother always floury, and her apron warm from the oven . . . and the dingy house not far from the Place Royale . . . the convent of Sainte-Aure . . . and Labille's and . . ."

"I told you those are the very things you must now forget."

"Ah," said Jeanne, continuing to smile, "but I go on . . . remembering."

3

JEANNE BÉCU

O a hot August day in the little town of Vaucouleurs
Anne Bécu gave birth to a daughter. That Anne Bécu
was not married, and indeed was not even certain as to who
was the father of her child, did not greatly worry her.

Anne was a beautiful girl, and no one expected her not
to have a lover. If the liaison was fruitful, that was Anne's
concern and, provided she asked no one to support her child,
there was nothing further to be said.

Hardy, independent, Anne was quite capable of bringing
up more than one illegitimate child, and this she would have
done, had her second, a boy, not died in infancy.

The little girl, Jeanne, was more healthy than her
brother; she was so pretty, even at an early age, that Anne
was certain she must have been the daughter of the handsome soldier and not of the wandering Friar whose love-
making—probably because of his ecclesiastical robes—she
had found so amusing.

When the little girl began to show such extraordinary good
looks, Anne was not surprised. Her own father when he had
lived in Paris—he had been a *rôtisseur* in that city—had been
reckoned one of its most handsome men, and the story went
that a grand lady, the Comtesse de Montdidier, had married
him. The marriage, it is true, did not last long; the Comtesse died and the devastatingly handsome Fabien Bécu took
service with one of the mistresses of Louis XIV; later, when
this lady was no longer in favour and could not afford the
services of Fabien, he left Paris for his native Vaucouleurs,

there married and had several children, one of whom was Anne.

Jeanne's first memories were of clinging to her mother's skirt as they went about the little town; she remembered how people, whenever they stopped to talk to them, would have a word for little Jeanne; perhaps there would be a *croissant* from the *boulanger*, a *gâteau* from the *pâtissier*. They would all have a word for her, would stroke her hair, or ask for a kiss in exchange for the small gift.

Jeanne's answer was always a radiant smile and an up-lifted face, red lips seeming eager to give what was asked.

"She's going to be her mother all over again," was the comment she heard often; it would be accompanied by a smile of something far from disapproval. Anne was a lovely girl and this was eighteenth-century France where austerity was frowned on and a girl like Anne Bécu, who was a target for masculine attention, was admired. As for the results of this attractiveness, well, in practical French minds that was life, and if Anne could feed and clothe her children, there was nothing more to be said.

Jeanne remembered being held in the arms of Grand-père Bécu, still handsome, still possessed of that sex magnetism which Anne had inherited and which, it was apparent even though she was so young, had been passed on in no small measure to little Jeanne.

Grand-père Bécu used to tell her of his glorious year as husband to a Comtesse; he told how later he had become cook to the Comtesse Marie Isabelle de Ludre who had, for a time, been loved by the King. Oh yes, Grand-père Bécu had caught glimpses of the King when he had come to visit his beautiful mistress.

The old man would stride up and down the room imitating the bearing, the manner of the King. "That, my little one, was great Louis Quatorze. Le Roi Soleil, they used to call him. There was a King! We don't see the like of that sort nowadays. This Louis . . . he's no Louis Quatorze."

Jeanne had said sharply: "But how could he be, Grand-père, when he is Louis Quinze?"

That had made Grand-père Bécu wheeze with laughter and place his wrinkled old hand on her shoulder. "You're a sharp one, Mademoiselle Jeanne," he told her more than once.

She used to climb on his knee and watch his mouth, waiting for the words to come out. There was no one like Grand-père Bécu who would tell her such tales, tales which conjured up pictures of a world far from Jeanne's own. There with him she could imagine splendour such as was outside the knowledge of anyone else in Vaucouleurs: flunkeys in scarlet and blue, food served on platters of gold and silver; apartments hung with velvet and brocade, and the two Comtesses—one whom Grand-père had married, the other whom he had served, looking rather like the china figure which stood on the mantelpiece and which was a relic of those fine old days.

But Grand-père Bécu could not live for ever, and when he died he took all the magic out of Vaucouleurs. "There is nothing to stay here for," said Anne to her daughter. "It is not easy to make a living here. Now, Paris, that is quite a different dish, I can tell you."

So to Paris they went, and Jeanne was glad, for in the big city it was easier to forget that she would never see her grandfather again.

Anne talked to her little daughter; for since the death of old Grand-père there was no one else to talk to.

"We shall not be helpless there," explained Anne. "Thank the saints that we have friends there. You have aunts and uncles in Paris, my little one, all doing well for themselves. They will see that we have a means of livelihood."

They were going, Anne explained, to a big house in Paris where she had been given the position of cook. It was a heaven-sent opportunity little Jeanne should understand, for, provided she, Jeanne, kept out of the way of the mistress and master of the house, she might accompany her mother and there would be no need for them to be separated.

It seemed an excellent prospect, and they left for Paris.

As soon as Jeanne set eyes on that city, as soon as she first smelt that sulphurous mud, as soon as she heard the shouts of the traders, had her first glimpses of the bustling markets, she loved it all. She knew she could belong here as to no other place.

It was Grand-père Bécu who had made Vaucouleurs enchanting, and when he had gone Vaucouleurs had become nothing but a dreary little town. Yet she knew that whatever happened to her in this great city, Paris would still be for her the most delightful place in the world.

During her first weeks there she would beg the servants of the household to take her whenever they had occasion to go out on some errand.

She longed to be out of doors all day, for each hour seemed to offer some fresh diversion. At nine o'clock the streets would seem to be full of waiters from the cafés carrying trays of coffee and rolls to people who lived in furnished lodgings. The barbers, their clothes white with powder, would be dashing from their shops to wait on their clients, and carrying wigs and tongs they would dart among the crowds in the utmost haste. Later the waiters and barbers would be replaced by other tradesmen or by the lawyers hurrying to the Châtelet and other courts, their gowns flapping about them, while those whom they were to defend ran behind them, trying to keep pace. There would be the financiers on their way to the Exchange; and all the men and women who had the morning to kill would be making their way to the Palais Royal, there to sit under the trees and talk over the politics of the country and the scandal of the Court.

Through the streets the carriages rumbled scattering refuse over the unwary, and it was necessary to walk on tiptoe to avoid ruining skirt hems and stockings with that poisonous mud.

Even at three o'clock in the afternoon when the streets were half empty they lost none of their charm; then it was possible to see the buildings, some magnificently noble, some pitiably sordid, but all exciting to the eyes of the little girl from the country.

Sometimes her mother would go to shop, and with her would go the little Jeanne. They would leave the house early that they might get the best of what was going. Then she would see the country folk arriving with their fruit and flowers, their fish, eggs and butter, and making their way to the Halles; and twice a week the bakers of Gonesse brought their bread into the town.

To buy from these country folk and to talk with them was a great pleasure, for they loved to talk, and they all had a smile, if not a small gift, for the beautiful little girl whose blue eyes shone with such joy in living and goodwill towards the world.

Jeanne was sorry for the country people because they had to go back to the country, and when she left them and went homeward with her mother, she would hug herself with joy.

Sometimes they would stop at the corner for *café au lait* in earthenware cups, bought from one of the women with the urns on their backs.

It tasted delicious to Jeanne, but Anne grumbled.

"Two *sous* the cup, and hardly a mite of sugar at that! These town people are robbers."

Jeanne nodded, drank her hot coffee and loved all the people of Paris, robbers or not.

.   .   .   .   .

54

Jeanne was of an adventurous nature. She had been told so often that her place was below stairs with the servants that she knew it well, but the staircase which led to a great hall was a continual temptation to her and, in spite of her desire to do as she was told, again and again she would find herself standing at the foot of that staircase, and it required a great deal of will-power to prevent her feet from carrying her up it. Frequently she would mount a few stairs, consider how wicked she was and then return to the kitchens and her rightful sphere.

She understood far more than the adults realised. She liked to sit in her corner, eating a hot roll or a piece of *gâteau* which had been thrust into her hands by one of the servants, for they all seemed to wish to give her something, a tribute perhaps to her beauty which was growing more remarkable each day. As she sat, they would talk, and she would remain silent, her eyes downcast, her ears alert.

One day she heard Nicolas Rançon talking to her mother as he so often did. In fact when they talked together the pair were so absorbed in each other that they forgot the presence of the child, and thus Jeanne was able to learn a great deal about her new home.

"*He* is a very rich man," Nicolas was telling Anne. "It's to be hoped he continues to love Mademoiselle. Alas, what would she do without him? What should we all do?"

"He", Jeanne knew from other conversations, was the great Monsieur Billard du Monceaux, whose name must be mentioned in whispers in this house. It was largely due to this great man that Jeanne must be careful never to mount those stairs. Monsieur Billard du Monceaux visited her whom Jeanne called "the lady". This was the mistress of the house, Mademoiselle Frédéric, who was very beautiful and whom the wealthy Monsieur Billard du Monceaux called every so often to see.

When he called there was bustle throughout the house.

55

The cooks were busy, Mademoiselle's personal maid would rush down to the kitchen to demand this and that, and there would be a general tension throughout the house. Perhaps he would stay a whole day and night—or even two days and nights.

It seemed to Jeanne that he stayed years, for at such times she must remain well hidden away, and as no one took her out to see the sights of Paris, she longed for the time when Monsieur Billard du Monceaux would go away and the house return to normal.

"A fortune," Nicolas was saying. "A fortune, I tell you. He made it out of the army. That's the way to make a fortune, Anne my girl. The army! It makes some of us soldiers; but the cunning make money out of it; he's the sort who makes money. Contracts for the army. Supplying clothes and food and everything. They say he got his contracts through the Duc de Choiseul himself. The Duke wants to make the French Army second to none, you see. Well, perhaps he has, and in doing it he's made *him* a rich man."

"Don't grudge *him* his money," said Anne practically. "We get our pickings."

Nicolas slapped Anne's buttocks and they laughed together. Anne went to the cupboard and brought out a pie. They sat down and began to eat, their heads close together, whispering. But they were not whispering of the things Jeanne wanted to hear. Jeanne knew this kind of whispering. It was a pretending to be angry with each other, and scolding, and really laughing all the time. It was not very interesting.

On that day they were so wrapped up in this pastime, however, that they did not notice Jeanne slip out of the kitchens.

Irresistibly she was drawn to the foot of those stairs.

She hesitated, put a small foot on the first and waited.

She listened. She could hear the mingling laughter of her mother and Nicolas Rançon. She had no wish to go back to the kitchens.

Then very deliberately she began to mount the stairs.

She reached a great hall which seemed to be full of beautiful things. There were pictures of men and women on the walls and from the centre of the ceiling hung great candelabra.

Projecting from the walls, it seemed to Jeanne, were the heads of animals, all staring at her. The people in the pictures seemed to stare also.

Jeanne smiled at them although they looked decidedly unfriendly. She made a closer inspection.

"You're dead," she said. "That's all you are."

An animal with a pair of ferocious horns looked as though he were ready to bite, so Jeanne put out her tongue at him and, to show she was not afraid, turned her back.

The floor was exciting; it was made up of black and white tiles; she stooped to examine it and trace the pattern with her fingers. As she was thus engaged, to her horror she heard footsteps—not coming from those stairs which she had mounted but on the tiles of the hall.

She leaped to her feet and made for the stairs, but she was not quick enough; someone was barring her way and she ran full tilt against a satin coat.

Her heart beating madly, she was afraid to lift her eyes, and suddenly she felt her chin taken and her face jerked upwards.

"What is this?" said the man who was holding her.

"It's a Jeanne Bécu," she answered, "that's what it is." When Jeanne was frightened she was apt to talk a great deal. She went on: "And I know who you are too."

"Who?" asked the man.

"You're *Him*."

"Well," said the man, "at least I'm not a *Her*."

57

"You're *Him* all right," said Jeanne. "And, you'll pardon me for telling you, you're hurting my arm."

"My apologies," he said.

He had released her and she hesitated for a second or so, debating whether to make a dash for it. He was less alarming in actuality than imagination, she decided; and in any case it was no use running because he had seen her.

"Shall we be sent away?" she asked.

"Why?"

"Because you've seen me."

"Do you think that possible?"

"They said I must not come up the stairs. Not here, where you are. But . . ."

"You are a disobedient child then?"

She nodded.

"And what were you doing here?"

"Looking."

"You are not frightened of me after all, are you?" he asked.

She smiled, because she had seen in his face that indulgence which she had never yet failed to arouse. She shook her head.

He touched her curls. "What did you say your name was?"

"Jeanne Bécu."

"And you live here?"

"My mother cooks for Mademoiselle."

"And you want your mother to go on cooking for Mademoiselle?"

Jeanne nodded vigorously.

"Then you would not want me to disclose what a disobedient daughter she has. What will you give me if I say nothing? A kiss?"

Jeanne was radiant. "Two," she promised.

He lifted her in his arms. She took his face in her hands

58

and gave him two kisses, one on each cheek, vigorous and conveying her relief.

He laughed and put her down on the floor; and she turned and fled.

At the foot of the stairs she crouched listening, for she had heard footsteps coming into the hall.

Then he spoke; and he quite clearly was a man who did not keep his promises, for he was talking to Mademoiselle herself and his first words were: "I have just seen that enchanting child. She belongs to the cook, she tells me."

But it was unimportant; he was not angry; that was quite obvious.

Jeanne had discovered what "he" was really like; she had made another discovery; a smile and a kiss were all that was asked of her—even by important gentlemen—when she was caught doing what she should not.

After that she would be sent for when "he" came to the house.

Mademoiselle laughed at his interest. "I do declare," she said on one occasion, "that you come here more to see little Jeanne Bécu than me."

Monsieur Billard du Monceaux denied this but Jeanne, listening intently as usual, was not so sure that he was telling the truth.

Mademoiselle bought her a dress and her own maid combed her hair so that she would be ready when Monsieur Billard du Monceaux called. She had an impudence, said Monsieur Billard du Monceaux, pinching her cheeks, which was to his liking.

What did she do all day? he wanted to know. She spent her time in the kitchens? But that would not do. She could neither read nor write, and he did not like to think of his bold little *gamine* being so ignorant. He had a plan for her. How would she like to go to school?

59

Jeanne considered. Yes, she would. She had seen books and had been irritated because she could not understand those queer black things which huddled together on the pages. She wanted to know what was in books.

Monsieur Billard du Monceaux talked to Anne; Anne by this time was very friendly with Nicolas Rançon and, since Monsieur Billard du Monceaux was so interested in Anne's daughter, some of that interest came Anne's way. She would marry Rançon; he would see that Rançon had a good position; and as for little Jeanne, she should go for a few years to the convent of Sainte-Aure.

This was great good fortune, Anne considered. The move to Paris had been a good one. Now she was to have a husband and an educated daughter.

The golden curly hair, the lovely eyes that were so serene, yet not unknowledgeable, gave many a qualm to the nuns of Sainte-Aure. Even when Jeanne was put into the convent uniform, with a black hood hiding the glory of her golden curls, and a band of white linen across her delicate forehead, she looked lovely. They could not hide the porcelain skin, the exquisite line of the face, nor those blue eyes which partly because of that mingling serenity and mischief appeared to be enigmatic. Her slender young body was garbed in rough serge, and her shoes were clumsy and made of yellow hide.

The girls she met at the convent were by no means highly born. The fees at Sainte-Aure were low, being only 210 livres a year. This was quite a different convent from those such as Fontevrault, to which the daughters of the King had been sent to receive their education.

The fifty-three nuns of the convent were of the Order of Saint Augustine, and the rules were strict. The day was devoted to duty and there were few pleasures; the food was adequate but of the simplest kind; and the pupils were not allowed to play or even laugh—laughter being considered a sin.

This was particularly trying for a child of Jeanne's temperament and she suffered continual reproaches and punishment. Even so it was impossible to curb her high spirits and all through her years at the convent they did not diminish.

Bitterly she missed the streets of Paris and often longed for them with passion; but she was eager to learn all she could and applied herself with enthusiasm to reading, writing and the keeping of household accounts, which appealed to her far more than needlework and cooking.

There was a philosophical streak in Jeanne's nature which made her adapt herself calmly to any change in her life and gave her that sunny disposition which was to endear her to all, except those in whom she aroused envy; Jeanne was completely without malice and vindictiveness, and it was to some extent that serenity, engendered by these traits, which was to make her grow into the most beautiful woman in Paris.

Life now became governed by bells. Instead of being awakened by the bakers from Gonesse entering Paris, or the voices of the traders on their way to *les Halles*, there was this ringing of bells. She must rise at five o'clock, wash in the coldest of water, take her place at the long refectory table, be ready to hear Mass at seven, read and write and force her unwilling fingers to sew.

Sewing might have been interesting if the materials she used were brocades and velvets such as Grand-père Bécu had talked about and she had seen in Mademoiselle Frédéric's hall; but what she must sew at the convent were shirts for the poor or black gowns for the nuns and children like herself.

And so the years passed.

When Jeanne was fifteen her education was considered to

be finished and Monsieur Billard du Monceaux, who no
longer visited Mademoiselle Frédéric, seemed to have forgotten all about the little girl who had once charmed him.
So when Jeanne left the convent she returned to her mother
and stepfather.

She was more beautiful than ever, and with her smattering
of education seemed like a lady in the humble household
which the Rançons had set up in the neighbourhood of the
Place Royale.

Jeanne presented a problem to them. She was an educated
young lady. Quite clearly she was not suited to become a
servant. But what else was there for her? Anne shook her
head over her daughter's future, and her husband Nicolas
did the same, because he had learned to think as Anne
thought.

Anne was uneasy, remembering her own youth when she
had been attractive; there had always been plenty to tell her
how charming she was and she was shrewd enough to see
that Jeanne would attract twice as much attention; moreover Jeanne's easygoing nature indicated that she would be
as generous with whatever she had to offer as she was with
a ribbon or a sweetmeat she was asked to share.

When they walked in the gardens of the Palais Royal, they
were continually reminded of the temptations which could
befall a handsome girl left unguarded in such a wilderness.
Under the trees the women paraded and the gallants
quizzed them. Many a fresh young girl from the country,
who had come to Paris to earn her living at the milliners' or
the dressmakers', would think to enjoy a richer life through
her promenades in the gardens of the Palais Royal.

"And what more natural," said Anne to Nicolas, "than
that young Jeanne should want to buy herself some gaudy
bit of ribbon to tie up her hair, or a glittering trinket, and
go the way of those girls to get it?"

"She wants looking after, that girl," agreed Nicolas.

"I always felt there was something very special waiting for her," said Anne. "Look at the way Monsieur Billard du Monceaux paid all that money to give her a bit of schooling."

"He could see what a beauty she was going to be."

"That's the point," said Anne. "She's more than pretty. By all the saints, I've never seen any to hold a candle to her."

To draw her attention from her daughter Nicolas pointed out the new hairstyles worn by some of the ladies.

"Why, they get higher every week," guffawed Nicolas. "Soon their heads will be taller than the rest of their bodies."

They sat down under a tree and while they were watching the passers-by a young man named Lametz, a friend of Nicolas, came along and sat with them for a while. He happened to be a hairdresser, and Nicolas chaffed him about the ridiculousness of the fashions.

Young Lametz defended himself and his trade good-humouredly and, when they rose to leave, Nicolas suggested that he should come home with them for a glass of wine.

Jeanne served them with the wine, and from the moment he set eyes on her the young hairdresser was unable to think of anything else. He remarked on her unusual grace and beauty, at which Nicolas and Anne confided their problem.

"She could learn hairdressing," said the young man. "Believe me, with the new elaborate fashions there's a fortune in it."

Anne looked at Nicolas, hope dawning in her eyes. She seemed to be saying: "Watch! Here it comes again!"

"We could not afford to have her trained," she said.

The young man smiled expansively. "My dear Madame Rançon," he cried, "you need have no thought of that. I would willingly help your daughter to become a hair-dresser."

Thus was Jeanne made an apprentice to hairdressing. It delighted her. The fantastic adornments which were

63

beginning to be worn in the hair were a source of never-ending amusement and excitement.

The business young Lametz had recently inherited from his father was a high-class one. He was interested in *ladies'* fashions. Not for him the hideous old barber's shop, the window-panes of which were spattered with pomade and powder, and the air filled with the smell of singed hair. He had his eyes on the fine ladies of Paris and eventually the Court.

Jeanne encouraged him in this. He would spend much time dressing her hair, piling up the golden curls in the new style which he planned to use on a Duchess.

"Naturally," he would say, "I shall be disappointed when I try this style upon her. She will not look like you, Jeanne."

He would take her face in his hands and tell her that such perfect features would have lent charm to any hair, and if he tried all his styles on her and she showed them to the ladies of the Court he would soon become a Court hairdresser, for these stupid ladies were as vain as peacocks. They could easily be made to believe that they would look as she looked, if they wore their hair dressed the same way.

"Our fortune is made, Jeanne."

"Ours, Monsieur Lametz?" she asked.

At that he took her hands and kissed them, and then her cheeks and her lips.

"We shall be married," he said. "For evermore we shall be together."

Jeanne was delighted. He had been so good to her, and Jeanne always wanted to give a little more than she received; but that was not possible because he had been so very kind.

Would she marry him? Of course she would, if that was what he wished.

"Then," said the ardent young hairdresser, "I am the happiest man in France."

. . . . .

But his state of happiness did not last long, for when the infatuated young man told his mother of his intentions, Madame Lametz was furious.

"Marry an apprentice!" she cried. "I'll never allow that. Anne Rançon sent the girl to you that you should fall into this trap! This is an end to your fine romance, my boy. I'll send that minx packing . . . back to where she belongs—and that is the gardens of the Palais Royal. Believe me, I know."

And eventually, after much anguish, the young lover, broken in heart and in spirit—for he was very young and had never been able to defy his strong-minded mother—was forced to give up the beautiful apprentice, and Jeanne was sent back to her mother and stepfather.

Anne was furious. She had thought her daughter settled, and nothing would have delighted her more than a marriage between Jeanne and Monsieur Lametz.

When she heard that Madame Lametz had referred to her as a schemer and a procuress, she went to the police and stormily demanded justice; the honour of herself and her daughter, she declared, had been defiled. Meanwhile Madame Lametz had brought in the *curé* and between them Church and State managed to settle the dispute.

But the final result was that Jeanne was once more without a settled future.

However, she continued to attract the attention of all with whom she came into contact, and it was not long before another well-wisher had found her a post. She was educated; she could read; therefore she should be reader to a certain Madame de la Garde.

This lady lived in a château quite near Paris—the Château Courneuve—in some style, for she was very wealthy, being the widow of a tax-farmer. This meant that her late husband had been granted a lease, called a farm, which enabled him to collect taxes; for this was the method which was used in France before the Revolution. The profits made by these *fermiers généraux* were very large; and consequently the household in which Jeanne now found herself was more luxurious than anything she had ever known before.

Jeanne settled happily into this luxury. She realised now that the emotion she had felt for Lametz was gratitude. He had been kind to her and she had wished to repay his kindness. Therefore she was not heartbroken by the separation and generously hoped that he had not loved her as much as he had said he did.

Now she enjoyed the pleasure of life in the château and she intended to please Madame de la Garde so that she might stay in these delightful surroundings for the rest of her life.

Madame de la Garde was pleased with the charming young girl, who could read quite adequately and seemed demure enough. All might have been well had not Madame de la Garde's younger son come to visit her.

The young man seemed bemused as soon as he set eyes on his mother's young reader; Jeanne found him waylaying her in the gardens, walking with her, talking with her, kissing her hands and her lips, telling her that she was indeed the most beautiful girl he had ever seen.

Jeanne was delighted to know that the sight of her gave him so much pleasure, and she was grateful for the many services he sought to bestow upon her. Again, as in the case of young Monsieur Lametz, she found her gratitude welling up within her and she longed to repay this young man, for all he had done for her, by doing all he wished her to do for him.

This affair was quickly rushing to an inevitable conclusion when Madame de la Garde's elder son came home.

Like his brother he quickly discovered in Jeanne the most beautiful young woman he had ever seen, and now when

Jeanne strolled in the gardens there were two brothers waiting to escort her, to glare across her at each other, to jostle each other for the pleasure of helping her along as though she were a frail invalid instead of a young healthy girl; and when these two brothers came to blows Madame de la Garde became aware of what was going on.

She summoned Jeanne to her reading, and when Jeanne demurely went to the table and was about to open the book Madame de la Garde was unable to contain her feelings any longer.

"To think," she cried, "that I have taken a scheming creature like you into my house. I must have been mad. One look at your sly face is enough. Go upstairs at once, and pack your possessions. You are leaving here immediately."

"But Madame . . . " cried Jeanne in dismay. "I do not understand."

"Do you not?" cried Madame, incensed. "Suffice it that *I* understand too well. It is not as though *one* of my sons is mad enough to want to marry you—when they both do so I declare there must be a streak of madness in this family and it has taken a schemer like you to bring it to light!"

"It was not I, Madame," said Jeanne with spirit, "who asked them to marry me. It was they who talked of it . . . and quarrelled together over which of them should be my husband."

"Scheming slut!" cried Madame de la Garde. "You have brought some witch's spell into the house. I'll not have you here a moment longer. Go at once. And if you are not ready to be driven back to your parents' garret in five minutes I'll have you thrown out."

Jeanne dropped a curtsy; she went to her room and packed.

She was desolate at having to leave the beautiful château;

and she was so sorry for the two brothers, both of whom had declared they would die if she would not marry them.

Yet again she accepted her fate with her natural philosophy. When events appeared to repeat themselves they could no longer be wholly unexpected.

Jeanne's next post was the most significant. Through it she was to step into a world quite remote from the one which she had known until this time.

Madame Labille, the fashionable dressmaker and milliner in the Rue Saint Honoré, was interested to employ young women, providing they were decorative enough. Her shop was one of the most fashionable in Paris, and each day it was thronged by people who lived on the edge of the Court. Women came to examine her fine brocades and velvets, and to buy her exquisite hats; it was the duty of her beautiful shop-girls to wear the hats or drape the fine materials about them and so tempt the rich to buy.

Women were not the only ones who came to the shop. They brought their men friends; and there were times when men came alone. They wished to buy some gift from Madame Labille for a friend, they would say; but Madame Labille knew that what attracted them far more than her beautiful gifts were her beautiful sales-girls, some of whom had left the shop to enter into lives of ease and luxury.

To take away Madame's beautiful sales-girls would have been to take away the greatest attraction in her shop. Therefore that shrewd business woman was constantly on the alert for attractive girls to replace those who left.

The girls lived on the premises and Madame Labille made a great show of keeping a very virtuous household; but she always allowed a girl, who was chosen to do so, to deliver a parcel, thus giving a client the opportunity of becoming better acquainted with the girl than was possible in the shop.

It was said of Madame Labille's shop that it was beginning to resemble more and more an apartment at Versailles.

It was to Madame Labille that Jeanne received an introduction, and one sight of Jeanne was enough to convince Madame Labille that this girl would be entirely suitable for her establishment.

Jeanne, up to this time, had been known as Mademoiselle Rançon, but when she joined the staff of Labille's she became known as Mademoiselle L'Ange. This was a suitable name, for with her exquisite colouring, her serene expression and that beauty which set her apart from even the most attractive of the girls, she could be compared with an angel by those who wished to make the comparison; while, for those who preferred to choose their company from less holy society, a gleam of mischief or sensuality could be discovered in her which provoked amusement because she was thus named.

Paris already had the reputation of leading the world's fashions, and living in this perfumed atmosphere of elegance made its impression on Jeanne. Naturally she loved beautiful clothes and it often seemed unjust that she, who was fashioned to wear them, should be obliged to sell them to people who were old and ugly and for whom they could do very little.

In the dressing-rooms, the girls would try on the garments, the fantastic hats, the gorgeous gowns, and pretend that they were being presented to the King in the state apartments or dancing in the Galerie des Glaces. Their acquaintance with the gallants of the Court meant that they had some idea of how life went on in the homes of the rich, and since they often by request carried purchases to young men's homes they had seen inside many great houses.

The atmosphere of Labille's was therefore like that of a hot-house; girls who entered it quickly lost their simplicity and began to learn a great deal about life in a society different from that into which they had been born.

Jeanne discovered in herself a taste for the new life. Now she could laugh at herself for having been sorry to have been turned out of the Château Courneuve, and ask herself how she could have endured the boredom of such a life in the country. There, it was true, two men had been desperately in love with her; but here there were at least twenty who were as ardently courting her. As for poor Monsieur Lametz, the *coiffeur*, the life she would have shared with him would have been drab compared with this exhilarating existence. Thus she felt intensely grateful to Madame Lametz in spite of all the insulting remarks she had made about her and her mother. In any case Jeanne always found it difficult to bear resentment against anyone for any length of time.

Madame Labille watched her girls with an eagle eye. Shrewd, clever, never for one moment allowing herself to forget the interests of the Maison Labille, she kept up an appearance of respectability whilst never offending a client. It was small wonder that the establishment of Madame Labille had become like a club for Court dandies and men of all ages looking for adventure.

They brought business, so they were welcome; and Madame Labille was delighted when she recognised some important gentleman of the Court.

One day the Marquise de Quesnay came to the shop. Madame Labille herself was at the door to greet her when the carriage drew up.

"It is long since we have had the great honour of receiving you, Madame la Marquise," twittered Madame Labille.

The Marquise accepted the homage with aristocratic grace and, inside Madame Labille's private room, she told her that she wished to buy new dresses and to see the very newest materials.

These were brought and the Marquise, after examining

them, asked that some of the girls should be brought in that she might see the material draped on them and decide how it should be made up.

Jeanne was one of the girls who were called in on this occasion, and Madame Labille noticed that the Marquise was more interested in the girl than the materials.

"Why, my dear," said the Marquise, patting Jeanne's golden curls, "you look delightful in that colour. Alas, I am not so golden, nor so slender."

"Madame la Marquise will look far more enchanting than my little Ange," Madame Labille quickly assured her customer, "because, pretty as Mademoiselle is, she lacks poise and elegance."

The Marquise pursed her lips and nodded. She signed to Madame Labille that she wished to be alone with her.

When Jeanne had gone she said: "That is a very pretty girl."

"All comment on her beauty," said Madame Labille. "'Tis a wonder her head is not turned by the flattery."

"She has the serene look of the true beauty who takes her charm for granted. I find her interesting."

"I am surprised that I have kept her so long," said Madame Labille. "It is not because she has been ignored that she is not the mistress of some very rich Court gentleman."

"She will come to it . . . in the end. Poor child! Here she is among all these beautiful things and she has to see women like me wearing them."

"Madame is too modest. These beautiful materials were fashioned for such as you, not for little Ange."

"One might say she has enough beauty without adornment. I could make use of a girl like her."

"At your gaming-house, Madame?"

"Exactly. Once it was known that I had such a beauty there, those gentlemen who seem to spend their lives in the

71

hunt for women like your little angel, would flock there . . .
and so spend their money. Lend her to me."

"I am at your service, Madame. Mademoiselle L'Ange
shall bring what you select to your house, and I shall give
her permission to spend the evening there."

"That is my good friend Labille. And . . . you will see
that she is adequately gowned. You may charge that to me,
of course."

"It will be a pleasure."

Madame la Marquise smiled, gratified. "Let her dress be
simple yet . . . exquisite. Not too fussy, you understand.
Let us not hide the sheer perfection of the youthful figure."

"It shall be as Madame requests," said Madame Labille;
and she sighed, for experience told her that very soon the
exquisitely beautiful and extraordinarily good-natured
Mademoiselle L'Ange would no longer be a member of the
Labille establishment.

The girls of Labille's clustered round Jeanne. They had
always known she was beautiful, but never, they assured her,
had she looked as she did on this day.

Her gown was of a pale lavender colour, cut low to expose
the white neck and breasts; the skirt was trimmed with yards
of satin ribbon; and with her fair hair piled high on her
head—she was very glad that she had had some small
experience with Monsieur Lametz—she looked, as Madame
Labille secretly thought, the most beautiful creature who
had ever stood in her *salon*.

The girls called their warnings to her.

"Don't run off to share the life of the first nobleman who
asks you, Angel!"

"Remember the love of noblemen is not lasting."

"We shall want to hear *all* about it."

Madame Labille hushed them to silence. "Remember,
Mademoiselle L'Ange," she said quietly, "you are repre-

senting Labille, and if any should ask where your dress was made, you tell them. You will bring whoever is interested along at any time they wish. And do not be bemused by all the flattery you will receive. Remember this: these gallant gentlemen are merely repeating their set pieces. They mean little. Do not be foolish. Remember what a good home you have had in this house.''

Jeanne's answer was to throw her arms about Madame Labille's neck in an expression of gratitude. She would never, never forget, she assured her. Madame Labille had given her the happiest time of her life.

Then she kissed all the girls and rode away in a carriage for the gaming-house of the Marquise du Quesnay.

That night Jeanne met the Comte du Barry.

This meeting was the most significant in her life as yet. The Comte was immediately attracted as were many others at the house of the Marquise; but in du Barry's case there was a difference. He was filled with wild hopes when he surveyed her, not at the prospect of gratifying his desire—but beyond that. He believed that in this exquisite girl he saw a great future for himself.

He asked her about her life, and in a short time she had confessed to him that she was from the Maison Labille.

This seemed to please him. It would, as a matter of fact, make everything so simple.

In a short time she had told him about her upbringing and how Monsieur Billard du Monceaux had had her educated at a convent, so that she was by no means as ignorant as some of the girls at Labille's.

"Yet," said du Barry, "there is a world of difference between you and a lady."

Jeanne, accustomed to hear nothing but praises concerning herself, was a little startled.

"Your face is beautiful," went on du Barry. "So is your

figure. But when you move, when you gesture, when you begin to speak . . . poof!—away goes the illusion. All know that the *faubourgs* have been your home."

"What I have suits me well enough," said Jeanne.

"It would not suit a gentleman for more than a week or two."

"I have often heard that it is impossible to suit gentlemen for more than a week or two, so that is no news to me."

"My poor girl, you have been misled. There are women who have suited gentlemen for twenty years—and that when they are no longer young and beautiful. Do not tell me that, in your ignorance, you have never heard of Madame de Pompadour!"

"Everyone has heard of Madame Pompadour. I spoke of gentlemen, not of Kings."

"I shall tell His Majesty what you have said. He will be amused to hear he is not considered to be a gentleman."

Jeanne, in spite of herself, was a little awestruck to be in the company of one who was on speaking terms with the King.

Du Barry noticed this and was gratified.

"Your trouble, Mademoiselle L'Ange, is that you see no further than your nose. Beautiful as that nose is, this means your view is very restricted. There is a great deal *I* could teach you."

"Now," said Jeanne, "we are on familiar ground. All my life I have been meeting gentlemen who assure me there is a great deal they could teach me. Yet what I learned from them did not seem so very much after all."

The Comte du Barry was more impressed than he wished her to know. She had a certain wit and, because it was without asperity, it held novelty. This girl, with the right grounding such as he could give, would be a great success.

He began to talk of himself, seeking to impress her with the grandeur of his background, exaggerating considerably in the description of his family's estates near Toulouse and his own position at the Court.

He wished her to be very careful, he said. If she were not, she would very soon become the mistress of one of the fine gentlemen, such as those who were watching her now in an almost carnivorous manner; she would become the mistress of one, then another. She would be handed down and with each change her position would worsen. She had seen the women in the meaner streets of Paris, had she not? Well, that was how she would become unless she was very careful.

He had a feeling that he would like to protect her. How did she feel about accepting his protection?

"I am young," said Jeanne. "I am strong; and each day I grow more aware of the world. If I did not need a protector two years ago, why should I need one now?"

"Because you are nearer to danger now than you were two years ago."

"Danger? I see no danger."

"That which is invisible is more to be feared than that which is seen."

"You amuse me," said Jeanne.

"You delight me. Amusement, delight. What could be a happier combination? I have a house in the Rue des Petits-Champs. I should like to show it to you."

"I have promised to return to Labille's tonight."

"Then I shall conduct you there."

He did, and bade her *au revoir* in an almost formal manner.

Jeanne, recounting her adventures to her friends, had to admit that the Comte du Barry was the most extraordinary man she had ever met.

He was at the shop next day—and the next. He ordered fine clothes, for his sister, he said; and Jeanne was to bring them to his house.

75

This she did and he showed her his establishment with the beautiful *salon* where he entertained his guests. He would be very happy, he told her, if she were one of his guests, but first he would have to give her a few lessons in deportment.

"Why," he added, "if you knew how to act and speak with some semblance of a lady, I might arrange an invitation for you to go to Court."

Her eyes sparkled at the prospect, and she thought of old Grand-père Bécu who had such tales to tell of the lady who had been visited by a King.

Du Barry, watching her, knew that he was gradually luring her into the trap.

So du Barry won. Jeanne left Labille's to the great regret of Madame, who could only shrug her shoulders and murmur: "That! Well, that is life. It had to happen sooner or later with one such as she is."

He did so much for her. She had lessons every day. She learned how to curtsy, how not to burst into loud laughter when she was pleased; how to hold a fan and put her hand to her lips when she yawned; she learned how to eat daintily.

It was the devil's own job though, declared the Comte, to teach her how to speak.

He was very patient, and she became very fond of him. There was so much to be grateful for, so that it was inevitable that when he desired to be her lover she should accept him as such, and that because he wished her to please his friends, as she had pleased him, she should feel in duty bound to do so.

She became known in certain circles as du Barry's beautiful mistress. She could be seen at the entertainments he gave at his house; and because of her charm and beauty there were many to clamour for such invitations.

He even allowed her to be known as Madame du Barry, to let the whole world know that, although he might allow

76

a certain dalliance where he considered it expedient, she belonged to him.

Four years passed and Jeanne still continued in this way of life.

When she reminded her lover that he had once talked of having her introduced to Court he bade her be patient. He did not despair yet of bringing that about. It was a matter of extreme delicacy, he assured her; it must not be hurried.

She was astonished to see the brilliance of his eyes when he thought of that possibility; she noted the edge on his voice.

Jeanne had laughingly said that she did not believe he would ever be able to keep his promise and introduce her to the Court. That was why, on that occasion when he had come in full of excitement and told her of his encounter with Monsieur Le Bel, she was unmoved; and when he said she must forget the past, she could only respond by remembering it.

4

SUPPER AT VERSAILLES

"I PERCEIVE, Le Bel," said the King, "that your thoughts are not with us."

Le Bel, who was stooping to adjust his master's shoe, looked up in startled horror.

"I am in a quandary, Sire," he mumbled, his face scarlet with the exertion of bending and with the mortification such an accusation aroused. "I dare not contradict Your Majesty; and yet if I tell the truth I must say that my thoughts are continually with you."

"You grow more and more of a courtier every day," retorted the King. "It's natural. How long have you been in my service? Oh, never mind. Suffice it that it is a long time. Of what were you thinking, Le Bel? Was it of some woman who pleases you?"

"Sire, I can in all honesty say that the women who have most persistently occupied my thoughts have been those who I believe would please Your Majesty."

"You have worked well in that direction, Le Bel. I should be the last to deny it. Now tell me, what is on your mind? Who is she, and why have you decided to keep her from me?"

Le Bel rose to his feet. "Your Majesty's perception is uncanny," he said.

"Well, I am waiting to hear."

"Sire, it is true that my thoughts were of a woman. But I am deeply perplexed. Should I dare bring her to Your Majesty's notice . . ."

"How many women have you brought to my notice in the past, Le Bel? Do you remember? I do not. Yet I should not have said that in the course of your business you were a very daring man."

"I have always selected these women with the utmost care, Sire. They have all been physically attractive, and they have all had some semblance of breeding."

"And this new one?"

La Bel shook his head.

"Tell me," said the King. "Does she squint? Has she a hare-lip? Such deformities could, I dare say, in very special circumstances provide a piquancy."

"Physically she is perfection, Sire."

"Yet you are perturbed with perfection!"

"Sire, I have seen her and was astonished by so much beauty and yet . . ." Le Bel lifted his shoulders.

"And yet?" prompted the King.

"Great efforts have been made to render her pleasing. . . ."

"And the result?" asked Louis.

"Alas, Sire. Although it would be impossible, I think, to find her equal in physical beauty, it would be equally impossible to make her presentable at Court."

"I am interested," said the King languidly. "Why is it impossible to instil a little breeding into this physically perfect creature?"

"I do not know her well enough to say, Sire. She is . . . of the people, perhaps. Her laughter is too loud . . . too sudden . . . too uncontrolled. She will greet one with a certain decorum, but this persists only for a few minutes; then she will appear to throw decorum to the winds and then . . ."

"And then, Le Bel?"

"Then we have nothing more than *une petite grisette*, Sire."

"But a very beautiful one. I'll see her, Le Bel."

79

"Your Majesty, I do not think you realise how tiresome the company of such people can be."

"Nonsense. I have known all kinds of women."

"I implore your clemency, Sire, but I must point out that although women of the lower stratum have sometimes pleased you—for a very short time—it has always been the endeavour of myself, and others, to shield you from the embarrassment of the . . . vulgar."

"You pamper me, Le Bel," said Louis sardonically. "You must allow me to make my own decisions, you know."

"Sire, forgive me. I think only of your comfort and pleasure."

"I'll see your *grisette*."

Le Bel's face lightened. "Perhaps she might amuse you for an evening. Yet . . ."

"I understand," said the King. "You would not wish her to know that her new friend is the King, for fear that even a small dose of her company might prove too astringent for the royal palate and it become necessary to dismiss her after I have endured five minutes of her too loud, too sudden and uncontrolled laughter."

"Sire, I would arrange a little party in my rooms."

The King nodded.

"And if Your Majesty would honour me with your presence . . ."

The King nodded again. "I shall come," he said, "as Baron de Gonesse. Then, if I find our *grisette* disappointing, I shall make some excuse and retire from your party . . . and no harm done."

Le Bel knelt and kissed the royal hand.

"Your Majesty has relieved me of a great dilemma."

The King waved his hand and dismissed the *valet de chambre*.

When he was alone he smiled. An observer would have thought that some weighty matter of State had been settled.

This is France, he pondered, in this eighteenth century, and this is France's King.

He went to a window and looked out on the Avenue de Paris. It was a view which never failed to fill him with a faint apprehension. The people of Paris were not fond of him, and he rarely went into the capital. The poverty which it was impossible not to see there set anxieties stirring within him.

He turned his back abruptly on the view. It was far more pleasant to think of the coming supper-party during which he could be amused, or disgusted, by Le Bel's new discovery.

A servant entered to announce that the Duc de Choiseul was asking for an audience.

She was ready. Her gown had been chosen with the utmost care. Du Barry examined her from all angles, while she posed in a manner which brought tears of exasperation to his eyes.

"Can you never be serious?" he demanded, in a tone which trembled with excitement. "Do you not realise that at last, after all these years, we are to be admitted to the Palace of Versailles?"

"I should be a fool if I did not," retorted Jeanne, "for you have talked of nothing else since the invitation came from your Monsieur Le Bel."

"Do not call him mine in that flippant manner. You would, if you were a wise woman, do your utmost to make him *your* Monsieur Le Bel."

Jeanne wrinkled her nose. "He was not to my taste. He is too old, and I liked not his prying eyes. I felt like a prize heifer put up for sale."

"I have already impressed upon you the need to ingratiate yourself with Monsieur Le Bel."

Jeanne shrugged her shoulders. "I have listened to enough scolding about my first meeting with Monsieur Le

F   81

Bel. Monsieur Le Bel does not like me. Very well, I do not like Monsieur Le Bel. You stormed at me. You said I threw away my chances. You threatened to send me back to Madame Labille. And you see, *mon ami*, you were wrong. You said Monsieur Le Bel was not interested. And now we have this invitation to the party."

"I think I know the answer," mused du Barry. "Monsieur Le Bel considers you such a beautiful young woman that, in spite of your bad manners, he is ready to give you another chance. So I beg of you, behave with decorum tonight."

Jeanne patted his cheeks. "You look so worried," she said. "I will do my best. But you know how forgetful I am."

He looked at her in exasperation. She was very lovely in her dress of blue lace. If only he could have grafted on to her the manners of a Court lady she would have been quite irresistible.

He was realising now the futility of trying to do that. He had picked up this flower, this rose—no, this orchid—from the streets of Paris, and because of her exquisite beauty he had believed that he could train and mould her into becoming another Pompadour.

It was only now, when the great chance was immediately before them, that he realised his folly. Le Bel, startled as he had been by her loveliness, was uncertain whether it would be wise to bring her to the notice of the King, who, charmed as he must be by her appearance, would surely be horrified at her manners which, for all the veneer that had carefully been laid over them, emerged in moments of excitement; and as one of Jeanne's characteristics was that irresistible *joie de vivre*, life was constantly offering her excitement.

Was it any use saying more to her now? No. The only thing was to trust to luck.

The carriage was waiting; they were both silent as they drove to Versailles . . . he with apprehension, she with excitement. Every now and then she would laugh aloud as though at her secret thoughts.

Monsieur Le Bel was waiting for them. He took one look at Jeanne and the worried expression in his eyes lifted a little. Her appearance was all that he could expect.

Jeanne gave him her too ready smile; her curtsy was short and quick and seemed to hold a trace of flippancy.

Du Barry was aware of the *valet de chambre*'s uneasiness, and inwardly he groaned while he greeted Le Bel with ceremonial formality, an unspoken reminder to Jeanne that she was in the Palace of Versailles and should be very impressed.

As they were conducted up a staircase, Le Bel said: "It is a very intimate supper-party. A few gentlemen of the Court . . . friends of mine."

Du Barry threw a glance at Jeanne which was meant to remind her once more that she was on trial and that she must remember that every minute she was in the company of these people they would be watching her for some fault, something which would label her a *grisette*, a girl of the people. Le Bel was clearly still uncertain and he wished for the opinion of his friends before he introduced her to the King.

That Jeanne had quite forgotten that she was on trial was obvious when she said frankly: "I never thought to take supper at Versailles!"

"Madame," said Le Bel hastily, "you understand that this party is taking place in my own small apartments."

Jeanne burst into her loud laugh. "You should not apologise to us for the smallness of your apartments, Monsieur Le Bel. They are Versailles—and that is enough for us. I did not expect to take supper in the state dining-room, or dance with the Dauphin in the Galerie des Glaces!"

Du Barry caught his breath in horror while Le Bel cleared his throat.

"Yet Madame," said the latter with dignity, "even in the

humblest apartment of Versailles we observe the etiquette of the Court."

"I hear His Majesty insists on that!" cried Jeanne. "Oh, what a life!"

Beads of sweat had appeared on the bridge of Le Bel's nose. He had come to a door, and he seemed to be seeking the courage to open it.

He believes, thought du Barry, that he is going to look extremely foolish in the eyes of his friends.

The door was opened. Four or five men were seated about a table, which was laden with food and wine.

Monsieur Le Bel announced: "The Comte du Barry and his sister-in-law, Madame du Barry."

The men had risen from the table and come towards the newcomers; one by one they took Jeanne's hand and bowed whilst she stood smiling at them.

"Let us be seated," said Le Bel, his voice high-pitched with nervousness. "Madame du Barry, I pray you, take this seat next to the Baron de Gonesse."

Jeanne took her seat, and surveyed the table; the food and wine looked good, and her eyes sparkled.

She turned and studied her neighbour, a man who, she guessed, was in his fifties; he was not handsome—far from it —yet he had an air of distinction such as she had never seen in any other man. It set him apart from the company and, even in the first few moments, Jeanne sensed that the others were aware of it. It was not his clothes, which were elegant but no different from those worn by the others; she was faintly intrigued and wondered what it was about the man which immediately caught her interest.

"Baron de Gonesse," she said, "I like your name."

"That pleases me," he said.

"Do you want to hear why?"

"If you would be so good as to tell me."

"Well, it's because it reminds me of the bakers of Gonesse."

There was an immediate hush around the table.

Monsieur Le Bel hastily signed to one of the servants to serve Madame du Barry, and Jeanne turned her dazzling smile from the Baron de Gonesse to this servant and thanked him with her usual good nature.

One of the gentlemen ventured nervously: "Madame, did you follow the hunt today? The Baron is a great hunter."

"No," said Jeanne, "I do not follow the hunt."

The Baron de Gonesse leaned towards her. "You were comparing me with the bakers," he said. "Pray go on."

"Oh, it was only the name." Jeanne burst into loud laughter. "You are not in the least like a baker, Monsieur le Baron. I should say no man could be less like one."

Le Bel laughed nervously.

"Madame du Barry," said one of the gentlemen, "tell me, what do you think of the new dances which have been introduced at Court?"

"It is safe to say that I like them very much for I like all dances," answered Jeanne.

She turned to smile at her neighbour, because she felt that he was the only one among the company who was at ease.

"You did not mind, I hope," she said, "that I said you reminded me of the bakers."

"Indeed not."

She leaned towards him and whispered: "I think I've shocked the others."

She laughed; his lips turned up at the corners. He was amused, but he did not laugh uproariously as she did. The others seemed to take their cue from him, and there were smiles all round the table.

"They come in, you know, with their bread," she said, "and they are not allowed to take any of it back through the barriers. They have to leave behind what they do not sell. It is sad when they don't sell it. I was always sorry for them when that happened."

"It grieves me," said the Baron de Gonesse, "that my name should have reminded you of them and your sorrow."

She patted his hand. "Now that *is* kind of you." She turned to him and her blue eyes were brilliant. "But it was not your fault. And I am far from sad. In fact I am very happy. It is a wonderful experience to have supper inside the Palace of Versailles. Do you not think so?"

"I am grateful to Monsieur Le Bel for inviting me to *this* supper-party," he said.

"Well, to me it is very exciting. I feel quite sorry for the poor King because he must have had supper so many times in the Palace of Versailles that it can no longer greatly excite him."

"I am sure you are exactly right in that."

She leaned her elbows on the table and as she did so caught du Barry's eye. Something was wrong with him for he was wriggling on his chair as though he was in great pain, his face slightly contorted, so that she realised he was trying to convey some message to her.

"What's wrong?" she demanded.

There was silence; everyone was looking from her to the Comte du Barry who, pretending he had not heard her, addressed a remark to his neighbour.

Jeanne shrugged her shoulders and turned to Monsieur de Gonesse.

She whispered: "He is eager for me to make a good impression on you all. I fear my manners bother him."

"He is churlish to be bothered by what should enchant him," said the Baron.

Jeanne put her hand to her mouth to soften her laughter.

"Tell me what amuses you?" said the Baron.

"The trouble with gentlemen of the Court is that they never say what they mean. Enchanting, my manners! Now you know that's a lie."

"I protest," he answered. "It is no lie. I swear I find your manners quite enchanting."

Her eyes had grown gentle. "I like you," she said. "You're a kind man. I know what you're thinking. This woman . . . having supper in Versailles . . . it's outrageous. Look at her behaviour. She does not belong to Versailles. You know, these other people do not like it at all; but because you're kind, you're pretending you do." Again she had taken his hand. "That's why I like you. You take good manners a step further, that's what you do. I bet you can bow and roll your head about as well as any of these—yet you can be kind too."

"You're flattering me, you know," he said. "I am not very kind."

"Nonsense!"

The others had heard the expletive escape from her, and again she was aware of the hush about the table.

She turned to him conspiratorially and, lifting her hand, shielded her face from the rest of them and grinned at him.

"Don't you dare to contradict me," she said, "about a matter which is so obvious." She leaned closer towards him. "Are you a very important man?"

"What makes you ask?"

"It's the way they look at you, the way they behave towards you. I believe they think I'm being impertinent to you. Am I?"

"You're being delightful to me. I am enjoying this party, and it is entirely due to your presence."

"Well, I'm enjoying it too and I think . . . well, no, it's not entirely on account of you, because I should have enjoyed it in any case. Supper at Versailles! It makes me laugh. Me . . . having supper at Versailles."

"Do you always enjoy life so much?"

She looked back over the years—to Vaucouleurs, the house of Mademoiselle Frédéric, her brief apprenticeship in the

87

hairdressing establishment, the Château Courneuve, Labille's
. . . even the convent: looking back on it, it seemed that she
had enjoyed it all.

She was laughing at the memory of it now; little incidents
from the past flitted before her mind's eye and even those
which had seemed tragic at the time seemed funny now.

She said: "Forgive me, Monsieur le Baron, but there is so
much to laugh at in life."

"In your life, you mean?"

"In everybody's, I imagine. Do you not agree?"

"There does not seem to have been a great deal of laughter
in mine."

He seemed so pitiable at that moment that she gave him
a friendly nudge in the arm. It was one of the gestures of
which du Barry had taken great pains to cure her.

"It's the way you look at it," she said. "If you go around
like a misery you can't expect life to be funny, can you?"

He agreed that this might be the case.

She was laughing again. "You are a queer one," she told
him. "You can never say Yes, or No . . . simply, like that.
Everything you say is like an important pronouncement.
Now look here, lots of funny things must have happened to
you."

"I am trying to recall them."

"You look as if you've had a lot of experience of life and
grown rather tired of it all."

"You have diagnosed my case correctly."

"Hark at yourself," she said. "Just hark! See what I
mean about not being able to say a plain Yes or No?"

Monsieur Le Bel had risen; he whispered into the ear of
the Baron de Gonesse: "If you should be in need of
rescue . . ."

"Certainly not," snapped the Baron. "I am in the middle
of a conversation which happens to interest me."

Le Bel returned to his place crestfallen, yet relieved.

Jeanne pursed her lips and nodded, not without a look of triumph at Le Bel; in doing so she caught du Barry's eye and saw that he was gazing at her in bewilderment.

A plague on them both, she thought. I like my Baron. He's the most interesting person at their supper-party.

"He meant he would rescue you from me," she whispered to the Baron. "What impertinence!"

"I agree whole-heartedly."

"As if you couldn't rescue yourself. Are you a baby? Do you have to he helped away from a woman who talks too much?" Again she nudged his arm. "Now *I* should say you were never one to have had any trouble on that score. Not with those lovely old phrases of yours." She laughed again. "Now I've got an idea that you like talking to me as much as I like talking to you."

"How discerning you are!"

"Now what were we speaking of before we were interrupted? Oh, I know. You were feeling that you had experienced most things and there was nothing of any great interest left."

"That's a sad state for a man to be in, is it not?"

"It's a foolish state. There's always something new in life, something that's going to be interesting to learn about. That's what I have always found."

"I do happen to have lived many years more than you have. It may be that I have undergone certain experiences as yet untested by yourself."

"You do make me laugh," she said. "Now, there must be a lot you don't know. And another thing, even if you are not young any more, which I see you're not, there are qualities which older people have and which the young ones lack."

"I have always thought that youth was one of the most desirable of all possessions."

She snapped her fingers. "Oh, Monsieur de Gonesse,

there is much you have to learn. I should like to take you on a tour through Paris. Yes, Paris . . . not very far from this Palace of Versailles. There you would see many poor people, all with something to be sad about and all young, and perhaps the sadder because they *are* young and have not learned that life cannot be *all* misery." A shadow crossed her face. "But we will not speak of them. This is to be a happy night."

He said: "You are right. We must allow nothing to spoil this night."

"But I do want you to understand, Monsieur Melancholy, that you have no reason to be sad because you have experienced so much and there seems little that is new left for you to do."

"You are a very charming mentor," he said.

She laughed and wagged a finger at him. "Then see you follow my advice."

"It is what I want very much to do."

She studied him intently. "Do you know, I think I have seen you somewhere before."

"I wish I had seen you somewhere before. Then this night would not have been the occasion of our first meeting."

"Do you mean that, Monsieur de Gonesse, or are you telling one of your flattering lies again?"

"I mean it," he said.

"Then I'm glad. I feel we've become too friendly to bother with the lies."

"I do not think I have ever seen anyone with a face and figure to compare with yours."

"And you have seen no one with manners to compare with mine either."

"That's true."

"I understand. The one pleases you—the other . . . it horrifies you. Go on. Admit it. You can say what you like.

Have a rest from formality because I can see you know as much about this Court etiquette as any of them."

"You must not ask me to admit what is not true. Did you not say that there should be truth between us? I find your person completely beautiful and your manners entirely piquant. You see, that is an irresistible combination."

"You know I'm doing all the wrong things and you're comforting me. But I like you for it. Did I not say you were kind? Kindness pleases me more than youth or good looks in a man."

"Are you telling me that *I* please you?"

For answer she patted his hand once more.

She caught du Barry's eye and grimaced pertly at him in a manner which made him hastily look away. She glanced about the room at the tasteful furnishings and the air of elegance displayed even in this small chamber. Supper at Versailles! she thought; and she wished that she could have boasted of this to the girls at Labille's or compared her experiences with those of Grand-père Bécu.

"Tell me your thoughts," said Monsieur de Gonesse.

"I was thinking of my grandfather. He would have liked to see me now. He once saw Louis Quatorze. He said he was a great King. I wish I had seen him."

"He was . . . impressive, even at the end."

"You knew him?"

"I . . . have seen him."

"Why, you could not have been more than a baby!"

"I was five and a half when he died."

"He died here . . . in this Palace, did he not?"

Gonesse nodded.

"Now I've made you gloomy," she said. "Versailles is not a place to be gloomy in."

"How can you know that, when this is your first visit?"

"What! All that splendour? What is it for, eh . . . the fine

91

marble, the glittering glass, the statues in the gardens . . . and the fountains and the flowers! What is it all for, if not to make people happy?"

"What indeed!" he said. "Tell me, which part of the Palace impresses you most?"

"I'll tell you. This part. This room. Because in it I am at a supper-party and I have made the acquaintance of my good friend Monsieur Melancholy de Gonesse."

He smiled again. "Tonight this is my favourite room in the Palace of Versailles. The Galerie des Glaces, the Salon d'Hercules, the Grotte de Thétis . . . what are these compared with the *petite chambre* of Monsieur Le Bel? And all because it is lighted by the presence of surely the most charming lady in France!"

"I believe," she said, "that you are on very familiar terms with the Palace. Tell me about these places . . . the Salon d'Hercules and the rest."

"How much better it would be if I were to show you . . . that is, show all that it is possible to show. You understand. . . ."

"Oh, I understand of course. There are places you couldn't show me."

"Certain difficulties might present themselves."

"Certain difficulties!" Her laughter rose to a high pitch. "I should say there were! I should not expect you to show me the King's bedchamber!"

"That might be achieved . . . in time," he said.

"Perhaps when he is away."

"He rarely goes away."

"They say he is afraid to show his face in Paris. And can you wonder?"

"I have ceased to wonder at anything."

"There goes the old cynic. There's a lot of poverty in Paris and the people hear these tales about him. No, he is wise to cling to Versailles and not show his face in Paris."

"Do the people hate him so much?"

She looked serious, then said quietly: "When things go wrong, people in high places are always hated. Those who lack possessions always hate those who do not."

"And you . . . what do you think of him?"

"I? Who should care what I think of the King?"

"Perhaps he would."

That provoked the loud laughter. She nudged him once more. "Did you really mean you could show me something of the Palace?"

"I did."

"When?"

"What is wrong with this moment?" He leaned closer to her and, imitating her gesture, he lifted his hand to shield his face from the company. "To tell the truth, I am a little weary of this party—I mean those guests who are not ourselves. Would you care to slip away?"

"I'm sure that would be a great breach of etiquette."

"Do you care if it is?"

"Not I. But you . . ."

"If you do not care, why should I?"

"But how?"

"Leave it to me."

He stood up. Jeanne was too amused to notice that everyone else stood.

"Madame du Barry and I have decided we will have a look at the Palace. I pray you all sit down and continue your supper."

They hesitated, and the Baron went on with some testiness: "I said, sit down." They sat; and offering his arm to Jeanne he led her from Monsieur Le Bel's apartment.

When the door closed behind them, Jeanne began to laugh. "Forgive me," she said, "but it was their faces. I'm sure they'll never forget it . . . as long as they live. That Monsieur Le Bel . . . I thought he was going to drop to the floor in a fit . . . and as for that other . . . that old one . . ."

"Richelieu."

"Was that his name? I thought he was going to faint right away."

So infectious was her laughter that the Baron joined in. Jeanne began to mimic him, his regal gesture, his cold clear voice: "'I have decided we shall have a look at the Palace. I pray you all sit down and continue with your supper.' If you'd threatened to blow them up with gunpowder they could not have been more astounded. It's this etiquette. . . . It's all etiquette at Versailles. You must admit it's comic."

"Yes," agreed the Baron, "I do admit it."

She looked at him with pride. "Who is Monsieur Melancholy now?"

"Not the Baron de Gonesse," he answered. "Madame du Barry, you may not be aware of it, but you are working a miracle."

She was serious suddenly. "I'm glad," she said. "In fact I'm happy . . . very, very happy. You are too charming a person to be melancholy—and let me tell you I like you better laughing than moping."

"So you find you are beginning to like me?"

"Of course I'm beginning to like you. I liked you the minute I saw you. Perhaps it was because I saw you liked me and that you were not going to care how much I shocked the company." She lifted her face to his suddenly and kissed his cheek.

"There, Monsieur de Gonesse. Now we'll explore." She took his arm. "But what," she whispered, "if we are discovered?"

He whispered back. "We must take good care not to be discovered. I spoke of the Galerie des Glaces."

"Yes," she said. "Take me there . . . if it is not too dangerous."

94

"I feel reckless tonight," said the Baron.

"That's a good sign," she told him. "It means you're forgetting all those melancholy thoughts about being old and having done everything."

"I am clutching at an illusion."

"It's no illusion. You're not old, Monsieur le Baron. Remember how you laughed a moment ago. That was young laughter. A man or woman need not be old . . . if they do not wish to be."

"I like your philosophy. I hope you will teach it to me."

"I will—in exchange for this glimpse of the Palace which you are going to give me."

He began to talk of Versailles, and she listened entranced. He cared passionately about Versailles, and he became almost animated as he discussed it with someone who knew so little about it that it must all seem fresh to her.

"The Palace of Versailles has been said to be one of the most beautiful palaces in the world," he told her. "The King had it built that it might express his greatness and the greatness of France in the eyes of the world. Everything in this building is the result of a great deal of thought. The King did not merely say, Build me a palace—and his artists, architects and workmen produced this. Oh no! The finest palace in the western world could not come into existence as simply and easily as that."

She nodded vigorously in understanding agreement.

He went on: "The King was *le Roi Soleil*, and the Palace was to represent those worlds which revolved about him. Everything was meant to display the glory of the sun; symbolism is in every column, every court and gallery."

"They don't have Kings like him any more, so my grandfather said."

"Alas," said the Baron, "his great-grandson resembles him in some respects—in his desire to create beautiful buildings.

95

He has spent too much time and money on his palaces and this is one of the reasons why, as you say, there is much misery only a few miles away in Paris."

"You're getting melancholy again. Tell me about the sun and his worlds."

"On the western side of the Palace there are three porticoes and each has four columns. These represent the twelve months of the year, and over the first-floor windows you would find scenes representing the four seasons. If you study the keystones over the windows you will see that they represent all the ages of man from infancy to old age."

As he spoke he had been guiding her with an air of the utmost familiarity, and they had reached the great Galerie.

Jeanne caught her breath at the beauty of the place. The Baron stood still, watching her ecstasy with quiet pleasure.

"The architect," he said, "was Mansart; the decorations are due to Le Brun, although of course one must not forget Tubi and Coysevox."

She was not listening; she could only look at the tall windows each of which was reflected in the mirror opposite. There were seventeen enormous chandeliers of crystal, and numerous other candelabra. Jeanne began to count them but gave it up. The curtains were of white and gold brocade; the *guéridons* lining the walls were made of glistening silver as were the tubs which contained flowers of all colours. The floors were covered with the most exquisite of Savonnerie carpets, and about the great gallery and on the ceiling were carved allegorical figures of the most breath-taking beauty.

Even Jeanne's natural exuberance was quelled by the sight of so much grandeur.

"It is surely the most beautiful place in the world," she said. "Oh, Monsieur de Gonesse, how can I thank you for showing it to me?"

"The public is allowed into Versailles, you know. You did not need me to bring you here."

"Ah, but to see it thus . . . with no one else here except us two! That is the way to see the Galerie des Glaces."

"I am beginning to wonder," said the Baron, putting his face close to hers, "whether it is not the way to see all things."

Jeanne turned to smile at him. He was growing fond of her, she knew. She was unperturbed. He appealed to her because he had been kind and had saved her from the solemnity of that supper-party. She felt gratitude welling up within her.

"Well," she said, "we did escape from the gloom of Monsieur Le Bel and his friends, did we not!"

He kissed her hand. "We did. I hope our escape may be permanent."

She was puzzled, but she did not ask what he meant by that. She turned from him to the splendour of the Galerie. "This is a place," she said, "in which to dance. It was made for dancing."

"You should see it on a ceremonial occasion," he told her. "Then you would say it really is splendid."

She had broken away from him and began to dance, her blue gown twirling round her, a solitary figure in the great Galerie.

The Baron watched her, and watching knew that she had wrought the miracle. He had forgotten he was fifty-eight; he had forgotten that he was old. She offered him no flattery, as did everyone else with whom he came into contact; and yet she had dragged him away from melancholy; for an evening she had made him share her glorious youth. Now, as he watched her, he was asking himself why he should not continue to share it for more than an evening.

He was growing impatient now of the masquerade. He wanted to hold that warm, young and, he was sure, passionate body in his arms.

He said: "It is enough."

And the command in his voice startled her in spite of herself.

She stopped dancing and came to him.

"You looked enchanting," he said. "I should like to watch you dance for hours but . . ."

"We must not be caught," she said.

"There are other places I wish to show you."

She was not alarmed by the urgency in his voice; she was experienced enough to realise his need of her and she wondered vaguely how this strange evening would end.

He was leading her up a staircase to a suite of rooms; she was aware of people who seemed to appear and disappear at a wave of the Baron's hand, and she began to suspect that the Baron was a very much more important person than she had at first believed.

"These," he said to her, "are the *petits appartements*. This is where the King of France spends most of his time. And here we have the King's own bedroom. What do you think of this, Madame du Barry?"

She had grown a little pale. "What right have we to be here?" she asked.

"As much right as any," he soothed her.

"What . . . if we should be discovered?"

"I have made arrangements that we shall not be disturbed."

She stared at him and took a step backwards.

"So . . ." she said, "I have been misled."

He spread his hands elegantly. "Perhaps . . . a little."

"And you . . . are not merely Baron de Gonesse."

"All the time I was myself, and remember, I did not displease you."

She laughed a little hysterically.

"I . . . I knew your face. I understand now. It was the plain dress. What . . . what should I do now? Fall to my knees or . . . something?"

98

He placed his hands on her shoulders. "We will dispense with all ceremony," he said. "I think that will be your wish and mine. . . ."

She drew back from him; her startled eyes looked towards the door.

He took her hands and kissed them with passion. "I am the same man as the melancholy Gonesse whom you made less melancholy. Madame, you delight me. You enchant me. You make me feel young again. It is my wish that you stay with me . . . that you show me how to be young again."

"You could command me," said Jeanne, "yet you seem to plead."

"I would not wish to command . . . in love," he told her. "I would have you come to me of your own free will . . . not because I am the King of France, but because I am poor Monsieur de Gonesse whose melancholy disturbed you, since you have a kind heart and wish to cure him of it."

Jeanne held up her radiant face, and the blue beribboned gown which had caused the Comte du Barry such anxiety was crushed against the somewhat sombre garments of the self-styled Baron de Gonesse who, as though at the waving of a wand, had been turned into the King of France.

5

CONSTERNATION AT COURT

THE Court was seething with excitement. The King had
a new mistress and was completely absorbed in her.

Who was she? everyone was asking. No one seemed to
be very certain on that subject, and wild rumours circulated
through the Palace.

The Duchesse de Gramont came angrily to her brother.

"I have been forbidden . . . yes, forbidden . . . the King's
apartments!"

The Duc de Choiseul looked pained. "It is intolerable
that you should be insulted thus."

"Who is this creature who is amusing Louis?"

"Some little light-o'-love. My dear sister, you take this
too much to heart. Think of Pompadour. Why, she first
stood aside for those who were younger and fresher, and then
became his procuress."

"One hears the most hysterical laughter coming from the
apartments," went on the Duchesse. "And, I regret to
say, the King's voice is recognisable."

"It may be that he is becoming unbalanced. But I agree
with you, sister, that it is humiliating for you."

"It was that scoundrel, Le Bel, who brought her to the
King, I hear."

"I doubt that not. Le Bel has been in charge of the
King's lighter moments for years."

"He should be ashamed!" cried the Duchesse. "They
should both be ashamed. Louis . . . at fifty-eight to behave
like . . . like a young shepherd! And as for that obscene

Le Bel, he must be seventy, and at his age should find more dignified ways of occupying his time."

"I will summon Le Bel and we will hear at first-hand what we must discover about the King's new *inamorata*. But, my dear sister, I am certain that you are unnecessarily disturbed. Louis has often had these little *affaires*. They mean nothing. In a week—or two weeks at the most—they are over, and he returns to companions more suited to his state."

Choiseul sent a page to ask Monsieur Le Bel if he would come at once to the Duke's apartments.

Le Bel stood before the first minister in the land and, as soon as he saw the stormy expression on the face of Choiseul's sister, he knew why they had sent for him.

"At your service, Madame de Gramont, Monsieur le Duc," he murmured.

"I pray you be seated, Monsieur Le Bel," said Choiseul graciously. "I expect you guess why I have asked you to come to see me. There is a great deal of gossip in the Court —somewhat disturbing gossip—and you are the man best informed of the truth."

"I gather you speak of the new mistress, Monsieur le Duc."

"Whatever possessed you to bring such a creature to Versailles?" burst out the Duchesse.

Le Bel spread his hands. "Madame, I have always searched far and wide to satisfy the King's pleasure."

"Never so far and never so wide as this time," snorted the Duchesse, "if one can believe all one hears."

"I will admit," said Le Bel, "that the lady is a little . . . different from those who usually amuse His Majesty."

"I should hope so," snapped the Duchesse. "I cannot imagine what the Court would be like if we had many of her sort at Versailles."

Choiseul interrupted soothingly: "My dear Duchesse, this upstart woman will soon have left Versailles and everybody here—most of all the King—will forget that she ever came."

Le Bel looked relieved. "Monsieur le Duc is right, Madame."

The Duchesse looked faintly relieved, but she went on: "Yet the *affaire* has lasted a week. Is that not rather long if this woman is all we have heard of her?"

"Madame," said Le Bel, "she is young and she is beautiful, even though her voice and manners seem to belong to *les Halles*. She is amusing . . . for a time . . . a very brief time. Believe me, I know His Majesty."

"We feel," said Choiseul with a hint of menace in his voice, "that you, Monsieur Le Bel, have treated your responsibilities lightly in bringing such a one into the Palace. It is not, you should understand, the *Parc aux Cerfs*. This is Versailles. Yes, there is no doubt of it, you have been very remiss."

Le Bel began to sweat a little. The most powerful man in France was angry with him, was threatening him. He remembered what had happened such a short time ago to Madame d'Esparbès. She had been in some sort of favour with the King and then—a word from Choiseul and she was whisked away to banishment and obscurity.

"I feel certain, Monsieur, Madame," stammered Le Bel, "that you overrate this little *grisette*. She cannot hold the King's attention. She has nothing but her beauty. I swear to you that when I brought her to the King it was to be just a light *divertissement*, you understand me. I thought she would be here one day and forgotten the next."

"Yet," said the Duchesse ominously, "she stays."

Le Bel smiled at her. "Madame, you cannot think that she would ever be acknowledged as the King's mistress."

"It seems incredible," said Choiseul; "yet he keeps her with him."

"It would be quite impossible," said Le Bel confidently.

"Such a woman could never be presented at Court, and how could she share the King's life permanently until that happened? He can only see her in private. Moreover, although she calls herself Madame du Barry, she is not married. And you know the King would never make an unmarried woman his permanent mistress."

Choiseul threw a triumphant look at his sister, as though to say: There! Did I not tell you that your fears were unfounded?

"That's true," said the Duke, his expression lightening considerably; "but, Monsieur Le Bel, I should consider it a friendly action if you could rid the Court of her presence as soon as possible. It is disturbing for those who care for the dignity of the Court to know that such people are allowed to pollute it."

Le Bel looked earnestly into the face of the most powerful man in France.

"Monsieur le Duc," he said, "you may be sure that I will do all in my power to have the woman removed."

Choiseul nodded, satisfied; and when Le Bel had gone, he and his sister were prepared to dismiss the upstart du Barry from their minds.

Le Bel sought a private audience with the King.

Louis had changed, the valet noticed; he actually seemed ten years younger; a faint smile curved lips which previously had rarely smiled. It is incredible, thought Le Bel.

"Well, what have you to say?" asked Louis, almost benignly; for when he looked at the lined face of his old servant he remembered that it was his endeavours which had brought the enchanting du Barry to his notice.

"I am deeply perturbed, Sire," said Le Bel.

"Well, well, what is it?"

"It concerns . . . Madame du Barry."

"What about her?"

"I fear, Sire, that I have committed a grave indiscretion, and that when you hear my fault you will be annoyed with me. I assure you that when I brought the young lady to you I had no idea that you would wish her to remain for more than a night or so, and . . . and . . ."

"Stop stammering," cried Louis. "What of Madame du Barry?"

"The young lady, Sire . . . is not what she seems. This I have discovered, and I feel it my duty to inform Your Majesty."

The King raised his eyebrows. "I feel convinced," he said, "that I know more of this lady than you do, Le Bel."

"Yes, Sire, yes of course. But her past . . . her status . . . I fear that I have been as guilty as any in deceiving you on these matters. She was introduced to Your Majesty as Madame du Barry. . . . You were led to believe she is a Comtesse. I have to disillusion Your Majesty."

The King smiled fondly. "You will find it difficult to do that."

"But this . . . this young lady, Sire, is no Comtesse. She is the daughter . . . not of noble parents, but of a cook. A cook, Sire! That was her mother. As for her father, it has not been possible to trace his identity. Indeed it is possible that even the young lady's mother is unaware of his name."

Louis smiled. "Why, Le Bel," he said, "you forget I am a King, and that both Comtes and Comtesses seem so far below my rank that even cooks cannot be much lower."

"Your Majesty is pleased to jest. There is one matter of graver importance than any. The lady, Sire, is not Madame du Barry but *Mademoiselle* Rançon or L'Ange. . . . It matters not what her name is except, Sire, that she is an unmarried woman."

The King was silent and Le Bel breathed more freely. Here was a true impediment. The memory of Louis

Quatorze and Madame de Maintenon had remained fresh in the memory of his great-grandson. "Never," he had said, "will I accept a mistress whom I could marry for, when one grows old and fond, how can a man be sure what follies he might not commit?"

"Sire," said Le Bel, seizing his advantage, "I will inform the lady that her services are no longer required. I will . . ."

"You will hold your tongue," snapped the King.

"But, Sire, Mademoiselle . . ."

The King began to laugh, as she had taught him to laugh.

"Mademoiselle," he said, "shall become Madame." He turned to Le Bel. "See to it . . . without delay. Arrange a marriage for her. It is unthinkable that she should remain unmarried."

"But, Sire . . ."

Louis was staring at his *valet de chambre* in amazement. Was the man daring to question the King's orders?

Le Bel felt the blood pounding through his veins, the pulse in his temple was hammering hard. He understood. He had lightly brought this woman to the King's notice, never believing that she could hold his attention for more than the briefest period. And now the King was determined that she should be married. This could mean only one thing: If this woman was not eligible to become *maîtresse en titre*, Louis was going to make her so.

This was defeat for the Choiseuls; and whom would the Choiseuls blame but Le Bel?

The valet bowed and assured the King that he would with all speed arrange a marriage for the young lady.

When he left the King's apartment he was feeling faint with fear.

He had reached that dangerous position in which he could not serve both the King and the Duc de Choiseul; and such a position could mean ruin.

The Comte du Barry haunted the Palace since Jeanne was now installed there.

Could it last? he asked himself. Was it possible? Could his wildest dream really be on the brink of realisation?

Yet it was understandable. Jeanne was undoubtedly the loveliest girl in Paris—in France for that matter. And why should not those manners of the markets entertain the King who must be jaded and weary with the formality of Versailles?

Could Jeanne become *maîtresse en titre*? By all the saints, if she did, she must not be allowed to forget the man who had put her in such a position.

He was a little nervous. Anxious to see Jeanne and yet afraid to present himself at the Palace and ask for her. That might offend the King, and once he had done that he could say good-bye to all the honours he hoped to achieve.

Jeanne lived in private apartments for as yet she could not go to Court, and her position was an extremely delicate one.

Still there was no harm in having an interview with Le Bel. That fellow should be grateful to him. Was it not possible that he, du Barry, had done that which every man at Court had striven to do: provided the King with a mistress who pleased him so much that he felt young again and, being in love with a beautiful young woman, in love with life?

Le Bel agreed to see him when he arrived at his apartments, and du Barry was astonished to note Le Bel's pallor. The man looked worried and much older than when they had last met.

"Why, Monsieur Le Bel," said du Barry, "you're a lucky fellow."

Le Bel groaned. "Lucky! It seems that I am a fool, and it does not greatly please me to see *you*, Monsieur le Comte, for you it was who led me to my folly."

"Folly! What is this folly? Is not the King regaining his lost youth through the tutelage of our little Jeanne?"

"Monsieur le Comte, this woman is causing a storm in the Palace."

Du Barry laughed. "The Duchesse de Gramont could not be expected to dance for joy, I dare say."

"And," said Le Bel sternly, "the Duchesse de Gramont has a brother."

Du Barry grimaced.

"They will make it their affair to discover the details of Jeanne's past," continued Le Bel.

Du Barry ceased to smile. "But . . . " he began.

"A milliner . . . a dressmaker . . . or whatever she was!" stormed Le Bel. "Unmarried! Did you not know that it is a firm law of the Court that the King's mistresses must be married? I speak of all those who are recognised as his mistresses and not of those, of course, who have been engaged in the past briefly to lighten His Majesty's burdens."

"The King knows these things?" asked du Barry, hoarse with anxiety.

"He does. I told him."

"Then you're a fool. On orders from Choiseul, I suppose. That man is determined to have his old mare of a sister neighing in the royal bed. I tell you . . . "

"Be silent awhile," said Le Bel, "and I will tell you how completely your Jeanne has charmed His Majesty. He does not care that her mother was a cook, her father unknown, and she a milliner—or dressmaker, or whatever it was—in this Paris establishment. She has so bewitched him that these matters seem of no importance to him. But there *is* a certain matter which is of the utmost importance. We have deceived His Majesty into thinking that she was a married woman. You know the rule of the Court. The King would never acknowledge an unmarried woman as his mistress."

Du Barry had turned pale. "But . . . but," he stammered,

"we must get her married. Without delay we must get her married."

Le Bel looked at him sardonically. "You echo the words of His Majesty."

Du Barry burst out laughing. "Then it shall be done!" he cried. "Little Jeanne"—he smiled determinedly at Le Bel—"my little Jeanne . . . has done that which every Court lady has been striving to do. She . . . without Court manners . . ."

"Say rather that it is this lack which has appealed to His Majesty."

Du Barry could not stop himself laughing for a few seconds. Then a thought struck him and he became very serious.

"You have not mentioned the King's orders concerning this marriage to anyone?"

Le Bel looked at him blankly. "I have not," he cried. "I dare not. I wonder what will happen to me when Monsieur de Choiseul understands that your Jeanne is to have a husband. He blames me. . . ."

"She shall have a husband," said du Barry. "Oh, curse it, curse it, why am *I* not free?"

"Because, like most of us, you commit indiscretions which later you would give years of your life to eradicate. Do you realise, Monsieur le Comte, what the enmity of the Choiseuls can mean to a man such as I am?"

But du Barry was not listening. "When it is known that the King has ordered her to be married, every unmarried man at Court will be competing for the honour."

Le Bel nodded. "If she can manage to hold her position that woman could become the most important in the country. In the future people may well mention her name in the same breath as that of Pompadour."

"Pompadour!" breathed du Barry. "Du Barry!"

Le Bel sneered: "Not Madame du Barry. You forget, my friend, that, already having a wife, you cannot marry her."

The gloom in du Barry's face disappeared suddenly. He cried: "You are right when you say I have a wife. But that shall not prevent our little Jeanne from becoming Madame du Barry. I have a brother. *He* has no wife. Monsieur Le Bel, in as short a time as can possibly be managed the King's orders shall be obeyed."

"A brother, you say?" said Le Bel. "That perhaps is the best solution. Then, as she came to Versailles as Madame du Barry, she may continue as such."

"It shall be done. Give me a few days . . . a week. I'll arrange it all. In the meantime, not a word to anyone about the King's orders. If it were known that a husband was wanted for Jeanne, the competition would be so intense that delay would be inevitable."

Le Bel nodded.

"A week . . . that is all I ask, and you shall have your Madame du Barry; and no one shall question her right to the name. *Au revoir* now, my good Monsieur Le Bel. Have no fear. This little matter is going to work out to the satisfaction of us both."

Le Bel went to his apartment and shut himself in with his gloomy thoughts. The marriage would shortly take place and the King would be pleased with his prompt obedience. Madame du Barry would continue to be Madame du Barry, the wife of a provincial nobleman. That should silence the critics.

Yet the valet was beginning to realise that in introducing that woman to the notice of his master he had done a very foolish thing.

The Choiseuls would remember the new situation was due to him. He might have the friendship of the King, but who could stand up against the enmity of the Choiseuls?

Le Bel felt suddenly very old and tired, and frantic with

anxiety. He made his way to his bed and lay down, for he felt too sick and giddy to stand.

This was the end, he told himself. The King was old; he would not need the special services of his *valet de chambre* much longer, and if this woman became a Pompadour his usefulness would be over. If that were all, it would not be of much significance. It was not. The most powerful man in the kingdom would never forgive him for shifting the sphere of influence from him and his family to the friends this woman would soon be gathering about her.

"Yes," said Le Bel, "this is the end of Le Bel, *valet de chambre* and pander to the King's pleasure."

He was right. He died that night; and later the story was spread through the Court that the old *valet de chambre* had died of the shock of seeing *une petite grisette* about to become the most powerful person in France.

6

THE MARRIAGE

IN the shabby old château in the village of Lévignac, the
morning seemed exactly like hundreds of others which
Fanchon remembered.

Her elder brother Guillaume had ridden off to inspect
what he was pleased to call the "estate"; in reality he would
be hunting the latest village girl to catch his attention and,
perhaps, if he had time, he would shoot a hare and bring
it home for dinner. Bischi would be telling the old servant
how to make cabbage soup for dinner, as though it had
not been the staple diet of the family for months. Fanchon
was at her table writing; and the mother and head of the
family was sitting in her chair recalling the good old days
when Antoine, her husband, had been alive—before taxes
and reckless sons had reduced the family to poverty.

The brilliant sunshine picked out the dust on the curtains
and the upholstery and showed the stains on the ceiling
which should have been re-washed years ago. Outside the
house, fowls scrabbled in the dust; every now and then a
hen would cackle and there would be a fluttering, a squawk-
ing as the cock proclaimed masculine superiority over the
female. The ducks waddled in and out of the dirty pond;
the geese went marching by, hissing at the fowls in their
silly way.

Fanchon remembered afterwards that the thought had
struck her: Thus it has been for as many years as I can
remember. Thus it will be until the end of my life.

She remarked on this when Bischi entered the room. Her

sister Bischi was a little younger than she was, and both were middle-aged; Bischi's name was Isabelle as Fanchon's was Françoise—but they appeared to be a family which was fond of nicknames; so appealing when their owners were young, but perhaps, thought Fanchon, a little ridiculous for middle-aged spinsters such as we are.

"So, Bischi," said Fanchon, "here is another day."

"Well," said Bischi, "what did you expect?"

"Nothing," said Fanchon. "I expect nothing. Nothing ever happens here. So should we expect anything?"

"Things do happen," said Bischi. "Sometimes we can pay our way—sometimes not."

"The limit of our excitement!"

"And you have had some of your poems printed."

"Oh yes . . . that. And we, because we're women, are supposed to accept this life. We are not like Jean Baptiste who can go off to Paris and make his fortune—or attempt to —nor like Guillaume who hopes one day to do the same. We must stay here and be content."

"It might have been worse," said Bischi. "I wonder whether Jean Baptiste has such a grand time as he would have us believe."

"At least it must be full of surprises. I wonder whether he will ever get to Court." Fanchon laughed. "He has said that if he does, and he can find a place for me, he'll send for me. He promised that years ago. No doubt I am a fool still to feel hopeful."

Bischi shrugged her shoulders. "Jean Baptiste cannot find a place for himself, so how can he find one for you?"

"How could he?" agreed Fanchon. "But perhaps our luck will change one day. Luck? Is it luck? Do you believe in luck, Bischi, or do you think that the way we live attracts certain events to us? Is the secret of luck or ill-luck in ourselves?"

"There's the subject for your next poem," said Bischi.

She had moved towards the window and looked out on the untidy yard. "This place gets worse as time passes."

"Which is natural," said Fanchon, "since no one does anything to improve it." She rose and, limping to the window, stood beside her sister. "Has it always been as bad as this?" she asked. "Did we imagine, when Papa was alive, that it was different, or was it really so? In any case, what can we do about it? There is no money. All we can hope for is an occasional hare or rabbit to enliven the monotony of cabbage or turnip soup."

"I think I hear Guillaume coming," said Bischi.

The two women listened. The sound of horses' hoofs was unmistakable. "It sounds as though he has someone with him," said Fanchon.

They stood expectantly at the window. Visitors were rare at the lonely château of Lévignac and the thought of a little change was exciting to both women.

Suddenly the riders came into sight, and they saw that Guillaume had a companion.

"I have never seen him before," said Fanchon. "Let us go and see who he is."

Bischi ran into the hall. Fanchon followed as quickly as her lame leg would let her, and when she arrived Guillaume was leaping from his horse, shouting at the miserable little stable-boy, and then to the family.

"News from Paris!" he said. "News from Jean Baptiste."

His voice seemed to be quivering with excitement. Fanchon knew then that she had been wrong when she had thought a little earlier that this was a day like a hundred others.

The excitement in Guillaume's voice told her that there was something very unexpected in this news from Jean Baptiste.

.   .   .   .   .

They sat round the table, which was worn by the platters of generations of du Barrys, and stared at Madame.

She was in her customary place at the head of the table, her grey hair pulled back from her wrinkled old face, her straight line of a mouth set determinedly. Ever since the death of her husband she had considered herself the head of the household. She had ruled her children, as she believed their father would have done and, as she went about the crumbling old house, her keys rattling at her waist (though there was no need to lock up the almost empty wine cellar or the cupboards which were bare), she managed to create an illusion of power and dignity. Shabby as she was—for her appearance matched that of the château—she had the air of a great châtelaine.

Guillaume, Fanchon and Bischi were all looking at her now, waiting for her decision. Before her lay the letter. In the kitchen the messenger was consuming a basin of cabbage soup and a piece of bread. Madame du Barry had graciously offered him this hospitality; and the messenger, who in Paris quite obviously lived on a scale which would have seemed sumptuous compared with that of the du Barrys, had meekly accepted it.

"This," said Madame, tapping the letter with a bony finger, "is another of the wild schemes of Jean Baptiste. I never heard the like. Leave everything, he says, and come to Paris. You are to be married, Guillaume. Married! You!"

"But, Mama," said Guillaume meekly, "I shall have to marry at some time. This seems a good opportunity."

"You will marry if and when the right moment comes," said Madame du Barry.

"Mama," cried Bischi, "do you not think that this could be the right moment?"

"It is fantastic," said the old lady. "'Leave everything and come . . . come at once,' he says. 'Do not delay.

114

Delay could cost me a future, the greatness of which you, who have lived so long in the country, could never understand.'"

"But we can understand," said Fanchon. "I understand perfectly."

"You are too clever," said Madame. "You think, because you have seen in print what you have written, that you are learned in the ways of the world. Guillaume is to go to Paris and marry a woman, and for that he is to receive a pension for the rest of his life. It seems to me like another of Jean Baptiste's wild schemes."

"Yet," said Fanchon, "he has sent the money for us to go to Paris."

"You long to go to Paris," said the old woman accusingly. "Never mind how you get there. Never mind if you get there and cannot return. Never mind. To Paris, you say. To Paris where fortunes are made. You forget that in Paris fortunes are lost as well as made."

"Jean Baptiste has proved to us that fortunes can be lost in Paris," said Fanchon demurely. "He should at least have a chance of showing us that they can also be made."

"What harm could there be in going to see?" muttered Guillaume sullenly.

"Harm! There's plenty of harm to befall those who go to Paris, my son."

"Jean Baptiste manages very well."

"Does he? Does he?"

"At least he can send the money for Guillaume and Fanchon to go to Paris when he wants them," put in Bischi.

"He would have done better to send money with which we could have repaired the château."

"But the repairing of the château cannot procure for him a place at Court," pointed out Fanchon. "The château, either in good order or as we know it, would still be 'my estate in the country' to Jean Baptiste."

"You are bemused," cried the old woman, "bemused by dreams of Paris and the sight of the money to get you there. It's another of Jean Baptiste's wild-cat schemes, I tell you." She rapped the table with her knuckles. "And you'll stay here, I say. You, Guillaume! You, Françoise!"

Guillaume was looking at Fanchon. She was crippled, but she had more spirit than the rest of them, and Guillaume knew that she was more fluent than he was, and that pungent words would be needed to win this round against the old woman who for so long had ruled all their lives.

Fanchon spoke then. "For the first time since he has been in Paris," she said, "Jean Baptiste has his great opportunity. He is our brother and we must not desert him now. To do so would be to ruin all that he has worked for. This marriage will not take Guillaume from you, Mama. He will return after the ceremony, for Jean Baptiste quite clearly states that it is to be a marriage in name only. The ceremony once per-formed, Guillaume returns to the château. You do not have to see his wife or know her; but, as a result of this ceremony, Guillaume will receive a regular pension. Why do you hesi-tate? Think of all that can be done to the château. What bliss to have something to eat which is not cabbage or turnip soup!"

"I do not believe that story," said the old woman. "It is fantastic. It is Jean Baptiste's way of luring you away from me."

"Why should he wish to lure them?" asked Bischi.

"Look at us!" cried Fanchon. "What use would we be to him in Paris?"

Fanchon laughed a little bitterly, a little hysterically. The letter and the prospect it held out to her had made her see herself more clearly than usual—a middle-aged spinster who had missed marriage, who had never been beautiful in her youth, a cripple. How differently had been equipped this young woman whom Jean Baptiste wanted to make Guillaume's wife! The unfairness of life was depressing, if one had been treated harshly. She supposed this young woman who was to be the bride had never considered how unfair life could be to others. Yet Fanchon had wit and a fluent pen, and had always had the reputation of being the clever one of the family. It was for this reason that Jean Baptiste had sent money for her—and not Bischi—to go to Paris with Guillaume. Now Fanchon was sorry for Bischi. Poor sister who had not even been invited to go to Paris!

Then suddenly Fanchon knew that she *was* going to Paris. Who knew—when she arrived she might find some means of staying there.

She might yet find escape from monotony, from boredom, from dirt, and squalor, from cabbage and turnip soup.

She glanced at the old woman at the head of the table, and for the first time in her life prepared to do serious battle with her.

She said in a cold clear voice: "This is no fantastic dream of Jean Baptiste's. The young woman whom he has introduced to the King can become as important in the country as Madame de Pompadour was. The King dotes on her. She is unmarried, and the King cannot acknowledge a mistress who is unmarried. Therefore there is a reward for the man who marries her." Fanchon permitted herself to wag a finger at her mother, who was so startled at the gesture that she was stunned into silence. "Make no mistake about it, many men will seek to marry her. Even now while we are sitting here round this table, hesitating, others may be taking from Jean Baptiste that prize which the obstinate provincialism of his family has snatched from him just as he was about to achieve it."

"Do not imagine," began Madame, "that you understand these things."

But Fanchon interrupted her. "We have the money, Guillaume. We must not desert our brother when he needs

117

us so urgently. Every hour we delay may be dangerous. We should leave at once for Paris."

"And why should it be necessary for *you* to go?" demanded Madame.

"Because Jean Baptiste has some work for me to do. Does he not say quite clearly: 'Fanchon must come also'? Guillaume, we waste time."

Guillaume said: "She is right, Mother. You must allow us to go."

The old lady was about to speak when Fanchon said: "There is no question of our being allowed, Guillaume." She looked at her mother steadily. "We must go. Mother realises that. She knows that, now we are no longer children, we know best in matters such as this."

The unkempt little serving girl was bringing in the cabbage soup and Madame lifted her hand, prepared to strike on the table as she had done for years, when she had been about to make some stern pronouncement. But Fanchon had caught her arm.

"Mama, you must not excite yourself," she said. "It is bad for you. Your children—your middle-aged children—know what is best for you and for them. Bischi will take great care of you while Guillaume and I are away. And after the marriage you will see a great change in the château."

The servant had set the steaming bowls on the table, and Fanchon released her mother's arm.

"We will eat," she said to Guillaume, "and then we must prepare for our journey—with all speed."

There was silence at the table.

The old lady knew she had been defeated.

Jeanne called at the house of the Comte du Barry in the Rue des Petits Champs. She was amused by the way in which he treated her nowadays. It was as though she were some precious piece of china which rough handling might destroy.

"Ah," she cried, "what it is to be loved by a King!"

"It is indeed a great blessing," agreed du Barry. "I trust you will always remember who obtained this great blessing for you."

Jeanne gave him that slight grimace which never failed to amuse the King. "Certainly I shall remember," she retorted, "if for no other reason than that I am not allowed to forget."

"*Sérieuse!*" cried du Barry. "How often have I had to say that to you!"

"Yet it was precisely because I was not *sérieuse* that Louis liked me."

Du Barry waved aside such idle gossip. "This is a serious matter."

"Where is my bridegroom?"

"Not yet arrived."

Jeanne put her hand to her mouth to suppress the rising laughter. "Do not tell me that I am going to be deserted at the altar!"

"If he does not come I . . . I will . . ."

"Challenge him to a duel?" suggested Jeanne.

"Now Jeanne, I pray you listen carefully. You will be at the church at five o'clock tomorrow morning."

"So early! And all for a bridegroom who may not be there!"

"He will be there. I promise you he will be there."

"Do not get so excited, *mon ami*. The King wishes me to marry, and if your brother does not want to be my husband . . . there are many at Court, so I am led to understand, who would be ready to step into the breach."

Du Barry turned pale at the thought, and Jeanne was immediately sorry for what she had said. She put an arm about du Barry's shoulder and lightly kissed his cheek. "It is my tongue . . . my mischievous old tongue. Do not heed it. No, I do not forget what you have done for me and I will marry your Guillaume and no one else."

She had not changed, thought du Barry. She was still the same good-hearted Jeanne. He was grateful for that. Oh, what great good was coming to him!

"There has been much to think of," he explained to her. "And I flatter myself that I have performed what is necessary with some skill. There will be many who will seek to pry into your affairs once the King has publicly acknowledged you. I want to be prepared for them. We do not wish these people to know that your mother was not married. Therefore you will appear as Jeanne Gomard de Vaubernier, daughter of Anne Bécu and Jean-Jacques Gomard de Vaubernier, a gentleman occupied in the King's business."

"He must have been the soldier my mother often talks about," said Jeanne.

"Your bridegroom is to be *Le haut et puissant seigneur, Messire Guillaume, Comte du Barry, Capitaine des Troupes détachées de la Marine.*"

"He sounds important—more so than his elder brother."

"He is in actuality merely the Chevalier du Barry. You, as a member of the family, must know such things."

"Then these statements you have made—are they not forgeries?"

"We cannot have our enemies putting stories about that you are the illegitimate daughter of a cook!"

"So you would commit forgery, Comte Jean, to save me from malicious scandal. Why, I do not think I should be able to accept the sacrifice if I did not know that what you do for me, you are also doing for yourself."

He took her by the shoulders and looked into her eyes.

"Never forget," he said, "that our fortunes are entwined about each other."

"As I said before, I cannot forget, for you will not allow it." She freed herself from his grip. "Everything is in your

hands—my future, my present and my past. You have even
taken charge of events which happened before I was born.
What more could anyone ask!"

As they were talking, the sound of a carriage pulling up at
the house, was heard and she and du Barry hurried to the
window.

"It is! It is!" cried du Barry exultantly.

Jeanne looking down saw a middle-aged woman, very
dowdily and shabbily dressed, getting out of the carriage
with some difficulty. She was followed by a man, who was
sufficiently like du Barry to be recognised as his brother.

"So that," said Jeanne, "is to be my husband. It is
strange to think that this time tomorrow we shall be
married."

"You need have no qualms," du Barry promised. "I have
said he shall leave you at the church door, and leave you
he shall. You must not stay long now they are here. We
cannot know who spies on us, and we must avoid gossip at
all costs. The King would not wish you to spend much time
in the company of your future husband."

The arrivals were shown into the room. Both of them,
exhausted by their journey as they were, appeared to be
quite bewildered at the sight of Jeanne.

Jeanne bowed with mock solemnity. The situation seemed
to her so comical that she could scarcely suppress her
laughter.

This man, who was prepared to be her husband at the
bidding of his brother and for a sizeable sum of money, was
hardly worth much more than a glance. She would bear his
name—but she had been doing that occasionally already.
After tomorrow she would have a right to call herself
Madame du Barry.

He was not unlike his brother—a coarser version, less
debauched perhaps, but lacking that grace and charm which
were his elder brother's.

"So . . ." he stammered, "so you are the lady I'm to marry." His eyes were wide with admiration. "Why . . . I . . . I did not realise . . ."

"There is no need for you to realise," said his brother curtly. "All you have to do is say and sign what is asked of you."

"I know that . . . but . . . er . . ."

"Mademoiselle Gomard de Vaubernier is in a hurry. Her carriage is waiting. . . ."

Jeanne smiled to hear herself so addressed. "We shall meet tomorrow at the church," she said. Then she noticed the woman.

For some seconds they looked at each other. Du Barry said: "This is my sister, Fanchon."

Never, thought Fanchon, had she seen such exquisite beauty. Never had she felt so aware of her musty old garments, her plain face and her deformed body. Never had she felt her complaint against the unfairness of the world so justified.

The Comte du Barry was uneasy; he knew he would not have a moment's peace until the wedding was over. He had arranged that Guillaume should be given a meal such as he knew he would never have tasted in the country château, and he had plied him with wine during that meal so that, as soon as it was over, Guillaume, already tired out by the exhausting journey, was eager to do nothing but sleep.

"Wise man," said Comte Jean. "I have a comfortable bed waiting for you. I shall take you to it now, so that you may have a good rest."

"I . . . I'm going to see the sights of Paris," mumbled Guillaume.

"All in good time," soothed his brother. "First rest so that you will be fit for tomorrow's ceremony."

Guillaume protested half-heartedly, but his brother had little difficulty in getting him to his room.

He returned to Fanchon who knew he wished to speak to her.

"He was fast asleep before I left the room," he said with satisfaction. "He'll know little until morning."

"And that, brother, gives you great relief."

Du Barry took her hands suddenly and pulled her to her feet. He looked at her steadily for some seconds. "My clever Fanchon," he said, "I am going to need you."

"You mean . . . I am to stay in Paris?"

"Versailles, my dear. Versailles."

"I . . . poor old Fanchon . . . at Versailles!"

"Listen, sister. You have seen her . . . my Jeanne. What did you think of her?"

"The loveliest creature I have ever seen."

"Fit for a King and a King of France, eh? He dotes on her, Fanchon. Oh, at the moment, no one takes this affair very seriously. But soon they will have to, and when they do, she will be surrounded by friends—or those who profess friendship—as well as enemies. Jeanne does not understand enmity. She herself is too light-hearted. She feels no enmity towards people; therefore she thinks they do not towards her. She has a great deal to learn."

"And you will teach her?"

"With your help. Listen to me, Fanchon. I have selected you to be her companion. There is no one else whom I can trust. You will guide her along the way she must go. You will advise her."

Fanchon nodded slowly. Then her face clouded. "I am fresh from the country, my brother. Have you forgotten that?"

"You have always had your nose in a book from the time you were a baby. You write with ease and fluency. You have always made yourself acquainted with the affairs of the country. In a few weeks after you have been at the Court, you will be fully conservant with the intrigues of politics and the bedchamber. You will work for me as Choiseul's sister works for him. Why, my Fanchon, I am learning from Choiseul. The only people one can trust in delicate matters such as this are the members of one's own family."

"So I am to be the companion of that glorious creature. What a contrast we shall make!"

"She has the beauty, Fanchon *chérie*. You have the brains. Both of you will see that I am not forgotten. What a combination I shall have working for me!"

"So . . . I remain in Paris," said Fanchon. She clasped her hands and stared blankly before her.

"Of what are you thinking?" asked du Barry anxiously.

"Of cabbage soup!" she answered.

Early next morning Jeanne's carriage rattled along the road between Versailles and Paris. It was the first day of September and, although warm, there was an autumnal mist in the early morning air.

It was not quite five o'clock when Jeanne arrived at the church of St. Laurent to find the du Barry party, under the command of Comte Jean, eagerly awaiting her.

The bridegroom's eyes gleamed as they rested on his bride; his brother watched him anxiously.

"Come along," he said impatiently, catching at Jeanne's arm.

Jeanne yawned. "Did it have to be quite so early?" she demanded of the Comte who was hurrying her into the church.

"It was necessary," he whispered. "I wish my brother to leave immediately after the ceremony, and he has a long journey to Lévignac. And it is well that there should not be too many people about."

"Several traders coming from *les Halles* stared into my carriage," she said.

"We will not let them disturb us."

Jeanne had turned to smile at Fanchon. "Do *you* like this early rising?" she asked.

"I do not," answered Fanchon, "but since it appears to be necessary I must accept it."

"What did you say your name was?" whispered Jeanne.

"It's Françoise, but I am called Fanchon."

"Chon Chon?" said Jeanne. "I like Chon Chon. You look far too clever to be a Chon Chon. But for that reason I like it."

The ceremony began. Jeanne looked at the man who stood beside her and whose hand was trembling as he took hers.

Jeanne thought of her mother, who had so dearly longed for her to marry respectably and had been so heartbroken when the marriage with hairdresser Lametz had come to nothing. What would Anne think of this marriage? She would be delighted to see her daughter rise so high. Married . . . at the order of the King. The King loved her and therefore she must be married to another man! It was so logical yet it seemed so extraordinary. But Anne was going to be very happy indeed. Jeanne had not forgotten her mother while she had lived under the protection of the Comte du Barry; nor would she when she lived under the protection of the King.

The last words had been spoken. She was married, and Madame du Barry in truth.

They came out into the morning air and drove with all speed to the house in the Rue des Petits Champs, where some refreshment had been provided for them.

Guillaume kept close to the side of his bride, his eyes admiring her, while they sat at the table; and immediately the meal was over Jean du Barry said: "This is the moment when bride and groom say good-bye to each other for ever."

"I object to that," said Guillaume. "A husband has some rights. I do not think I shall return to Lévignac for a day or so."

"You will return this day," his brother told him sternly.

"It is a decision I shall make on my own account."

"You have forgotten the terms of the agreement?"

"Agreement! I was told I should marry a young woman. I was not told she was the most beautiful in Paris."

"Poor Guillaume," said Jeanne. "But you must go back, you know. That is the King's command. If you did not . . . What would happen to him if he did not?"

She looked from du Barry to his sister, and her gaze continued to rest on Fanchon's face.

"*A lettre de cachet* most likely," suggested Fanchon. "A long, long stay in the Bastille."

Guillaume looked alarmed. "A harsh punishment for a man who merely wants to make the further acquaintance of his bride."

"Dear Guillaume," said Jeanne, leaning towards him, "it is sad, I know, but you must understand that ours is no ordinary marriage."

"I will give up the pension. I will stay in Paris . . . anything . . . Anything . . ."

"Stop!" thundered Comte Jean. "Guillaume, you are more of a fool than I thought you. At this moment we may be spied on. How can I be sure that my enemies have not set spies in my own household?" He strode to the door and called to one of his servants.

"My brother, Monsieur le Comte, is unexpectedly called away," he said. "Have his carriage brought at once to the door."

Guillaume flashed a look of hatred at his brother.

"So," he began, "I have been used, and now that I have played my part I am to be fobbed off with a pension. . . ."

"It shall be a very good pension," whispered Jeanne

soothingly, determined to make it as high as she possibly could because she was so sorry for poor Guillaume, who had been brought from the country and now was being sent back to it. He had had a glimpse of the fascinating city; he had a notion of what life in Paris could be like; and he had been married to herself who, it would have been falsely modest to deny, was a greatly desirable woman. She longed to comfort him, but she realised that by so doing she would only make his departure the more depressing.

"I will give up the pension," he answered.

But she shook her head. "Your sister is right. It would be a *lettre de cachet* and the Bastille."

Comte Jean filled his brother's glass and made him drink; and when the servant appeared, poor Guillaume made a maudlin exit, looking all the time at the radiant face of his beautiful bride while his brother dragged him away to his carriage.

"Poor Guillaume," said Jeanne to her sister-in-law. "I fear it has made him very sad."

"He has come very well out of it," was the rejoinder.

Jeanne walked to her sister-in-law and looked at her intently. "You look . . . sharp as vinegar," she said. "But I do not believe you are, Chon Chon."

"So you are going to persist in calling me that name?"

Jeanne nodded. Then characteristically she kissed Fanchon on both cheeks.

"I'm glad you are to be with me. Your brother has told me of his plans. I think we are going to like each other."

Fanchon tried to feel cynical, but oddly enough she could do nothing of the sort. She felt absurd tears pricking her eyelids. This was folly. She was clearly overwrought.

Jeanne had noticed her emotion. "It means," she said, "that we are going to be friends, we two."

So, thought Fanchon, she casts her spell not only over Kings but over sour old spinsters.

Later that morning Jeanne drove back to Versailles where her royal lover was waiting for her.

He kissed her hands.

"The deed is done," she told him. "Your Majesty sees before you a respectable married woman . . . Madame du Barry in truth."

"I rejoice. I hope you have lost none of your gaiety in your newly found respectability."

"Oh no, Sire," she said. "Respectability and Jeanne du Barry will not get along very well with each other, I fear."

"I hope," he said. "Now that this little matter is settled and you need no longer live quite so obscurely, I thought that if you had the apartments recently vacated by Le Bel you would be very near my own, and that, my dear, would mean that we could communicate with the greatest ease. Mind you, these apartments are unworthy . . . quite unworthy, and I would have you understand that they are but temporary."

"I shall enjoy being there. There are two reasons. One is because I shall be near my old Louis; the other is because that is where I first met my dear old Baron de Gonesse."

He lifted her hand and kissed it. What would seem gross flattery in others came so naturally to her lips.

"How you delight me!" he said.

Then he led her to the apartments which had belonged to the late *valet de chambre* and she saw that they had been hung with elaborate curtains of rich blue velvet. Her colour, the King called it.

And as they stood in that room where the supper-party had been held, the King showed her a diamond necklace and asked her gracious permission to clasp it about her neck.

"And that," said Jeanne, her eyes sparkling to challenge

the diamonds, "is a request I cannot find it in my heart to deny Your Majesty."

Then she examined herself in the mirrors from all angles, embraced the delighted King, and revealed in many ways that she found life an amusing and delightful adventure.

But as the lovers embraced, news was carried throughout the Palace that the new favourite had been installed in apartments close to the King's. The Duc de Choiseul heard it and he immediately discussed the affair with his sister.

In the Palace of Versailles, Jeanne's envious enemies were beginning to realise that she might be a formidable adversary.

7

APARTMENTS IN VERSAILLES

JEANNE revelled in the apartments of the late Monsieur Le Bel, while the King remained devoted to her and the Court watchful. Even though it was some weeks since Louis' infatuation had begun, few took the relationship seriously. It could not last, was the opinion of many. The woman might be as beautiful as a goddess but she had about as much idea of the etiquette of Versailles as a market woman, and etiquette was the breath of life at Versailles.

As for Jeanne herself, she would have been completely ignorant of the whispering if Chon had not told her of it.

"We are like a child taking our first steps," said wise Chon. "We are managing very well, but later we may have to do more than totter along. We shall have to hop and skip, jump and dance—but it must be to our tune, not to theirs."

"I shall have you, Chon, to be my partner," said Jeanne complacently.

"Nay, His Majesty is to be your partner, I shall merely whisper my advice."

Chon had met the King. It was necessary, she knew, to do so, for if she were going to live close to Jeanne at Versailles, how could it be otherwise?

Chon had been anxious, for she realised how important this meeting would be to her future.

"What will he think of me?" she asked Jeanne. "I who have no beauty to charm him!"

Jeanne laughed at her fears. "Oh, but Louis is the kindest of men. You must forget he is the King . . . as I do."

Chon looked helplessly at her sister-in-law and continued to think apprehensively of the inevitable meeting.

Thanks to Jeanne it was less of an ordeal than she had feared.

"And here is my dear Chon Chon," Jeanne had said, "whom you must love because I do. She is terrified of Your Majesty, so I pray you be most especially kind to her."

Chon, overcome with embarrassment, had knelt at his feet. His eyes quickly perceived her lameness, but easily and charmingly he ignored it.

"Rise, my dear," he said. "So you are Madame du Barry's friend and sister, eh? Chon Chon—now that is an interesting name."

"I gave it her," cried Jeanne. "Before that she was merely Fanchon. His Majesty," went on Jeanne turning to Chon, "has a penchant for nicknames. You must have heard what he calls the Princesses. Madame Adelaide is Loque, Madame Victoire is Coche, and Madame Sophie is Graille. That will show you how wicked His Majesty can be!"

Chon met the King's eye and Louis smiled as though to say: How enchanting is this Jeanne of ours!

Sharing their delight in her made them friends. A strange experience this, thought Chon: I, a middle-aged spinster living in the country such a short while ago, am now at Court exchanging friendly glances with the King.

"I have decided," said Jeanne, "that Your Majesty shall have a nickname, and there is only one which is worthy of you. This is my name for you, Louis: It is La France. What do you think of that?"

"I shall cherish it, since you gave it to me."

Jeanne looked at Chon as though to say: Listen to him! Does he not talk in the most charming way?

So nicknames became the custom between them, and

Jeanne would chatter light-heartedly to La France, and the King showed his friendship to her sister-in-law—largely, Chon believed, to please his cherished mistress—by calling her *Grande Chon Petite Chon*.

And as Chon continued to marvel at the strangeness of life, she was full of hope for the future of the du Barrys.

That important Minister of France, the Duc de Choiseul, had too many matters of State with which to concern himself to give a great deal of thought to the King's new mistress; and when he considered the great events of his career which had brought him to his present eminence he could not believe that an ignorant woman could possibly harm him.

Enamoured as the King might be he was not so foolish as to turn against the man in whose hands he had entrusted the conduct of the affairs of France for so long. Louis was no fool. He was conscious of the changing temper of the people. He was fully aware that the philosophers, who had sprung into prominence during his reign, expressed their thoughts with a lucidity which was having its effect.

It was not many years ago when Louis had one of the greatest frights of his reign—to compare perhaps with that occasion when the would-be assassin Damiens had attacked him.

Choiseul smiled complacently, thinking of the frailty of the King which put him into the hands of such clever women as Madame de Pompadour and astute statesmen such as himself. The King's sensuality was his weakness. The *Parc aux Cerfs* was a byword throughout the country; and the affair of little Mademoiselle Tiercelin, although important because of the publicity which had accompanied it, was no isolated incident.

Louis was very fond of young girls—children, one might say—and he had one day seen this child, accompanied by her governess, in a crowd when he was riding through the city. Deeply impressed by her unusual beauty he had dispatched one of the lieutenants of the police to discover who she was and have her brought to him. The little girl was carried to Versailles where the King made much of her, allowing her to share his meals and even his prayers. Such favour was a great honour. Unfortunately when Mademoiselle Tiercelin was fourteen she bore the King a child, and Louis, who had always found pregnant females slightly distasteful, sent her away, providing her with an income of 30,000 livres a year. This was not considered enough by the young lady who, during the years she had spent under the King's patronage, had developed extravagant ideas; and at brief intervals she appealed to the King for more and more money. Louis paid; but because Mademoiselle Tiercelin was not discreet, the story of her adventures at Versailles became known first in Paris and then throughout the country.

It was stories like this which detracted from the little popularity which remained to the King and which placed him, to some extent, in the power of scheming ministers.

Louis was in conflict with his parliament, for he believed in the divine right of Kings and this was an age when the people were in revolt against that doctrine. More than a hundred years before it had been rejected in England and a bloody civil war had been the result. Louis was not unmindful of the affairs of the country across the water, and consideration of the fate of Charles I could always render him reflectively melancholy.

The precarious position of the country had been brought home to him by the recent upheaval concerning the Jesuits. During the last decade, members of Ignatius Loyola's Society of Jesus had become unpopular in Spain and Portugal, chiefly because they had put themselves in command of large parts of the New World and had acted contrary to the wishes of the Kings of these two countries.

"Expel the Jesuits" had been the cry, and efforts had been made to deprive them of their growing power.

When young King Joseph of Portugal, visiting his mistress, the Marchioness of Tavora, had been set upon and wounded by assassins this crime was traced to the Jesuits, and the Marquis of Pombal, the First Minister, had arrested several concerned in the attack on the King. Many lost their heads; others were broken on the wheel; and the help of the Inquisition was called in, with the result that Father Malagrida, the Jesuit Principal, was accused of heresy, found guilty and condemned to be strangled and burned.

Rome could not ignore such treatment of the Jesuits and protested strongly, whereupon Pombal exiled them from Portugal and sent them to Italy.

Although, in France, there was a section of opinion which was very much against the Jesuits, it was considered that Pombal's treatment of them was very severe indeed; and the Dauphin had put himself at the head of their cause.

Madame de Pompadour had always been afraid of the influence of the Jesuits because she knew that if they inspired the King with religious feelings he might feel it incumbent upon himself to dispense with his mistress. Thus she set herself firmly on the side of those who wished to accord to them in France the same treatment as they had received in Portugal.

Choiseul, up to that time favouring neither side, had then thrown in his support on the side of Pompadour.

Finding themselves persecuted the Jesuits asked that the King's *acquits au comptant* should be made public. Louis was horrified at the suggestion of letting his people know the amount of money which had gone into promoting and maintaining such an establishment as the *Parc aux Cerfs* and supplying the needs of young ladies such as Mademoiselle Tiercelin.

Such affairs must not be brought to light when, only a

short distance from Versailles, the people of Paris were suffering such misery. It was during times such as this that the astute Choiseul realised to what extent the King must lean on a cunning minister. The indolent but shrewd King knew his position in relation to his people. Did he not avoid entering his capital whenever possible, and when he was obliged to leave Versailles take a route which was not through Paris?

The people at that time had been ready to march on Versailles; the King had been wavering in his decision against the Jesuits; and when Choiseul, determined to get his way, had made out a case for their dismissal, he had put it in such a way that the King dared not refuse.

"If we exile the Jesuits, Sire," was Choiseul's sly comment, "the people will become so absorbed in this matter that they will forget the enormous amounts which have been spent on the *Parc aux Cerfs*; they will forget the little scandal created by that indiscreet young lady, Mademoiselle Tiercelin."

And Louis, who could not deny his senses what they craved, and who realised that Choiseul's shrewd manœuvres could keep the peace a little longer, gave way.

Thus Choiseul had, in one brilliant stroke, bound himself more closely to Pompadour, and, while keeping the confidence of the King, had set himself on the side of the *Parlement*.

Choiseul smiled to recall his triumphs, to remember the Edicts which had been published against the Jesuits. The royal family, headed by the Dauphin, had been deeply disturbed, for this, they had declared, was a blow at the Catholic Church. The King, who enjoyed his periods of devotion to religion between debauches, would have liked to stand with them against those who wished to exile the Jesuits, but Choiseul held the King in the palm of his hand, so he had believed then; so he believed now.

If he did not rid the country of the Jesuits, Choiseul told Louis, he must come into violent conflict with the *Parlement*. Choiseul did not talk openly of revolution, but he implied that this was what the disbanding of the *Parlement* would mean.

There was too much scandal attached to the King's name; his people were already murmuring against him; he remembered continually that history often repeats itself and could never forget the fate of Charles I of England who had tried to rid himself of his parliament, which had in consequence rid him of his head.

Louis might realise that the attack on the Jesuits brought him no good; but he had no alternative but to accept it.

What triumph! thought Choiseul. From December 1764 the Society of Jesus was disbanded in France, and Jesuits could only live there if they abandoned the dress and habits of the order. They had been treated in a much more civilised manner in France than they had in Portugal or were a few years later in Spain; but this was a triumph for a clever minister and it was an example to be remembered when little fears beset him that this new upstart mistress in Versailles might affect his position there.

Choiseul snapped his fingers. This little slut from her milliner's shop affect the great Choiseul! It was a ridiculous thought.

All the same his dear sister had been humiliated by the woman, and it would be a pleasant gesture towards his beloved Duchesse if he had the woman sent away.

It was not a matter about which he cared to approach the King. It was far too undignified. He smiled suddenly, for an idea had occurred to him. Why should he not approach Madame Adelaide? The elderly Princess was constantly trying to insinuate herself into State matters. Here was one little mission she could perform.

Let her reproach her father for so far forgetting the

etiquette of Versailles; let her remind him of his duty to her so recently dead mother. In other words, send Madame Adelaide into battle against the woman of the streets. What a contrast! Poor faded Adelaide, royal to the finger-tips, lover of etiquette to such an extent that she added new rules even to those which were already existing in Versailles—and the brazen, beautiful courtesan on whom all the glittering diamond gifts of a besotted King could not disguise the aura of the *faubourgs*.

Madame Adelaide was greatly excited when she heard that the Duc de Choiseul wished to call on her. She was with her sisters when the news was brought to her, and Victoire and Sophie stared into her face, as they always did at moments of excitement, awaiting the cue she would give them.

"Ah," said Adelaide, fanning herself vigorously and looking extremely haughty, "so Monsieur le Duc de Choiseul is requesting an audience, is he? Tell him that I will consider whether I can see my way to granting it."

"Madame," said the messenger, "Monsieur le Duc says the matter is of the utmost importance."

Madame Adelaide continued to fan herself; Victoire and Sophie exchanged quick glances after which they fixed their eyes on their sister's face.

"Very well," said Adelaide. "Matters of State, I understand, cannot wait. You may tell the Duc de Choiseul that I will receive him immediately."

When the messenger had gone Victoire and Sophie ran to her, but Adelaide held up a hand. "You must leave me at once," she said. "I have no doubt that Choiseul wishes to consult me with regard to a new war. It will be with the English."

Victoire and Sophie exchanged nods.

"He knows," went on Adelaide, "that I hate the English."

The sisters nodded again. Adelaide knew that when they were alone they would remind each other of the time when, during war between France and England, Adelaide had run away from Versailles to join the French Army. When she had been brought back to the Palace she had bitterly complained that if she had been allowed to carry out her plan of action the war would have been over in a very short time, victory for the French being certain. Adelaide's intention had been to invite the English leaders, one by one, to her apartments, seduce them, and when they slept cut off their heads.

Remembering this, the sisters told themselves that it was natural that Choiseul, who must be contemplating war with the English, should wish to consult Adelaide about it.

"Now," said Adelaide, "go away. You must not disturb us." She waved her hands and her younger sisters hurried to obey, as they always obeyed Adelaide. But they stood on the other side of the private door listening, while Choiseul entered by the main door and, taking Adelaide's hand, kissed it with apparent devotion.

Adelaide was delighted. She had not liked the man until this moment, for he had not treated her with the respect which she considered her due; but now that he had come to her she was ready to be his trusted ally.

"You wished to consult me, Monsieur de Choiseul?"

"Very earnestly, Madame la Princesse."

"You may be seated."

"Thank you."

"Now tell me what troubles you, Monsieur le Duc."

"That which, I fear, troubles a lady as pure and noble as yourself."

Adelaide hesitated and a suspicious look came into her eyes. She was remembering an occasion long ago when, during a performance in the theatre at Fontainebleau, she had fainted. There had been rumours—wicked rumours—

at that time, Adelaide remembered. Years later it was said that the Comte de Narbonne had a royal princess for a mother. Such scandals gave her great prestige with Victoire and Sophie, but she did not wish to hear any insolence from Monsieur de Choiseul. But the Duke was smiling at her in his winning way, and she dismissed her suspicions.

"His Majesty, your royal father, Princesse, is falling into evil hands once more, I fear."

Adelaide nodded. She remembered Madame de Pompadour whose influence with her father she had tried to break. The Comte de Maurepas, that mischievous man, had referred to Pompadour as her *Maman Putain*, and she had repeated the expression in the presence of her father and his favourite.

She had not known at that time that she was calling the woman a prostitute; but she was not sorry afterwards that she had done so. She was the enemy of all those light women who sought to obtain a hold over her father.

"Madame la Princesse, there is one whose tact, whose discretion, whose wit, could help to disentangle His Majesty from the meshes which the evil woman is preparing to weave about him."

"You may leave this task to me, Monsieur de Choiseul."

"I knew I could rely on you. The woman must be sent where she belongs—back to the streets of Paris."

Adelaide wrinkled her nose. "It is unthinkable that she should remain another day at Versailles," she declared.

"If Madame la Princesse could speak to her father . . ."

"She will do so, Monsieur le Duc, at the first opportunity. And . . . I assure you . . . if opportunity does not present itself soon, she will *make* it."

"The Court expects His Majesty to be in mourning for his Queen," went on Choiseul.

"My poor mother! She will be looking down from heaven, watching him. I will tell him that. But, Monsieur de

Choiseul, there is nothing to fear. This woman will never
be presented at Court."

"Never!" echoed Choiseul. "Yet it is distasteful to
think of her polluting the air even of the private apartments."

"I shall stop it," said Adelaide fiercely. "And, Monsieur
de Choiseul, if you should need my help in other matters . . .
War with England . . ."

Choiseul bowed over her hand. "I shall never forget,
Madame, the great part you once prepared yourself to play
against the enemy."

Adelaide bowed her head, smiling with delight; and as
soon as he had gone she went to the other door and opened
it sharply; as she expected, her sisters almost fell into the
room.

Adelaide put her fingers to her lips.

"What do we do now?" asked Victoire.

"Yes, what do we do now?" echoed Sophie.

"You," Adelaide told them severely, "will do what you
are commanded to do. *I* will plan our campaign against this
odious du Barry."

Three heads remained close together, and there was whispering in the apartments of Madame Adelaide which were
so close to those of the King himself.

Louis looked sourly at his daughter.

"My dear Loque," he said, "I consider this a somewhat
impertinent intrusion on your part."

"Someone must speak to Your Majesty on this delicate
matter. And who better than your daughter?"

Louis retorted coldly: "I regret that my daughter should
so far forget her good manners as to attempt to discuss with
me matters which are no concern of hers."

"Oh, but there you are wrong, dear Papa. This *is* my
concern. I think of my dear mother . . . scarcely cold in her

grave. Imagine her looking down on you now . . . with that woman."

"She has looked upon me with women on various occasions," said the King lightly. "That which she did not greatly object to when she was alive could scarcely worry her now she is dead."

Adelaide raised her eyes to the ceiling. "I think," she began, "I think . . ."

"I am delighted," interrupted Louis, "that you are at last mastering that very useful occupation."

Adelaide threw herself at his feet. "Let me plead with you, Papa."

"I would prefer you to continue in the more useful occupation of thinking. Go back to your sisters. I doubt not that, listening as they have been at some not very distant spot, they may have missed a few of the words which have passed between us. Go, my Loque, and enlighten Coche and Graille. And tell your holy sister Louise . . . tell Chiffe . . . how you have tried to make me renounce my wicked ways. It will at least keep you occupied."

"Papa, you are tempting Heaven. What if you were to die tonight . . .?"

"I have not felt less like dying for years," said the King, "and for that my thanks are due to the lady you would ask me to give up. If you were really fond of me, you would rejoice in my happiness."

"Oh . . ." shrieked Adelaide.

Louis looked at her and was suddenly sorry for her. Had association with Jeanne made him a little tender-hearted? Poor Adelaide, he thought. She ought to have been married. It is the unnatural life she has led with her sisters that has unbalanced her. He remembered that she had once been a pretty girl and that in those days he had been fond of her.

He said: "I'll make some coffee and you shall summon

your sisters to drink it with me. And we will have no more of this nonsense."

"First swear you will not allow her to live in the Palace," cried Adelaide. "She . . . she pollutes the place."

"Are you daring to offer terms to me?" asked Louis in exasperation, his tender feelings evaporating. "Oh, get out of my sight. I cannot bear to look at you . . . you nor your sisters. And another time, before you come demanding favours of me, you might try to look more like the lady whom you appear to hate so much, and to show a temperament as sweet as hers."

Adelaide stumbled to her feet. "Father . . ." she cried, "you . . . you are turning from your family for the sake of this . . . woman. I cannot prevent my distress from showing itself."

"What cannot be prevented must perforce be endured, but there is no reason why I should suffer your folly any longer. I have asked you to go. I now demand that you obey me."

Adelaide gave him a formal curtsy and hurried out to join her sisters.

With them she clenched her fists and muttered: "It is war . . . war. We will fight and save him from a *putain* . . . even as, had they let me, I would have saved France from her defeats at the hands of the English."

Victoire and Sophie looked at each other and nodded; then they fixed their eyes on their sister's face, waiting for instructions.

Jeanne was as yet unaware of the storms which were rising all about her. She felt happy and secure. No one could have had a more devoted lover than La France, nor a more instructive and friendly companion than Chon Chon. Several members of the Court were beginning to regard her with friendship, and some of these people were in very high places.

One of these was the old Duc de Richelieu whom, being the First Gentleman of the King's Chamber, she saw now and then. His lewd old eyes would twinkle as they surveyed her, and there was a promise of friendship in them. The Duc had no wish to offend her. If she were going to remain the King's favourite, then he would be foolish to do so; and if the King discarded her, Richelieu would be ready to show her that there were other gallant gentlemen at the Court prepared to offer protection to such a charming creature.

Jeanne was shrewd enough to understand the motive behind those twinkling eyes; and if she had not been, there would have been Chon at her elbow to point it out.

"Go warily with Richelieu," was Chon's advice. "We may find him useful. For it would appear that Monsieur de Choiseul will, if we should become too powerful, set himself up against us in earnest. I should not like to see that, for Choiseul is the most formidable enemy we could have. However, if we gather about us our own friends, we shall be a better match for him than if we try to fight him alone."

"Leave him to me," said Jeanne, "and rest assured that old Richelieu will be on our side."

But Jeanne was not interested in political intrigue. Choiseul was a tiresome fellow. She had smiled dazzlingly at him on the rare occasions when she had caught his eyes upon her, but she had met nothing but a stony stare with which the man tried to make her feel that he did not see her at all.

But Jeanne did not propose to waste time on such unpleasant subjects as the possible enmity of Choiseul; there were far more interesting things to be done. In the first place she had installed her mother in a grand house in Paris; and how delighted Anne was in her daughter's good fortune! Then there was the matter of Monsieur Billard du Monceaux. That had been a very pleasant incident.

She had summoned him to her quarters at Versailles, and

poor Monsieur Billard du Monceaux had come in bewilderment, telling himself that there had been some mistake.

She would never forget the look on his face when he had entered the room. She had had the curtains drawn, because she did not want him immediately to recognise her as the little girl whom he had discovered in the house of Mademoiselle Frédéric.

She had received him with the utmost charm. "I pray you, Monsieur Billard du Monceaux, sit beside me," she had said in that best Court manner, which she could assume by taking a little pains and keep up as long as she remembered to do so. "Tell me, do you remember a little girl whom you once sent to the convent of Sainte-Aure? Her name, I believe, was Jeanne Bécu."

"Why, Madame," answered the bewildered man, "I remember her well. The loveliest child I ever saw."

"You were kind to her," went on Jeanne. "You made her your little god-daughter and paid for her education; then, you wicked man, you forgot all about her."

"She was but a child," said the man, "and time passed. . . ."

"Time passed," said Jeanne, "and the child grew into a woman. That woman will never forget what a kind gentleman once did for her. I am that woman, my friend and god-father, I, Madame du Barry."

Then Jeanne leaped to her feet and threw herself into the old man's arms. There were tears in her eyes and laughter on her lips as she said: "It is I who may be able to do good for you now, my friend. Do not think, Monsieur Billard du Monceaux, that I am the sort to forget a kindness."

Then did Monsieur Billard du Monceaux fall on his knees before her, overcome by his emotion.

She had fulfilled the promise of her childish charm and beauty, he told her, and it was reward enough to have had a hand in making her the delightful creature she was today.

And afterwards Monsieur Billard du Monceaux had gone away, and he could not stop talking of that beautiful creature who was now the beloved mistress of the King. Not only was she the most beautiful of women, she was also the kindest.

How much more pleasant it was to arrange reunions with old friends such as Monsieur Billard du Monceaux than contemplate battles to be fought with such as Monsieur de Choiseul!

There was, however, one jaunt which Jeanne could not resist the pleasure of giving herself.

She said to Chon: "Prepare yourself, we are making a short journey."

"Is this to be another reunion with old friends?" asked Chon.

"Not friends . . . exactly," said Jeanne.

She was smiling with grim pleasure as she instructed her coachman to drive to the Château Courneuve.

Madame de la Garde was amazed to see such a splendid carriage. She was even more amazed to see the sumptuously clad young woman who stepped out of it, followed by the more sombrely dressed companion; almost immediately she recognised the young girl who had once been her reader and whom she had dismissed so ignominiously.

"Mademoiselle . . . Bécu," she stammered.

"Madame du Barry now, Madame de la Garde. And I have brought with me my sister-in-law, Mademoiselle du Barry, who lives with me at Versailles and is my dear friend and companion."

"Madame du Barry," echoed the woman. "I . . . I have heard of your good fortune. I am honoured that you have called on me."

"Our reunion," said Jeanne, "takes place in very different circumstances from those of our last meeting."

"I pray you come into my little *salon*." Madame de la

Garde was clearly nervous. "And I will offer you some refreshment."

"Come, Chon," said Jeanne; and they followed their hostess while Jeanne savoured the pleasure of coming back to this house, as an honoured guest with the power to strike terror into her hostess, instead of as the humble little reader who could be—and who was—turned out at a moment's notice.

There was the room in which Jeanne had sat and read to Madame de la Garde. It seemed very small, very unimpressive now; yet it has not changed at all, thought Jeanne. It is I who have changed.

"And your sons, Madame de la Garde. . . . How are they?" asked Jeanne.

"They are very well," said Madame de la Garde; and a look of fear came into her eyes. It was clear that she believed the magnificently clad young woman, sitting opposite her and regarding her mischievously, had come to repay an old debt, and her hands trembled so that her wine was spilt on her gown. She was realising the great power which would be Jeanne's now. Even here in this old château she had heard of her fame and the esteem in which she was held by the King, so that a word from her could make or mar the careers of men such as the sons of Madame de la Garde.

Jeanne, who had come to flaunt her power and position before this woman who had once humiliated her, suddenly felt sorry for her. It seemed to Jeanne that what she was doing was somewhat mean and petty, and immediately she had one wish, which was to put Madame de la Garde out of her misery and reassure her that she had nothing to fear.

"Madame de la Garde," said Jeanne, "I merely came to call on you as an old friend. It is so long ago I was in your house that I have almost forgotten what happened to me here. I do remember how good your two sons were to me."

146

She laughed. "They caused you some anxiety, did they not? You feared they would marry your little reader, and you were alarmed for their future. Ah, Madame de la Garde, you were right. Of course you were right. I should have been a most unsuitable wife!"

Madame de la Garde was staring at her unbelievingly, and Jeanne went on: "I came but to tell you that, now I am in a position to be of some use to my friends, I shall not forget them; and your two sons made me very happy while I was under your roof. If I can be of any use to them"—she turned to Chon who was watching her intently—"and I fully believe I am in a position to be so . . . rest assured I shall."

"Madame, your kindness amazes me," stammered Madame de la Garde. "I do not know what to say."

"Then I will say it for you," cried Jeanne. "You must no longer feel distressed because you turned me out, for if you had not, the great good fortune which is now mine might not have come to me. Therefore, Madame de la Garde, I must be grateful to you as well as to your sons."

Chon stared in astonishment as Jeanne went to Madame de la Garde, laid her hands on her shoulders and kissed her on either cheek.

When they were driving back to Versailles it was Chon's turn to laugh. "I thought we were going to preen ourselves before that odious woman," she said. "I thought we were going to say: 'See, Madame, what a fool you have been in insulting Jeanne Bécu who became Madame du Barry!'"

"One does not always achieve what one sets out to do," answered Jeanne gravely.

Although Jeanne was contented in the rooms of the late Monsieur Le Bel, the King was less pleased with her apartments. As the days passed his pleasure in his mistress increased and he decided that he would no longer allow her

147

to remain in rooms which had once belonged to a *valet de chambre*.

Louis was realising that in Jeanne du Barry he had found a companion who could give him all the pleasure he had found in Madame de Pompadour. Jeanne had not the same interest in politics; but Louis was discovering how pleasant it was to have a mistress who did not meddle in State affairs. He told himself that had Madame de Pompadour been a Jeanne du Barry the *Parc aux Cerfs* need never have come into existence, and there need not have been those somewhat humiliating backstairs adventures. Jeanne, full of youth and vitality, was healthy—as Madame de Pompadour had not been. He had enjoyed the Pompadour's friendship and had to look elsewhere for physical satisfaction. How different it was with Jeanne! She rejuvenated him; she had taught him how to laugh, not only at others but at himself.

Unfortunately she could not accompany him on all the occasions when he would have liked to have her with him. He—more than anyone at Versailles—was bound by its etiquette. Until Jeanne was formally presented at Court she could not appear at his side in public.

This was irritating, particularly as he realised that it was not going to be easy to find a sponsor who would make the formal presentation.

But in the meantime he meant to give her a more elaborate apartment and one which was nearer his own, so that he could have the pleasure of reaching her with the greatest of ease; and, recalling his daughter's impertinence in daring to remonstrate with him, he decided what he would do.

He sent for Adelaide.

When she came, her manner was so triumphant that Louis felt more irritated than usual at the sight of her. The foolish old woman believed that her father had sent for her in order to patch up their quarrel.

How could a sensible woman, like their mother, and a

man such as myself who, I venture to believe, am not entirely lacking in intellectual power, have created such a daughter—three such daughters! wondered the King.

Adelaide curtsied while her father watched her sardonically.

Louis came straight to the point. "The Dauphine's apartments are very pleasant, daughter; do you not think so?"

"My dead brother's dead wife's . . ." began Adelaide.

"Certainly," interrupted Louis testily. "I said the Dauphine, did I not? Whom else could I mean? I said, do you not think the apartments she used are very pleasant?"

"Why yes, Papa."

"I am glad, because they are now to be yours."

"Mine! But thank you, Papa. That is good of you." She was smiling that foolish, triumphant smile which indicated that she believed that he was sorry for the way he had behaved, was planning to take her advice and that this was his way of telling her that their little quarrel was over. Adelaide often lived in the past. It was so comforting to let her mind wander back to the days when she had been a pretty girl and her father had favoured her, for, if she had been devoted to him then, he had certainly been indulgent to her.

She, poor lady, imagined that life was going to be as it used to be, when courtiers had sought her favours and her father had liked to joke with her and make her play to him. When she had played the violin or the harp or cornet he would applaud her wildly and all the courtiers would follow his lead; she had then believed herself to be a great musician. Later Louise, her youngest sister who had dared more than Victoire and Sophie ever would, told her that the noises which came from the instruments were so discordant that everybody was laughing at her lack of musical talent, encouraged to do so by the King. Louise implored her sister not to allow herself to be made to look so foolish; and at length they had all tired of the joke—except Adelaide who longed to be asked to play again.

Now she let herself imagine that soon she and her father would frequently drink coffee together in the *petits apparte-ments*, and that he would ask her to play for him and applaud her—and insist that the courtiers did the same—while she played.

His next words shattered her dreams.

"You will leave your present apartments immediately."

"Leave them, Papa . . . but they have been mine so long. They are nearer to your own than any. There is only the little staircase which separates them. And . . . what of Victoire and Sophie? Their apartments are close to mine, you know."

"Victoire and Sophie will no doubt manage without your being so close. In any case they will, I imagine, be able to find their way to your new apartments."

"Papa, I . . . I must look after Victoire and Sophie."

"Let them look after themselves, Adelaide. And be ready to vacate your apartments immediately."

"Papa . . . but why?"

"Because Madame du Barry will be moving in as soon as you leave."

The King waved his hand and Adelaide, never for one moment forgetting the etiquette of the Court, curtsied and stumbled out of the room. Her two sisters stared at her disconsolate face, and for once poor Adelaide was unable to speak to them.

Meanwhile the King was smiling. Everyone, from the highest to the lowest, must be taught that Madame du Barry had come to Versailles to stay as long as he was there to protect her.

8

TO BE OR NOT TO BE—PRESENTED

CHON was thoughtful as her carriage took her from her brother's house in the Rue des Petits Champs towards Versailles. Jean, Comte du Barry, had conveyed to her the fact that he was growing a little uneasy.

"You see, Fanchon," he said, "I have worked hard for this over many years, and if I failed now I could not hope for such good fortune again. Jeanne pleases the King, but as yet she is little more than one of those girls who used to be smuggled up the backstairs by Le Bel. She has the apartments of Madame Adelaide and that is good, but until she has been presented we cannot feel secure."

Chon had agreed whole-heartedly. She, who lived in the Palace and had quickly learned the etiquette of the Court, realised more fully, even than did her brother, the necessity for that presentation.

She had clenched her hands and declared: "It shall come to pass and without much more delay. It must; and when it does, brother . . . oh, when it does, then we must be prepared for the full force of Choiseul's enmity."

Du Barry nodded. "But let us negotiate our fences when we are close to them. At the moment let us concentrate on Jeanne's presentation. You must insist that she makes Louis arrange it."

Chon had smiled grimly. He knew Jeanne even as she did; but she believed she had a greater understanding of the King's character. Louis realised the difficulty of getting one such as Jeanne presented, and Louis shirked what was difficult; as for Jeanne, she could be told to ask for her presentation, but if the King brushed the matter aside and showed that he did not wish to discuss it, she would be ready to fall in with his mood.

Oh, this Court etiquette! sighed Chon as her carriage rattled her along. It might be comic if it were not so irritating. Jeanne is installed in the Palace; she actually lives in apartments which were once occupied by Madame Adelaide but, because she has not been presented, officially she is not there. And until she has been presented she has no right to be seen in any of the royal carriages, to eat in any of the royal apartments or to share in the public life of the King in any way.

There was only one solution: Jeanne must be presented. And if it did not happen soon (and this was that for which Jeanne's enemies were hoping), in time she would become merely the King's light-o'-love, with no power at Court whatsoever.

She left her carriage and made her way into the Palace. It was very unfortunate that she should meet the Duc de Choiseul with the Duc de Richelieu and a few of their attendants.

Chon curtsied. The Duc de Richelieu acknowledged her as did those of his party; the Duc de Choiseul and his men looked through her as though she did not exist.

Chon went on her way. Well, she assured herself, I am but a menial in the Palace—companion to the King's mistress—but wise men, if they believed Jeanne's fortune was on the rise, would surely consider it worth while to treat me with courtesy.

When she reached the apartments she was told that Jeanne was with the King; so she sat rehearsing what she would say to her, how she would impress upon her the importance of obtaining this honour from the King without delay.

Before she saw Jeanne again she encountered the Duc de

Richelieu who, in his capacity of First Gentleman of the King's Chamber, was more often seen by Jeanne and Chon than any other nobleman at Court.

"Why, Mademoiselle Chon Chon," cried the Duke, his twinkling eyes showing her a certain respect, "our friend Choiseul was somewhat churlish this day, was he not!"

Chon lifted her shoulders. "I have never found the Duc otherwise," she told him.

"It is because he thinks you have no right to be here."

"He behaves as though I am such a familiar part of the surroundings that he does not see me."

"He does not see you because it is a breach of etiquette in the ducal mind that you are here at all. He prefers to ignore you, for to accept you is against the formality of Versailles. Mademoiselle Chon Chon, you have been remiss. The young lady *must* be presented."

"You are right, Monsieur le Duc."

"Then . . . explain to our charming friend . . . what must be, must be."

"I will do so."

The Duke nodded. His glance implied: I am behind you, offering support. I am your friend.

So there were some shrewd people in Versailles, thought Chon, who believed in the rising star of Madame du Barry.

When the old Duc de Richelieu left Chon he sought the company of his nephew, Emmanuel, Duc d'Aiguillon, for he was very eager to discuss certain matters with him.

Aiguillon looked at his uncle with interest. The old man was continually intriguing and, in spite of his age, still dreamed of becoming the most influential person of the Court and the power behind the throne. Aiguillon shared his ambition and was wise enough to know that, working together, they could go further than they could hope to alone.

"Good day to you, nephew," said Richelieu, his lined old face wrinkling with mischief. "I have been talking to that woman of our young lady's."

Aiguillon looked languidly at his elegant hands. "Are you not being a little premature, my uncle, in claiming her?"

"My boy, I am an old man; I have been twisted and turned this way and that by the winds of fortune. I fancy I am therefore capable of recognising a favourable wind when it blows my way."

"Well, you old weather-vane, so Louis has been completely entangled this time, has he?"

"He becomes more devoted every day."

"Well, you should know. You have always understood what the King looked for in his mistresses."

Richelieu laughed; he knew that his nephew was referring to the affair of the Duchesse de Châteauroux who, years before, when she had been merely Madame de la Tournelle, had been his, Aiguillon's mistress. Louis had greatly desired her, but she had been deeply in love with Aiguillon until Richelieu had offered to separate them so that she would turn to the King. The wicked old Duke had arranged that an ex-mistress of his own should write passionate love letters to young Aiguillon, and as the letters continued to arrive, Aiguillon fell into the temptation of writing to her and promising to be with her in order to comfort her. This letter Richelieu gave to the King, who in his turn gave it to Madame de la Tournelle, and she, believing her young lover to be faithless, became the mistress of the King.

Richelieu read his nephew's thoughts and, laying his arm about the young man's shoulders, said: "That is ancient history. We are older and wiser men now."

"I but recall the incident," said Aiguillon, "to assure myself that you are an adept at discovering those women who best please Louis."

"Louis and his women!" said Richelieu. "Let us be

thankful that we have a King who is so enamoured of the charming creatures. This penchant of our King's can bring much good to such as we are."

"What are your plans for this one?" asked Aiguillon.

"To watch. To be ready. To offer the hand of friendship ... tentatively. So that, if she achieves this presentation, she will then find two powerful noblemen ready to guide her: Richelieu and Aiguillon."

They eyed each other significantly.

Aiguillon was thinking: He does not forget that he is the great-nephew of Cardinal Richelieu and longs to play that part with Louis XV which his distinguished relative played with Louis XIII. Richelieu, considering his nephew, thought: He longs for power. Good soldier though he is he has been slighted and ridiculed by his enemies. He hates the *Parlement* and more than any man in France he hates Choiseul.

If the two Dukes were being shrewd over this matter of Madame du Barry, then Choiseul was being a fool. If the woman came to real power, it was not wildly improbable that a new party could be formed about her, a party which would send Choiseul into obscurity and set itself at the head of affairs.

The Duc de Richelieu and the Duc d'Aiguillon had dreamed of being head of such a party.

So, while the fate of the mistress was in the balance, it was politic to show her that she had friends at Court in the two noble and ambitious Dukes.

The Court was buzzing with the news. Madame du Barry was to be presented. The King desired it. Even so, it was going to be no easy matter to bring about the ceremony. The etiquette of Versailles was so rigid that even the King could not dispense with it, and the presentation did not depend on him alone.

In the first place the great Choiseul was very much against it; he had even gone so far as to protest to the King, and had told his friends that if it took place he would retire from a Court life which must necessarily become debased by the admittance of such a creature. However, it was generally believed that Choiseul would not retire unless forced to; he was deeply in debt and needed the great revenues which came from his duties to the State.

Another enemy to Jeanne had appeared. This was the heir to the throne. Louis, Duc de Berry, was a quiet boy who spent more time with his favourite locksmith than in social activities; shy, diffident, aware of his inability to shine in company, he had, unlike his grandfather, no desire for the company of women. They embarrassed him; and his grandfather's blatant adoration of this vitally attractive young woman of the people seemed to him shameful.

Although the Dauphin had little to say against the King's favourite, his dislike and disapproval carried some weight. He was, after all, the heir to the throne, and the King, approaching sixty, could not, considering the life he had led, be expected to live many more years.

Therefore, feeling there was the antagonism of the chief minister and the heir to the throne to be considered, there were many who were sure that it was going to be no easy matter to find a sponsor for Jeanne du Barry.

It was a situation to provoke much amusement in a Court such as that of Louis Quinze; bets were made and the subject openly discussed in the ante-rooms of the great Palace. "Will she?" "Will she not?" "What are the odds today?" Those were the questions heard more frequently than any others, while an amused and cynical Court awaited the outcome.

Louis was disturbed. Before Jeanne was presented she must be accepted as a lady of noble descent, and although the Comte du Barry had produced a very cleverly forged birth certificate and a certificate of marriage, Jeanne's powerful enemy, Choiseul, had sent his spies into Paris and the country to gather information, and he was fully aware of her origin. Moreover, he was determined that no one should remain ignorant of it.

The King wondered whether he could buy the principality of Lus en Bigarre and give it to Jeanne so that she could be presented as a foreign Princess. This would eliminate major difficulties; but already Choiseul had done his work, already even the people of Paris were aware of the period spent at Labille's.

No! Jeanne must have a sponsor; she must be presented at Court in the normal manner. But who would be her sponsor?

It was Richelieu, First Gentleman of the Bedchamber, who provided the answer, as he had to so many of the King's amatory problems.

"I know the very lady, Sire," he said. "She is related to the Duchesse d'Aiguillon who, with her husband, as you know, is ever ready to serve Your Majesty."

"A friend of the Duchesse?" said the King; and his look said: If the Duchesse is so ready to serve me why does she not offer herself for the task?

Richelieu's wise old face wore an expression which implied: Far as we would go in the service of Your Majesty, we could not go as far as that. What if you discard the lady? Think of the ridicule which would fall upon the shoulders of the Aiguillons for having sponsored her.

Louis saw the point; he was not a man to ask impossibilities of his subjects, and he appreciated the wisdom of Richelieu and his nephew who were ready to give certain help, provided it was not to be too ostentatiously given. In any case the King's need of a sponsor was so dire that he must accept what was offered.

"I speak," said Richelieu, "of the Comtesse de Béarn.

157

She is old and therefore would add dignity to the proceedings."

"Presumably she suffers from poverty as well as old age," said Louis. "And she would wish to be amply rewarded for the part she plays."

"Sire, let us face the truth that no woman would undertake this task without some reward. There will be certain expenses. This Comtesse is verging on insolvency. She would need funds . . . ample funds."

Louis lifted one shoulder. "Well," he said, "if she is prepared to serve us, she shall have her reward."

The King congratulated himself and sent for Jeanne. When he had embraced her he told her: "I have some pleasing news for you. We have found your sponsor."

Jeanne seized her lover by the shoulders and kissed first his cheeks, then his lips.

"Now," she said, "I may be with you on all occasions. No more of these meetings which are supposed to be secret but which everybody knows about."

"Once you have been presented you will accompany me on all my journeys. You will have your rightful place at Versailles. I shall acknowledge you in the eyes of the Court and we shall put an end to all the humiliations you have had to suffer. My dearest, I have asked Pompadour's brother, Marigny, to have those apartments which she occupied at Bellevue, Marly and Choisy refurnished in readiness—for they will be yours. Now, I may hope to give you all that I have wished to during these past weeks."

Jeanne was filled with joy. She could not pretend that she was not going to enjoy all the glitter of Court life, for she knew she was.

"There is one matter," said the King warningly; "when you have been presented, it will be necessary for you to show a little more decorum. In public, I mean. In private . . . everything must be as it always has been."

Jeanne realised afresh all that this man had done for her and, in a rush of emotion, she knelt, took his hand and kissed it with tenderness and courtly respect; and when she lifted her eyes to his, there were tears in them.

The Duc de Choiseul and the Duchesse de Gramont were furious. The seemingly impossible had been achieved. A sponsor had been found for the du Barry! A poor old woman —but they had discovered that she had a serpent's tongue and was well able to defend herself verbally—had been found to perform the ritual.

Choiseul discussed the gravity of the situation with his sister, and they both realised that the presentation would be a great victory for the enemy.

"The old woman is desperately in need of the money," said Choiseul, "otherwise she would never undertake the task."

"Nevertheless she has undertaken it," retorted the Duchesse.

"What alarms me is that the Duc de Richelieu has taken it upon himself to order her a Court dress," went on the Duke. "You know what this means, my dear. The sly old fox is coming out into the open. This is not a gesture of friendliness towards the woman so much as an insult to me. I tell you this, if that woman remains in power, they'll be forming a little group about her, and it will be headed by old Richelieu with that idiot Aiguillon beside him."

"There is nothing much to fear from them. Richelieu's too old and Aiguillon is known throughout Paris as a fool."

"There will be others. Maupeou, for one."

"Maupeou! But he owes his appointment as Chancellor to you."

"He'll forget that. If he sees a new sun beginning to rise he'll be stretching out his grasping hands to its warmth, never fear. And forget not, sister; he is at the head of Justice

—a powerful man. So do not think it will be merely old Richelieu and foolish Aiguillon with whom we have to contend. There are Bertin, St. Florentin. I have seen the signs and, sister, we shall doubtless find the religious party supporting her."

"The religious party supporting a harlot—a harlot from the *faubourgs* at that!"

Choiseul took his sister by the shoulders and looked intently into her eyes. "They do not forgive me for expelling the Jesuits. They would support the Devil himself if it meant striking at their enemy. I am their enemy, sister. I tell you that if this presentation takes place we shall be in the most uncomfortable position we have endured since we came to Court."

"So," said the Duchesse, "this little affair is more than the presentation of a harlot, it is a matter of high politics."

"I see that you understand our predicament perfectly."

"And what do you propose to do?"

"Firstly, Madame de Béarn must be made to see how very unwisely she is acting. Secondly, we must stir our friends to action. I will get Voltaire to write a little satire on the du Barry. He is very anxious to curry favour with me and there is venom in his pen. In fact, sister, we shall use the pen as one of our sharpest weapons. We'll have people singing in the streets, and the burden of their song shall be Madame du Barry, the slut who, by the tricks she has learned in her brothel, brings to a *paillard* the sensations he craves."

In the streets they were singing songs about the King's latest mistress, for Choiseul had lost no time in calling together his *chansonniers*; and as the songs were written so singers were sent out into the streets to interest the public in them.

The people listened eagerly to the new songs, for Paris

loved its songs and most events of importance and interest were commemorated thus. Usually the songs had a certain wit and irony, for such qualities appealed strongly to the Parisian.

Soon the tune of the old folk-song, *La Bourbonnaise*, had a new set of words, and everywhere the refrain was heard; it was whistled and hummed; but more frequently it was sung, because it was in this case the words which caused so much amusement.

Quelle merveille!
Une fille de rien,
Une fille de rien,
Quelle merveille!
Donne au Roi de l'amour,
Est à la Cour!

Elle est gentille,
Elle a les yeux fripons;
Elle a les yeux fripons;
Elle est gentille;
Elle excite avec art
Un vieux paillard.

En maison bonne,
Elle a pris des leçons;
Elle a pris des leçons;
En maison bonne,
Chez Goudan, chez Brisson;
Elle en sait long.

Que de postures!
Elle a lu l'Arétin;
Elle a lu l'Arétin;
Que de postures!
Elle fait en tous sens
Prendre les sens.

Le Roi s'écrie :
L'Ange, le beau talent !
L'Ange, le beau talent !
Viens sur mon trône,
Je veux te couronner,
Je veux te couronner.

This was the favourite song; it was sung in the cafés and lemonade shops, in the gardens of Palais Royal; the traders coming into *les Halles* at the break of day were singing it; those wending their way homewards after a midnight carousal sang it also.

Choiseul had already set abroad the rumour that Jeanne had lived in a brothel before coming to Court—hence the allusion to the "*maison bonne, chez Goudan, chez Brisson*", Mesdames Goudan and Brisson being two of the most notorious brothel-keepers of the day.

How could Louis allow the heroine of *La Bourbonnaise* to be presented at Court! Choiseul cherished great hopes of his songsters.

New songs appeared and although *La Bourbonnaise* remained the favourite, people were singing:

Lisette, ta beauté séduit
Et charme tout le monde.
En vain la Duchesse en rougit
Et la Princesse en gronde ;
Chacun sait que Vénus naquit
De l'écume de l'onde.

To which the friends of Choiseul had added the verse:

De deux Vénus on parle dans le monde,
De toutes deux gouverner fut le lot :
L'une naquit de l'écume de l'onde,
L'autre naquit de l'écume du pot.

162

Lampoons were smuggled into the Palace. Often the songs would be heard in the gardens, even below the windows of the King's apartments. Excitement ran high; and the questions continued to be asked: "Will she? Won't she? What are the odds? For? Against?"

The date for the presentation was fixed. The dress was ready. Jeanne had spent hours practising the ritual. The Duchesse d'Aiguillon was very helpful, and Jeanne had begun to look upon the lady as her very good friend, in spite of warnings from Chon that the Duchesse's friendship was not entirely disinterested.

Jeanne was determined that when Louis received her in the presence of his relations—Adelaide, that wicked old daughter of his, for one, who she knew hated her—he should not be ashamed of her. She would curb her exuberance; she would behave as though she had spent her lifetime at Versailles, and with such meticulous care that none should be able to sneer at her deportment. She was taking lessons of Vestris, the famous dancer, so that she would curtsy in the perfect Versailles manner and perform the very difficult circular kick without mishap. She would look so beautiful that every other woman would seem insignificant—that was the least difficult task she had to perform.

The Duchesse d'Aiguillon was at hand to advise her, as was her husband, the Duke, and the old roué Richelieu. Monsieur de Maupeou, that important man, had indicated that he was ready to give her his support. It was comforting, so said Chon, that these important gentlemen should be looking her way with approval.

"Nice kind gentlemen," Jeanne had called them; to which Chon had replied shrewdly: "Let us not take too seriously their niceness or their kindness; but rather let us pin our hopes on their far-sighted wisdom."

Jeanne was certain that all would go well with the

presentation; she refused to be intimidated by her enemies; Chon had even heard her hum *La Bourbonnaise*, and savouring the words with some amusement. Jeanne, Chon decided, needed someone to look after her—someone like herself who loved her for her personal charm and simplicity rather than the good fortune her friendship might bring.

It was two days before that fixed for the presentation, and Jeanne was practising the curtsy and the kick, with Chon playing the part of the King, when a messenger arrived from the Comtesse de Béarn.

Chon turned pale as she leaned over Jeanne's shoulder to read the letter. Her lips moved as she read:

". . . hence, having sprained my ankle so that it is impossible for me to walk, I shall be unable to present you at Court. . . ."

"Poor old creature!" cried Jeanne. "I hope she is not in pain."

"In pain!" cried Chon. "The coward! The dissembler! She no more has a hurt foot than I have two sound ones. Do you not see, she is afraid . . . afraid at the last moment to do what she has promised and what she is being paid well to do!"

"You think that this is deliberate?" asked Jeanne.

"I know," said Chon firmly.

There was nothing to be done but postpone the presentation. The King was angry, fearing that he was being made to look ridiculous, but the Choiseuls were gleeful, and the odds against Madame du Barry's presentation were raised, while the Court awaited the next move.

At length a noblewoman, a certain Madame d'Alogny, who was entitled to go to Court but who until this time had been living in obscurity, was found; she was promised a great reward if she would go to Court and, after a short stay there, present Madame du Barry to the King. This Madame d'Alogny agreed to do.

Adelaide, still smarting from the loss of her apartments, had placed herself firmly on the side of Choiseul; she declared to her sisters that they must stand together, that the evil woman must never be presented, so that they might save their poor father from his folly.

Adelaide had her opportunity when Madame d'Alogny was presented to her. It was a matter of etiquette that Madame d'Alogny should kneel and kiss the hem of the Princess's robe, when Adelaide should either graciously extend her hand to be kissed or bid her rise; and until the Princess responded, Madame d'Alogny must remain on her knees. Such was the etiquette at Versailles.

Adelaide was waiting in the *salon*, her sisters clustered about her, when she saw the woman enter. One of Adelaide's women whispered to her: "Madame la Princesse, the woman who now approaches . . . she it is who is to act as sponsor to Madame du Barry."

"What an odious creature!" said Adelaide quietly.

"Odious creature," whispered Victoire to Sophie, and Sophie's lips were forming the words as Madame d'Alogny was presented to Adelaide as the eldest of the Princesses.

Adelaide inclined her head and Madame d'Alogny fell to her knees, slightly lifted the hem of Adelaide's gown, and kissed it.

She waited for the hand to be extended, or at least for permission to rise. Neither occurred. But without a glance to right or left Adelaide walked away leaving the woman kneeling there; Victoire and Sophie, imitating their sister's expression and walk, followed her; and poor Madame d'Alogny continued to kneel, not knowing what else she could do, only being aware of the rigid etiquette of Versailles which forbade one to rise until given a sign or permission to do so.

She was aware of the amused glances, the titters.

It was all part of the game which was being played at Versailles: To be or not to be presented.

And as the mortified woman remained uncertainly on her knees there were many in the *salon* who murmured that Madame du Barry would never be presented.

After her humiliating experience it was impossible for Madame d'Alogny to remain at Court. Even Jeanne became gloomy.

"I see," she said, "that there is a plot against me. Too many powerful people are determined that I shall never be presented, that I shall never share your life. Alas, La France, we shall have to continue with our meetings, which are supposed to be secret, and when I meet people at Versailles they will continue to look at me as though I am a ghost whom they cannot see."

Louis cried: "It shall not be so. I am the master here. You *shall* be presented."

He sent for the Comtesse de Béarn.

She was told that she would present Madame du Barry at Court and that this time there should be no hurt ankle, no excuse whatsoever for disobeying the orders of the King; she should receive 100,000 livres for her services; but perform them she should or feel the displeasure of His Majesty.

The Comtesse de Béarn knelt before the King; she wished to hide the gleam in her eyes; 100,000 livres! It was a goodly sum.

"There can be no question of disobeying a command from the King," she said.

Louis nodded; and once again preparations for the presentation began.

The day arrived. The story of the great efforts to present Madame du Barry at Court had spread to Paris and the roads between Versailles and the capital were crowded with people of all classes who were determined to see the favourite and take a share in the betting which was still going on.

Many declared that, even now, something would happen to frustrate the desires of the King and this daughter of the people, for Monsieur de Choiseul was still at the head of affairs.

The King had come from evensong in the Chapel Royal and made his way to the Galerie des Glaces. Louis had caught the general uneasiness; he would not be happy until the affair was over. There had been too many hitches for comfort.

He himself was feeling a little shaken from a recent accident in the hunting field; it had been nothing much but at such times he was aware of the speculation in the eyes of those about him. He is an old man, they thought; he cannot last much longer. And at such times he needed Jeanne; he needed her as he had never needed a woman before; she restored his youth and scoffed at his fears; thus, when he was with Jeanne, and then only, could he feel the power to banish death far . . . far into the future. Naturally he wanted to keep this beloved creature with him at all times. She *must* be presented.

He wished her to arrive in the great Galerie in all her breath-taking loveliness, so that she could put to shame those of her enemies who had sought to destroy her. He grew angry when he thought of the calumnies which were being spread about, the suggestive songs which were being sung in the streets. But once she was presented, once she was acknowledged as *maîtresse en titre*, her enemies would be more careful.

Therefore this time the presentation must take place.

Last night he had sent her diamonds to the value of 100,000 livres, and he was longing to see her wearing them. In the Galerie the crowds were assembling. At any moment now she would be announced; she would come towards him.

167

He glanced at those near the throne. Choiseul was looking gloomy, and so was his sister. He would warn Choiseul that if the persecution of Madame du Barry did not cease he would dismiss Madame de Gramont from the Court. It was impossible to dismiss Choiseul so easily, but that family should have a warning. Adelaide was looking angry and her sisters were watching her to get the cue as to what they should be feeling. Foolish Adelaide! How did she hope to pit her wits against his! And Richelieu had a triumphant glance or two to throw in the direction of Choiseul, as had Aiguillon. There were other statesmen who were not looking displeased. That meant that Choiseul had his enemies.

Choiseul had been in power too long. It was a mistake for a minister to imagine himself to be indispensable.

Meanwhile the time was passing.

Choiseul, who was close to the King, whispered: "Sire, the lady is a little late." And try as he might he could not keep the note of glee out of his voice.

The people who were crowding into the ante-chambers were making bets. She will? She will not? And even at this time there were many who were ready to stake their money on a further postponement of the ceremony.

The King was showing signs of strain.

The Duchesse de Gramont whispered to a friend: "If it fails this time, it will never happen. Louis, besotted as he is, cannot risk looking ridiculous twice."

Louis' foot was tapping impatiently; a fixed smile was on his face but he was alert all the time for the announcement of her arrival.

He signed to Richelieu who, he knew, had done a great deal to make the presentation possible.

"What can have happened to her?" he asked.

"Your Majesty, have patience a little longer, I beg of you. She will be here. There must have been some slight mishap."

"If she does not come soon there will be no help for it but to abandon the ceremony. How can she have allowed this to happen after all our difficulties?"

Richelieu had begun to sweat uncomfortably; he was conscious of the cynical eyes of the Duc de Choiseul fixed upon him. What fresh mischief had that man been working? wondered Richelieu.

This presentation was no ordinary, frivolous ceremony. It was a matter of politics. This *fille de rien* carried with her all the hopes of the new party; that was why, as the minutes ticked away and the King grew more and more anxious, Richelieu, Aiguillon, Maupeou, Bertin, St. Florentin and many another feared that their hopes had been too sanguine, and that by supporting Madame du Barry they had made themselves very vulnerable to their enemies.

Jeanne was seated before the mirror. The hairdresser had piled up the fair curls and had powdered them so that their whiteness enhanced the delicately tinted complexion. Jeanne's blue eyes sparkled.

"It must be perfect . . . perfect!" she cried. "Nothing less than perfection will do. They will all be watching . . . for one sign of vulgarity, one little thing to which they can point with scorn."

Chon, who had been watching the proceedings, assured her: "You look beautiful. There is no one at Court who can compare with you."

"I think that if the curls were piled a little higher they would be more becoming," insisted Jeanne.

"Madame," said her hairdresser, "to alter the coiffure—that means that we must begin again."

"Then begin again," cried Jeanne recklessly, and she pulled the long hairpins from her hair and shook it about her shoulders.

Chon gasped in horror. "The time . . ." she began.

"I tell you," said Jeanne, "that there must be perfection
. . . nothing less will please the King . . . or me."

And the hairdresser, who knew that his reputation might
well depend on what he achieved this day, began once more
to build up the tower of hair.

Chon paced the room. They should be at the Palace now.
Chon could picture it all so clearly; the hopeful sniggers of
those enemies whom Jeanne refused to take seriously; the
anxiety of their friends which must turn to annoyance when
they learned that such a frivolous matter as the dressing of
her hair might ruin all they had worked so hard for.

"Hurry, hurry," said Chon to herself. She dared not say
it aloud; she feared to disturb the hairdresser, who must
work with the utmost skill and speed.

So the minutes passed; and when Jeanne was ready in
her white gown, blazing with the diamonds which the King
had given her, her hair, as Chon had to admit, now that it
was piled higher on that exquisite head, did add to her
beauty.

"But there is so little time," cried Chon frantically, as she
hurried Jeanne into the carriage where the Comtesse de
Béarn was waiting. She lectured her as they drove.

"You must encourage a sense of the most correct conduct
if you are to succeed at Versailles," said Chon. "Dearest
sister, never be so foolish again. What use all these elaborate
preparations if, when we arrive at Versailles, there is no
ceremony?"

"Surely Louis would not allow that."

"Louis is devoted, but he is in the grip of Madame
Etiquette no less than any of his subjects. Jeanne, I must
impress upon you once more that after this reception you
must be more serious. You will have to understand your
new position."

Madame de Béarn nodded. "Your sister is right in all she
says," she added.

Jeanne turned to Chon and gripped her hand. She said solemnly: "It shall be so. You shall have no cause to complain, I promise you. In public I shall be discreet. I am learning my lessons of deportment from Monsieur Vestris and a little wisdom from you. Have no fear."

"I could wish," said Chon a little tartly, "that you had developed this wisdom a little earlier. Today for instance. Then I should not be riding to Versailles in a state of extreme anxiety."

"Poor Chon Chon," murmured Jeanne. "Louis will be waiting for me, never fear."

Louis was beginning to feel angry.

"The little wretch!" he said to Richelieu. "Has she still no sense of the ways of the Court? I cannot much longer endure the sly looks of Choiseul!"

"A little longer, Sire," said Richelieu. "Another five minutes . . ."

"Another five, then I must abandon the presentation."

Now there was a distinct titter in the crowds farthest from the King.

"I wouldn't have missed this for all the jewels Madame du Barry will get from Louis in the future," was a languid comment.

To Choiseul and his sister it seemed that the minutes would never pass; to the King, Richelieu, Aiguillon and their friends it seemed that never had minutes flown more swiftly.

"Another five minutes, Sire," begged Richelieu.

"It cannot be more than five," answered Louis.

Then there was a shout from someone near a window. A carriage had arrived. It was . . . Madame du Barry.

Now there was the excitement of watching the King inform his mistress of his displeasure, for there was little good humour on his face.

171

She came into the Galerie following Madame de Béarn. Poor Madame de Béarn! Never had she looked so old and raddled as she did in the company of the dazzling Jeanne; and at the sight of Jeanne, so exquisitely lovely that she must draw grudging admiration even from her enemies, all Louis' annoyance faded.

His eyes gleamed as he watched her. Could this be his little *grisette*? Adorable as she had been, he had had to admit that the thought of her as the central figure on an occasion such as this had given him a qualm. But there was nothing to fear from this new Jeanne. She had learned her lessons perfectly. There was no gleam of mischief in her eyes now. She was sedate and, miracle of all miracles, serene.

To her beauty—the like of which had never been seen even at Versailles—she added grace and dignity, accepting the King's salute, being greeted by the Princesses and the Dauphin, all as though she were a young lady of the noblest family in France who had prepared all her life for this inevitable moment.

Forgotten was her unpunctuality. Louis could only rejoice that in his old age he had discovered the perfect mistress.

As for the spectators, they realised that there was a new power at the Court. Jeanne du Barry had been acknowledged as the uncrowned Queen of France.

9

MAÎTRESSE EN TITRE

How could Jeanne do other than enjoy the life which
was now hers? As the acknowledged mistress of the
King, who had more influence over him than any other
person, she was courted and flattered on all sides.

She was quite happy, not only because a life of absolute
luxury was hers, but because it was in her power to give
others almost everything they asked her. Her generosity soon
became well known with the result that there were many
calls upon it.

In vain did Chon and the Maréchale de Mirepoix, whom
the King had appointed to be her chaperon at a handsome
salary, warn her; as for the King he merely laughed at her,
for he seemed to find everything she did quite enchanting.

She had even tried to make friends with Choiseul, for, as
she said, it was natural that he should be annoyed with her
because she had taken the place which his sister had hoped
to fill. She would have been ready to forget past grievances;
it was Choiseul and his sister who were too proud to accept
her friendship and preferred rather to run the risk of
destroying themselves than do so.

Jeanne at last could only shrug her shoulders. If the
Choiseuls were determined to be her enemies, then so it
must be. There were plenty ready to be her friends.

Her fine clothes, her jewels—and especially her diamonds—
delighted her, as did her exquisitely furnished apartments at
Versailles and Louveciennes. Here were installed many
pieces of furniture, the work of craftsmen which had taken

several years to complete. There were pictures by great artists such as Boucher, Vernet, Teniers and Wynants. She was particularly delighted by a Van Dyck portrait of Charles I of England.

Chon had told her that the Barrymores, an old Irish family, were connected with the du Barrys and, as the Barrymores were connected with the Stuarts, the Stuart King of England could be said to be related to Jeanne through her marriage.

Jeanne delighted after that to refer to the picture, mischievously, as "my royal relation".

The sun streaming through her windows awakened Jeanne. She enjoyed savouring those first seconds on waking, putting out her hands to touch the brocade coverlet and the lacy pillows to assure herself that she really was in her apartments at Versailles, and not a little girl again in the convent of Sainte-Aure wakened in the early hours of morning by the first bells.

"It's true," murmured Jeanne. "I am truly here."

Then she laughed at her folly before she began to think of the coming day.

Two of her maids entered at her call. They came confidently assured of her good temper. Madame du Barry, they had discovered, was the best mistress at Court; she was generous, always good-tempered and particularly gay in the mornings.

"Madame's bath is prepared," Jeanne was told as she was helped into robe and slippers.

Lying in her scented bath she thought once more of Sainte-Aure, while the maids hovered and, when she was ready, dried her, perfumed her and helped her to dress.

"Let Zamor bring in my coffee now," she said; and in came Zamor, a rather beautiful boy, a native of Bengal not much more than seven years of age, gorgeously attired in scarlet and gold. He was a graceful little creature and Jeanne was very fond of him. He could dance in his odd little way, and she liked to show him to her visitors; Zamor knew that he was no ordinary servant and had come to expect to be treated as a little pet.

"Good morning, Madame," he said, his white teeth dazzling in his dark face.

He knelt before her with the tray and while she was drinking her coffee he seated himself at her feet and leaned his head against her skirts. Louis had often noticed the familiarity of her servants. "You treat them as your friends," he said. "Well," she had retorted, "it is better to have friends than servants." Louis had smiled his approbation. Did he not approve of all that she said and did? "How happy I am," she had told him, "to have a lover who is also the King, and to have servants who are also my friends."

While drinking her coffee she opened a letter which had been brought to her. It was from a Monsieur de Mondeville who implored that he be allowed to see her; it was a matter, he wrote, of life and death.

"Monsieur de Mondeville," she repeated; and Zamor told her: "He presented himself yesterday when you were with the King. He said it was a matter of life and death."

"I should have been told," said Jeanne.

"Madame, can a lady in your position see all who come calling?"

"You are impertinent, my dear Zamor."

Zamor's answer was to snuggle against her knees.

"If he should call again see that he is brought at once to me," she said.

Visitors began to call. As a lady of such importance she received them in her bedchamber, where they would remain while her *toilette* was attended to and place themselves about

175

her toilet table watching her reflection in the huge mirror—
a gift from the King—on which was mounted a coronet in
pure gold and decorated with sprays of rose and myrtle also
in gold.

The *coiffeurs*, the *parfumeurs* and those who wished to show
certain wares to Madame du Barry came at this hour of her
dressing. It was like a public *lever*. The beautiful hair was
pomaded, powdered and piled high above that exquisite head
under the gaze of courtiers and tradesmen, all chattering
excitedly in the meantime.

On this morning there came Monsieur Böhmer of Böhmer
and Bassenge, who, knowing the Comtesse's passion for
diamonds, had new specimens to show her as well as a
drawing of a diamond necklace yet to be made, which, he
declared, would be the most elegant and beautiful of its kind
ever known to the world. Jeanne studied the drawings and
declared that such a necklace would surely cost a fortune,
and she did not think that the King, who had given her so
much, could be asked for such a present.

"But for the most charming lady in France!" cried Monsieur Böhmer; and he left the drawings of the necklace on
her toilet table.

The hairdressers had finished with her hair, and the
powder which had fallen from it had been removed from her
face, which was now being treated with the cosmetics from
the little china jars on her table; her eyebrows and lashes
were being darkened, her lips touched with carmine and
her finger-nails with a faint rose colour when Monsieur de
Mondeville came into her apartment. Zamor hurried to her,
and catching her white hand with his little black one told
her that the gentleman who came the day before about his
matter of life and death wished to see her.

"Come forward, my friend," said Jeanne. "What is this
matter of which you wish to speak to me?"

Through the mirror she smiled at the man who seemed

startled by the sight of her beauty. He did as he was bid, and bowed over her hand.

"I come to you, Madame," he said, "because I have heard that you have a kind and generous heart. I know a member of your sex who is in urgent need of kindness and generosity. Could I speak to you alone?"

Jeanne was cautious. She knew that Choiseul's spies came to her rooms, that they reported and distorted conversations which took place there; she believed, now that Chon and the Maréchale de Mirepoix had made her understand the vulnerability of her position and the enmity it aroused, that Choiseul's minions might at any moment be waiting to trap her. She was not therefore going to allow this man to be alone with her.

"What you have to say to me, Monsieur," she told de Mondeville, "must be said here and now, for shortly the King will be arriving and I must be ready to greet him when he comes."

Monsieur de Mondeville looked perplexed for a while, and then he told the reason for his visit.

A young girl in his native town of Léancourt, who had been the mistress of the *curé*, had become *enceinte*. The *curé* had died, before the girl, sick with grief and anxiety, had given birth to a stillborn child; because she wished to avoid scandal which would involve her dead lover she did not declare the birth in accordance with the *Ordonnances*. This was discovered and the girl was then accused of murdering her child and condemned to be hanged.

"Madame," declared Monsieur de Mondeville, "this poor girl must have justice. She is no murderer. You, who have a kind and generous heart, will do something to save her, I am sure. This girl, who has sinned perhaps—as who has not?—is to die, unjustly, Madame. Unjustly. And unless someone of power can plead with the Chancellor, her sentence will be carried out."

M   177

Jeanne's blue eyes softened. "Monsieur," she said, "you are a good man to concern yourself with this poor girl, but I have no power to alter her sentence."

"Madame, it is said that nothing you ask is denied you. A word to the Chancellor from you . . . and it is certain that he would show mercy to this poor girl. Here, Madame, is a statement which I have had drawn up. It is signed by several people who are aware of this injustice. If you will glance at it you will see that the story I have told you is true. This girl is to die for not declaring the birth of her dead child."

Jeanne read the statement. The Maréchale was frowning and Chon had come quickly to stand beside Jeanne.

"Do not forget that His Majesty will arrive shortly," murmured Chon.

Jeanne retorted: "I could not be happy even with His Majesty if I had to think all the time of that poor girl. There is only one way of preventing myself from doing that. I will write to the Chancellor."

Chon laid her hand on Jeanne's shoulder—which was meant to be a warning; she was advising caution; but Jeanne had already risen and gone to her writing-table.

Monsieur Le Chancelier [wrote Jeanne],

I know little of your laws, but if they condemn a poor girl merely for having been delivered of a still-born child and not declaring it, then I say that they are barbarous, unjust and against reason and humanity. I enclose a petition which has been sent to me, and from this you will see that the girl in question is condemned either for being ignorant of the law or through understandable reticence. I leave the affair to your sense of justice, and ask for a mitigation of this poor girl's punishment.

She signed the letter while Chon and Madame de Mirepoix stood on either side of her reading it.

Their eyes told her that she was too impulsive. But

Jeanne's indignation was aroused. More than anyone in this room she understood the injustice which could be the lot of the poor, and no unfortunate person was going to ask her help and not be granted it.

Monsieur de Mondeville bowed low over her hand, shed tears of gratitude, and retired; after which Jeanne went back to her magnificent mirror that her *toilette* might be completed in readiness for the coming of the King.

When Louis arrived, the visitors bowing and curtsying made a passage for him; and one by one they disappeared from the apartment knowing that he wished to be alone with Madame du Barry.

Louis had left her; he had been amused by her account of the affair of the poor girl. It would be interesting to see how the Chancellor reacted.

"If," said the King, "he rescinds the sentence, that will show the way the wind blows."

"That poor girl's life must be saved. I can tell you, I shall be very angry with Monsieur *le Chancelier* if it is not."

"He knows that," said Louis with a chuckle. "I wonder if he also knows the measure of my love for you. If he does, that girl will go free."

Chon was relieved that the King was not displeased. It was a delicate matter, Chon thought, meddling in affairs outside Jeanne's personal interests; but Jeanne, irrepressible as ever, had told the King of Chon's fears, and this had amused Louis, who had called Grande Chon Petite Chon to come and tell him what she feared so much. It was a very pleasant meeting that morning and there would be another later in the day.

In the meantime Chon and Jeanne would have their midday meal together, and afterwards Jeanne would go into the park, Zamor walking discreetly behind her carrying her train, if that was necessary, or perhaps her sunshade.

But Jeanne decided that on that day she would take a ride in her fine new carriage. It was so splendid that it was amusing to watch the people passing by who were now so eager to catch her eyes, to bow, and call a good day to her. It seemed to Jeanne that there was no one in the world who did not wish her well—except of course the Duc de Choiseul and his sister.

It was while she was riding in the park that she met her brother-in-law, the Comte du Barry. He greeted her with delight, but she detected that proprietary look in his eyes which, even now when she was the King's mistress, he could not lose. She could not object when her sense of fairness reminded her that she owed her position to him.

"Lovelier than ever!" said the Comte when her carriage had pulled up beside him. "I guessed I should meet you. I have a surprise for you." He turned, and a young man came forward from a clump of trees. He bowed over Jeanne's hand and she exclaimed: "Why, it is little Adolphe."

"No longer so little," said du Barry.

"Madame . . . Jeanne," said Adolphe, "you are even more beautiful than when you lived in my father's house."

"My son was most eager to meet you again," said the Comte. "He talks of you continually."

"And what are you doing now that you are in Paris, Adolphe?" asked Jeanne.

"Alas, that is our trouble," the Comte answered for his son. "We want a good place for young Adolphe."

"At Court?" said Jeanne.

"Where else?"

"If you could speak to the King on my behalf, dear Jeanne," said Adolphe, "I should be grateful all the days of my life."

Jeanne smiled, warm-heartedly. "Of course I will do all I can to get you a place at Court."

"Then, my son," said the Comte, "you are as good as

there, because our Jeanne has but to ask and what she asks is given to her."

"Jeanne . . . how can I thank you?" asked Adolphe.

"There should be no thanks. You are my little nephew now, are you not? I doubt not you will be hearing from me ere long."

The Comte and young Adolphe were well satisfied, and as the carriage drove away the Comte laid his hand on his son's shoulder. "There," he said, "goes the best investment I ever made in my life."

Jeanne, riding back to Versailles, was smiling tenderly. Little Adolphe, she was thinking. He was always such a charming little fellow. And he is handsome still. Certainly he shall have his place at Court.

She must not stay long riding in the park, for the King would expect to see her in the afternoon, and she must return to her apartment where her women would help her change her dress and freshen her *toilette*.

Louis hated to be kept waiting, and after the business of the day he was eager for her company. She was determined to please him in every way, not only because she wished to retain her position but because of the gratitude and affection she felt for him.

When he came to her that afternoon she took the first opportunity to mention her meeting with Adolphe and to express the hope that some place could be found for him at Court.

The King promised he would think about it and what would be best for her young nephew.

He must leave her soon, for these meetings during the day could not be of long duration; but with the coming of the evening there would be a fresh *toilette* for Jeanne, and she would emerge in real magnificence, wearing the diamonds which the King had bestowed upon her and which she

181

admired beyond all stones; then she would sit beside the King at the banquet, and play cards with him and a few friends in the card *salon*; or perhaps there would be a ball or a theatrical performance.

With her beside him Louis showed his contentment to the Court; and Chon was able to report to her brother that young Adolphe's future was assured and that in time Jeanne would be able to do all that the Comte had hoped for the family which had adopted her.

It was some days later, when Jeanne was seated beside the King while they took dinner, resplendent in a gown of blue and gold, ablaze with diamonds, her lackeys in attendance magnificent in their gold-embroidered satin, that the King whispered to her: "I have two pieces of news which should please you. One is from your friend the Chancellor. I am certain that I am not wrong in calling him your friend."

"Your Majesty means that the girl's life is to be saved?"

Louis nodded. "He suspended the case until he had examined the evidence. Now he has pardoned the girl. No doubt he knew that it was your wish that he should do so."

Tears came into Jeanne's eyes. "Oh, Louis, I am so happy tonight."

"The good fortune of others pleases you better than your own, it seems. You show more pleasure in saving this girl's life than in your diamonds."

"But I do not forget that the power to save the girl *and* the diamonds comes from Your Majesty."

Louis pressed her hand fondly.

"Now you must hear the other piece of good fortune." He glanced along the table and smiled at his grandson, the heir to the throne, who was seated a few places from them. "Berry has a vacancy in his household. Have you not, Berry?"

182

The boy looked sullenly at his grandfather. "It is so, Sire," he said.

"Then cheer up, Berry, because I have found someone to fill it. The Comtesse's nephew will be your new equerry. I have already made him a colonel in the cavalry."

The Dauphin looked down at his plate, and the King turned to Jeanne. "It is his way of expressing his pleasure," he said ironically.

And as Jeanne looked at the young Duc de Berry she thought: There is another to set side by side with Choiseul. Why do they dislike me so much when I only wish to be friends with them?

10

THE DAUPHINE AT VERSAILLES

IT was impossible for Jeanne to stand aloof from politics.
A new party had begun to form, consisting of those men
who were determined to support her and bring about the
downfall of Choiseul. This party was even known as the
Barriens, and it was led by Richelieu, d'Aiguillon, Maupeou,
the Duc de la Vauguyon and the Abbé de Terray—all men
of some influence.

The indifference of Jeanne towards the insults which
Choiseul continued to send in her direction was a source of
some annoyance to the *Barriens*, whose great aim was to use
her influence with the King to oust Choiseul and his supporters from the positions they had held for so long, that
they themselves might take them.

Every word Choiseul spoke against Jeanne was immediately carried to her, and at length Jeanne was forced to
face the fact that this man was fighting for her destruction.

On occasions when the Court was assembled to await the
arrival of the King, two groups would be formed, one surrounding Choiseul, the other about Madame du Barry; and
it was noticed that gradually the group supporting the
minister diminished and that of the mistress increased. How
could it be otherwise when, on the arrival of the King, all
his attention was given to Madame du Barry, and those
who wished to be in the King's company must also be in hers.

Choiseul watched with growing concern. He was aware,
not so much of the Court sycophants as of the powerful
adherents who were being won over to the *Barrien* party.

In public he maintained an insouciance, feigning not to notice the way things were going. His conversation was as brilliant as ever, his quips as witty; but the close observer might detect a certain tension in his expression when he was caught off his guard.

Louis was sorry for him and went so far as to remonstrate with him.

"You should not dislike Madame du Barry so much, my friend," he told him kindly. "It is not very wise of you. Let me tell you this: Madame du Barry herself is aware of your capabilities. She asks nothing but that you do not concern yourself with her, and then she would not concern herself with you. She is very beautiful. I am very fond of her. That should be enough to make her your friend."

Choiseul answered: "Sire, she plots with her friends for my dismissal, and seeks to set Aiguillon in my place."

"Aiguillon! You know that he has been ridiculed too much ever to replace you."

"Your Majesty has a fondness for the man."

"Ah! Long ago a trick was played upon him concerning a certain lady. I owe him something for that, and it makes me fond of him. But your place! Come, Choiseul, do not be foolish. A smile . . . a gesture . . . a word of kindness . . . that is all that will be necessary. I can assure you that Madame du Barry has the most forgiving heart in the world."

But Choiseul, in spite of the King's warning, could not bring himself to give that smile or word of kindness, and the breach widened.

Eventually Jeanne grew tired of offering friendship. When she found that Choiseul was her partner at cards she would grimace with distaste and show her displeasure, and Choiseul responded with cold looks of disdain or witty asides addressed to others though aimed at her.

It was a position, said the Court, which could not last;

and Choiseul continued to believe that his astute statesman-ship would mean eventual triumph over the favourite.

Negotiations for the marriage which he had been arranging between the Dauphin and Marie Antoinette were nearly completed, and he was sure that once the bonds between France and Austria were strengthened, everyone must realise who had forged them and who was the best man to keep them intact. How could the fondness of an old rake for a woman—whom many believed to have been little better than a prostitute—compare with the country's need of the man who had guided France's foreign policy for so long? In a very short time he hoped to bring the little Austrian Archduchess to France.

The news of Jeanne's intervention, which had saved the life of the young girl of Léancourt, was spread abroad and other people in difficulties began to seek her help, which Jeanne was ever eager to give for, more than anyone else at Court, she could sympathise with the poor. When the mother of a soldier, who had deserted from the army and had consequently been condemned to be shot, came to her imploring her to save the young man's life, Jeanne promised to do all in her power; and so great had that power become that the soldier was saved from the firing squad.

There was much publicity concerning another affair which took place at this time, and in which Jeanne played the part of an angel of mercy.

Parc Vieil was an old château in Champagne between Montarges and Joigny, and belonged to the Comte and Comtesse de Loüesme. The fortunes of the family had deteriorated during the preceding generations, and they were so deeply in debt that one creditor took proceedings against them and the Comte and Comtesse were in danger of imprisonment. Gendarmes arrived at the château to take possession of it and to carry away the Comte and his wife to prison, but they were met with armed resistance. The Comte had the moat filled with water, but the gendarmes procured beams of wood, set them across it and thus reached the gates of the château which they began to break down. Firing took place with the result that one of the gendarmes was killed.

More gendarmes arrived, but when one of the family's servants was killed, the Comte and his wife surrendered. They were taken first to a prison in Montarges and then brought to Paris. There they were to be tried by the *Parlement*, for in killing a gendarme they had been guilty of rebellion against the King. The result of the trial was that both the Comte and the Comtesse were condemned to be beheaded.

The Comtesse de Moyon, their daughter, obtained an audience of the King and implored him to spare her parents.

Louis replied that he was sorry for her, but her parents had broken the law and must take the consequences. The poor woman was led half fainting from his presence, when suddenly she remembered the Comtesse du Barry, who had intervened more than once in what had seemed hopeless cases.

She sent a heartrending message to Jeanne, who, having heard a great deal about the case, could not refuse to see her.

Jeanne's tears mingled with those of Madame de Moyon. She swore that she would stop the execution of the Comte and Comtesse, and, just as she was, her dress disordered, her eyes wet with tears, she hurried to the King.

"I implore Your Majesty to grant me a favour," she cried.

Louis was disturbed to see her in such a state and, always equally enchanted by her tears as by her laughter, by her dishevelment as by her elegance, he raised her in his arms and admitted that it was going to be very difficult for him to deny her what she asked of him.

"So, you must tell me what it is you need so desperately, my dearest."

187

"The lives of the Comte and Comtesse de Loüesme," she answered.

Louis looked startled. "But you must understand. Sentence has been passed upon them. The matter is settled. They have broken the law."

"They were greatly provoked," cried Jeanne; "and their daughter is heartbroken."

Louis shook his head; whereupon Jeanne threw herself on her knees and gazed up at him imploringly.

"This I ask," she said. "I want this more than anything you could give me. You have said you want to please me. Then please me now."

But Louis still looked grave. "Come, rise, my dear," he said. "I will explain the law to you."

"Nay!" cried Jeanne. "I shall not rise. I shall stay here until you give me the lives of those two people."

Louis hesitated. Then he smiled. "I doubt not," he said, "that you will always have your way with me."

"So you grant my request?"

"I will do all in my power to meet your wishes."

Jeanne had leaped to her feet, and thrown her arms about him.

He held her to him tenderly. "This," he said, "is the first such favour you have asked of me. I am glad that it should be an act of mercy."

He would have kept her with him to caress her, to make love to her.

"But there is one matter I must attend to at once," said Jeanne. "I must tell Madame de Moyon that her parents are not to die."

Thus it was realised that the power of Madame du Barry equalled that of Madame de Pompadour, and that the King was finding more pleasure in Madame du Barry than he had in her predecessor.

Jeanne was delighted with her position. She learned Court manners; she was becoming the most elegant as well as the most beautiful of Court ladies; her apartments were scented with the most exquisite perfumes which came from the crystal bottles placed about the rooms; amber, carnation, musk and the scent of roses hung about her. But not only was she determined to enchant with her person—she would develop her mind. Books appeared in her apartments; she had a great admiration for Shakespeare, who was not at that time very popular in France, and she deeply regretted that she could not read his works in English and must rely on translations. She became conversant with the classical writers such as Cicero, and Homer; she enjoyed the wit of Voltaire; but she found something very disturbing in the works of Jean-Jacques Rousseau which were causing a stir in intellectual circles.

She was in fact showing the Court that, although it was true that she was a *fille de rien*, that applied to her origins and not to her mind.

Her apartments and her carriage were as magnificent as those of Madame de Pompadour had been. The King allowed her an income of 300,000 livres a month, and there were occasions, such as a state ball, when she would appear bedecked with gems to the value of 5,000,000 livres. The modiste, Pagalle, who made her clothes, kept many seamstresses working on nothing but creations for Madame du Barry. She enjoyed every moment of this glittering existence and, while delighting in all the good things which came her way, she never lost an opportunity of sharing her good fortune with others.

When the King expressed his amusement at little Zamor's antics she asked him why, since the little boy so pleased him, he did not show his appreciation with something more substantial than words; the result was a handsome present for Zamor, who, after the departure of the King, kissed her hand fondly and told her no one ever served a more kindly mistress.

It was true. Jeanne had no desire but to enjoy life and for everyone else to forget their grievances and do the same.

This was the state of affairs when the Archduchess Marie Antoinette arrived in France for her marriage to the Dauphin.

From the moment Marie Antoinette saw Madame du Barry she was determined to hate her. For one thing Marie Antoinette knew full well that she owed the great position in which she now found herself to the Duc de Choiseul, that great ally of Austria and friend of her mother's; and she had been well grounded by her mother in the line of conduct she must follow. Therefore the enemies of Choiseul were her enemies. The little Dauphine, somewhat spoilt by her mother in spite of that lady's sternness, expected immediately to win the affection of the King and the Dauphin. The Dauphin seemed a somewhat sullen boy, almost indifferent to her. As for the King he was charming indeed, but Marie Antoinette soon discovered that all his attention was directed to a young woman who seemed to be constantly at his side and to whom almost everyone—one outstanding exception being the Duc de Choiseul—paid great respect.

Madame du Barry appeared at the banquet, sitting beside the King; she was not, the Dauphine knew, a member of the royal family; yet she was accorded honour as though she were.

"What position does Madame du Barry occupy at Court?" she asked one of the courtiers whom she found beside her. "What are her duties?"

"Madame la Dauphine . . ." The man hesitated; he was clearly a little embarrassed. "Madame du Barry . . . she . . . er . . . her duties are to amuse the King."

The young girl studied the beautiful woman. There must be some reason why kind and clever Monsieur de Choiseul disliked her so much. She was unsuitable to take a place right in the centre of the royal family.

She smiled at the courtier with girlish enthusiasm. "I swear I will take her place," she said.

The courtier bowed his head very low to hide his embarrassment.

Marie Antoinette could not long remain in ignorance of the position held by Madame du Barry at the Court.

Adelaide took it upon herself to tell the young girl, and in the company of her two sisters she explained that Madame du Barry was a wicked woman who was causing a great deal of trouble at Court. Marie Antoinette was ready to be on very friendly terms with the three Princesses and immediately called them "the aunts", to their great delight. Adelaide told her sisters that she was going to take the Dauphine under her wing and train her in the way she should go. Victoire and Sophie were as usual overcome by their sister's cleverness; and the three of them would take Marie Antoinette to the apartments of one of them and there talk to her at great length concerning Court affairs, never forgetting to speak with great venom of the woman whom the King so blatantly adored.

The young girl listened and believed all she heard. Horace Walpole, who visited the French Court, had described them as "clumsy plump old wenches with a bad likeness to their father". He had explained how they "all stood in a row" with black cloaks and knotting bags, trying to look good-humoured and not knowing what to say. But Marie Antoinette saw them in a different light; they were allies against the terrible woman from whom she wished to free the King who had been so much more gallant to her than had her young husband.

Every light comment which was made by Jeanne was conveyed to the Dauphine. In a moment of exasperation, caused by the sullen manners of the Dauphin, Jeanne had

remarked to the King that he was a "*gros enfant, mal élevé*";
and when this was conveyed to Marie Antoinette by way of
the aunts she was furious. It seemed to her intolerable that
a woman of Jeanne's class should be allowed to pass comment on the royal family at all; but that she should dare to
speak disparagingly of the heir to the throne, and Marie
Antoinette's own husband, was not to be borne.

She was determined to carry her war against the King's
mistress into the open and ignored her on every occasion,
while she tried her utmost to charm the King and turn his
attention from his mistress to his granddaughter-in-law.
Louis was, of course, not indifferent to the attentions of a
young girl, but he was too deeply in love with Jeanne to do
anything but take her side in any quarrels which might
ensue.

Jeanne smiled indulgently at the young girl. She had too
high an opinion of her charms, was Jeanne's comment. If
she were not the Dauphine, and had to work for her living,
she would be a somewhat ordinary little girl. She had
gingery hair and no eyelashes. "Poof!" said Jeanne. "They
would not take her very far if she had not happened to be
born royal."

With what glee Adelaide and her sisters passed on such
comments to the angry young Dauphine!

Knowing their mistress's determination to flout the
favourite on every occasion, the ladies of Marie Antoinette's
entourage never lost an opportunity of inflicting little pin-
pricks.

On one occasion, when Jeanne was attending the little
theatre at Choisy, she found the seats which had been
reserved for her and a companion taken by two ladies of
Marie Antoinette's suite, one of these ladies being the
Comtesse de Gramont, a relation by marriage of Choiseul's
sister the Duchesse.

Jeanne's companion immediately pointed out that the seats had been reserved at Madame du Barry's request; whereupon the Comtesse de Gramont replied that these seats had been reserved at the request of the Dauphine.

Jeanne, bringing her Court manners into play, remained aloof from the argument and at length decided it was more dignified to leave the theatre. Nevertheless she could not allow such a deliberate snub to pass, and she told the King what had happened. The result was the dismissal of the Comtesse de Gramont from Court.

Madame Adelaide, followed by her sisters, immediately went to the Dauphine.

"You cannot allow your women to be dismissed in this way," said Adelaide. "It is an insult directed at you."

Marie Antoinette, determined to uphold her dignity, listened eagerly and asked what she must do.

"You must go to the King and beg him to allow the Comtesse to return to Court," she was assured.

When Marie Antoinette left them, the three sisters chuckled together. Adelaide felt that her life was given new meaning since the coming of the Dauphine, and she could now meddle in state affairs; her sisters, nodding and applauding, shared her triumph.

Louis received the Dauphine kindly; she was a dainty creature and her youth was very appealing. Humbly she explained her mission. Louis listened with attention and made many excuses. He could not, he said, bring the lady back after she had been dismissed . . . not at the moment. His dear little granddaughter would understand in time that the etiquette at Versailles was observed by all—even Kings, even charming little Dauphines—and it could not be tampered with.

The aunts were waiting when Marie Antoinette returned. They shook their heads and murmured epithets of hatred against "that *putain*"; and when news came that the

Comtesse de Gramont was ill, they advised the Dauphine once more to appeal to the King.

"Tell him," said Adelaide, "that that poor woman is near to death. Our father is always thinking of death—although he pretends not to. That will touch him. Tell him the woman cannot die in disgrace."

Marie Antoinette did as she was told; the King was beginning to be exasperated, but the young Dauphine pleaded so prettily that in a weak moment he agreed to give way.

Here was triumph for Marie Antoinette. The aunts twittered with glee. Adelaide felt like a successful general, and her sisters basked contentedly in the reflected glory. Marie Antoinette flaunted her success and took the Comtesse de Gramont with her on every possible occasion.

"You could have that woman sent away from Court again, if you insisted," Chon told Jeanne.

But Jeanne had forgotten the affair. What did it matter now whether the young Gramont was at Court or not? Let the little Austrian enjoy her triumph. Moreover it would make an embarrassing situation for Louis if she insisted.

Louis understood her feelings, and the affair of the Comtesse de Gramont did not lessen her influence with him, but rather did it increase it.

11

THE DEFEAT OF CHOISEUL

WITH the marriage of the Dauphin the hopes of Choiseul
had risen. His enemies, he knew, were waiting for the
chance to ruin him, but he believed that his position had
been considerably strengthened by the alliance with Austria;
and the little Dauphine was his firm ally.

He had watched the affair of the theatre seats with amusement. It was such trifles which were an indication of the
way in which the wind was blowing. Louis was growing
older. He was sixty; surely a man who had lived such a
dissipated life could not expect a great many more years.

The Dauphin would be entirely in the hands of his
charming little wife, and the Dauphine was one of Choiseul's
most ardent supporters.

"Very soon, my dear Madame du Barry," said Choiseul
to himself, "you and your *Barriens* will be feeling less pleased
with yourselves."

He was haughtier than ever when he met the favourite;
he turned disdainfully from her efforts to shrug aside their
differences. She seemed to look upon him as a mildly disturbing element in her surroundings; she should find that he
was more than that.

He had heard that recently during dinner she had picked
up two oranges and thrown them carelessly into the air
crying as she did so: "Fly away, Choiseul! Fly away,
Praslin!" At which all those about her, including the King,
had expressed some amusement. She should one day,
Choiseul promised himself, regret her slight to his dignity.

He did not waste much thought on the woman; she was absurdly lacking in vindictiveness, which meant that she gave little thought to him and all the unpleasantness he had brought to her. His songsters were still singing about her in the streets; she was a fool if she would not look at what was unpleasant. Therefore he need waste little time on her, and his thoughts were now directed towards Aiguillon, for Aiguillon would be at the head of any new party which would take command if he, Choiseul, were to fall; and it was Aiguillon who would step into his shoes.

Aiguillon was a fool too, it seemed to Choiseul, and he was a man who in the past could not have been said to have a great deal of luck in his affairs.

He had made himself an object of ridicule to the country, largely because of his activities as Governor of Brittany during the Seven Years War and afterwards. Although in truth he had been a good general, he had so many enemies in Paris and at Versailles that stories, derogatory to his powers as a soldier, had been circulated about him.

For instance it was said of him that when at Sant-Cast where the English had landed in Brittany, he was ostensibly directing operations from a windmill, while in reality he was making love to the miller's wife; and while her husband fought for France, the Duke, more gallant in love than in war, was covered in flour while his men were covering themselves in glory.

That his troops had scored a victory over the English was forgotten; the story of his adventure with the miller's wife being so much more interesting to his enemies in Paris. The *Parlement* of Paris was against Aiguillon because the *Parlement* of Brittany was independent of it.

When the Duke attempted to enforce certain decrees in Brittany, the *Parlement* of Rennes opposed him and he came into conflict with La Chalotais, the Attorney-General. Aiguillon was not a great ruler and in consequence the state of Brittany was far from happy; therefore the Rennes *Parlement* had a good case against him for they declared that the unhappy condition of Brittany was due to the inefficiency of its Governor.

When Aiguillon learned that La Chalotais had written certain letters in which he had set down charges against him, he ordered that the Attorney-General be arrested on a charge of sedition. The *Parlement* of Rennes, however, would not hear the charges brought against the Attorney-General and decided in its turn to take action against Aiguillon. They brought an accusation against him of using public money for purposes for which it had not been intended.

Aiguillon, made furious by the way in which he was being treated, snapped his fingers at the provincial *Parlement* and put his case before the King. Louis, knowing the Duke to be a fool, but refusing to believe that he had deliberately misappropriated funds, commanded him to write an apology to the *Parlement* of Rennes, and insisted on the resignation of La Chalotais.

The Duke obeyed the King but the Rennes *Parlement* were determined not to close the case against Aiguillon and, refusing to accept his apology, they insisted that he be brought for trial on the old charge. Meanwhile Aiguillon's enemies in Paris had not been idle, for Choiseul realised that here was that golden opportunity for which he had been waiting. The *Parlement* of Paris, under his direction, decided to support the *Parlement* of Rennes, and the trial of Aiguillon was arranged to take place at Versailles in the presence of the King.

The new party which had been forming itself with Jeanne as its figure-head—the *Barriens*—immediately placed itself on the side of Aiguillon, who was one of its most influential leaders. Choiseul, with the *Parlement*, was on the other side.

Excitement was intense. To many people it seemed that

the minister and the favourite stood face to face, prepared for battle.

There were two sittings, but Louis was half-hearted. He had had a fondness for Aiguillon ever since he had stolen Madame de Châteauroux from him, and he knew that Jeanne was eager that the case should go in favour of Aiguillon. This was natural enough, Louis conceded, because the Aiguillons had befriended her even before her presentation, and Choiseul, who was the chief of Aiguillon's enemies, had also, in spite of Jeanne's repeated endeavours to end the state of war between them, deliberately flouted her on every possible occasion.

Bored with the wrangling, eager to please Jeanne, Louis stopped the trial, and, ordering the Chancellor to confiscate the documents, stated that Aiguillon should be freed and declared innocent of the charges brought against him.

The *Parlement*, which had for some time been struggling for its rights against the Monarchy, immediately declared that the Duc d'Aiguillon should not be allowed to resume his privileges until he had cleared himself of the charges brought against him.

It was necessary for Louis to take his soldiers into Paris to secure the documents concerning the case. Gun-fire was heard in the capital on that occasion, and there was some tension since it was known how dangerous disagreement between a king and parliament could be. Louis secured the documents and announced that there should be no more proceedings against the Duc d'Aiguillon.

Choiseul had at last realised his peril. The King had withdrawn that support without which he could not exist in his present position. Louis was throwing in his lot with the *Barriens*; and it was no difficult matter to understand why. If Choiseul was dismissed from his high office it was because Louis believed he had others who were capable of taking his place. Aiguillon might be dubbed a fool, but behind Aiguillon was old Richelieu, still a shrewd old man, Maupeou, a man devoted to work and with three times as much energy as most, and the Abbé Terray, an able man. There were others, too, thirsting for office. Choiseul was not, after all, indispensable.

There was only one thing which could save him. If there were war, the King would be afraid to dismiss him. Choiseul felt that he was fighting with his back to the wall; to save himself he must plunge France into war.

There was at this time an argument in progress between Spain and England over the possession of the Falkland Islands. The Treaty of Utrecht had put these into Spanish hands but a fort had been built there by the English, who were now staking a claim. The Spaniards had sent three frigates to ensure that the islands should be retained by Spain, but when the English heard what was happening they immediately dispatched a squadron.

This was a small incident, not a matter for a major war, but Choiseul believed that if France offered herself as an ally, either to the English or the Spanish, war would be declared by the country to which he offered France's support.

These plans he laid before the King, and Louis watched his foreign minister begin a game of double dealing—first coquetting with the English ambassador, then with the Spanish.

Louis was eager to avoid war with England, and he feared that this was a course to which Choiseul was recklessly leading him. Louis was still smarting from losses in Canada and India, and he could remind himself that these losses had occurred during Choiseul's ministry. Now Choiseul, fearing that his infleunce was on the wane, was desparately seeking some means of reviving it, and this, in the eyes of a King determined on peace, seemed a criminal action.

Meanwhile Choiseul's enemies were closing in on him. Richelieu and Aiguillon explained to Jeanne the need for Choiseul's dismissal, and Jeanne, learning of Choiseul's criminal desire to plunge the country into war for the sake of his own position, added her voice to others and discussed with the King the danger of Choiseul's policy to the throne and the country.

Louis nodded grimly. He had made up his mind. He wrote two letters; one was to his cousin, the King of Spain, in which he wrote:

"Your Majesty is not unaware of the spirit of independence and fanaticism which is spreading through my kingdom. I have so far borne this with patience, but I am beset in the extreme and my *Parlements* endeavour to take from me my sovereign power which I hold from God only. I shall use every means in my power to command obedience. War, in our present state, would be disastrous to us. . . ."

He went on to stress the family feeling between the two countries whose kings were close relations, and he added that, if he should find it expedient to change his ministers, his views and aims would remain the same.

Having written the letter to the King of Spain, Louis wrote another to the Duc de Choiseul in which he said:

"Cousin, the dissatisfaction caused me by your services forces me to banish you to Chanteloup, for which you must leave within twenty-four hours. I should have sent you farther away but for the regard I have for Madame de Choiseul, in whose well-being I feel a great interest. Have a care that your conduct does not force me to alter my mind. I pray God, cousin, to have you in his holy and worthy keeping."

This letter was handed to Choiseul by the Duc de Vrillière on Christmas Eve of that year, 1770. Although it was an end to fame and fortune and everything which he had striven to keep in his grasp, he received the letter without any show of disappointment; and the next day he left Versailles for Chanteloup.

The people of Paris and Versailles, who had sung the songs he had caused to be written and who had been taught to hate the King and his mistress, crowded about his carriage which was drawn by six horses, for he travelled with his wife and sister, the Duchesse de Gramont, in royal style.

At Chanteloup he lived in the utmost extravagance, entertaining lavishly, keeping open house, welcoming all who were discontented with the King, his mistress and the new Triumvirate which consisted of the Duc d'Aiguillon as Foreign Minister, Abbé Terray as Controller-General and Maupeou as Chancellor. The writers and philosophers were made particularly welcome, and as there was an open house and luxurious hospitality for all, Choiseul continued to be a power in France. From Chanteloup the campaign against Jeanne du Barry continued. Scandals were circulated, stories invented, and singers in the streets of Paris were still singing the songs which had been written at the instigation of the Duc de Choiseul.

12

ENEMIES AT CHANTELOUP AND VERSAILLES

A FEW months before the downfall of Choiseul, that enchanting little house close to the Palace of Versailles, which was called Petit Trianon, had been completed; and to show the Court in what esteem he held his new mistress (for Petit Trianon had been intended for Madame de Pompadour) Louis presented the house to Jeanne.

Jeanne was enchanted; the house had been built to represent a country house, and here she and the King would, she declared, lead a life of rustic simplicity far from the formal etiquette of the Palace.

Simplicity was the theme of Petit Trianon; it was however carried out in exquisite taste and this simplicity was as costly as the most ostentatious magnificence would have been, and Gabriel who had designed the façades had achieved great beauty with the honey-coloured stone.

It was August of that year 1770 when Jeanne first entertained Louis at Petit Trianon. He, no less than Jeanne, was delighted with the house. In the first-floor rooms, which had been built in the design of a small reception suite including an ante-room and two dining-rooms, they could look over the Jardin Français, and Louis could discuss with Jeanne how he intended to have the gardens laid out.

Petit Trianon, they agreed, was to be that little country house which might have belonged to a nobleman and his wife, both passionately interested in horticulture and determined to lead the simple life. Even the interior decoration was largely in delicate floral patterns, lilies formed in the shape of circles and bunches of roses; and in the dining-room patterns of fruit had been carved on the wall panels.

Both Jeanne and the King were delighted with the table which had been installed in the dining-room, for it seemed to them an ingenious invention. Attached to the table were four pieces known as "*postillons*"; these "*postillons*" descended and ascended to and from the kitchens which were immediately below; this device eliminated the need to have servants in the room, and thus the much-desired privacy was achieved. The inventor, Loriot, was to be thanked for the invention, and his *table volante* had been previously installed in the Petit Château at Choisy-le-Roi; but this one which the King had had put into the dining-room at Petit Trianon was a great improvement on that at Choisy.

To this most delightful of residences, only a stone's throw from the Palace of Versailles, the King and Jeanne often went accompanied now and then only by their most intimate friends.

The Comte du Barry was somewhat dissatisfied by what he had achieved. He had believed that in providing a mistress for the King he would have attained that power in politics on which he had set his heart; and now on the dismissal of Choiseul it was others who stepped into high places. Chon, since her sojourn at Court and her understanding of affairs, had long realised that her brother was not the man to hold any such position, and that Jeanne would have been foolish to press for it. Jeanne, in any case, could never greatly interest herself in the continual jostling for places. Moreover, she was well aware of the Comte's mercenary motives which had existed with regard to herself from the very beginning of their relationship. There was nothing Jeanne could do for the Comte except have him admitted to Court and throw occasional small honours his way. It was different with his son who was known throughout the Court as Vicomte Adolphe; for this young man Jeanne had a real affection.

Having no children of her own she grew very fond of Adolphe and soon began to look upon her nephew as her son. Often she would discuss his future with Chon, and all that she would do for him if it were in her power.

Chon too had a fondness for Adolphe; he was, after all, her own nephew. He was very good-looking, and he in his turn had always been fond of his beautiful aunt Jeanne and his wise aunt Fanchon. He was often in their company, and everyone at Court believed that the future of Vicomte Adolphe would be very bright indeed. The Comte du Barry had to content himself with seeing all that he had hoped for for himself go to his son. At least, he could assure himself, it was in the family.

The first thing that must be done was to provide a good marriage for Adolphe, and Chon and Jeanne put their heads together over this.

Marie Antoinette, who had hated Jeanne more than ever since the dismissal of Choiseul, for unfairly she blamed Jeanne for this, did all in her power to interfere with Jeanne's plans for the marriage of Adolphe; as for the Dauphin, he listened to his wife and declared that if, as his equerry, Vicomte Adolphe attempted to take off his boots he would feel the Dauphin's foot in his face.

Jeanne merely laughed at the Dauphin and Dauphine as though she considered them to be two spiteful children, and went on with her efforts to find a suitable wife for her nephew. First she selected Mademoiselle Saint André, an illegitimate daughter of the King; but Monsieur de Saint Yon, whom the King had made the girl's guardian, was so incensed at her being given to one of the upstart du Barrys that when the King explained to Jeanne that Saint Yon had acted as father to his daughter for many years and that for that reason he wished to consider his feelings, Jeanne readily understood.

Jeanne's next discovery was Rose Marie Hélène de Tournon, an exceptionally beautiful young girl who was related to the Prince de Soubise, and connected with the great family of Rohan. That the girl had no fortune seemed of little account, for naturally the nephew of Madame du Barry had a brilliant future.

Her family demanded that Adolphe should present his wife with a marriage settlement of 200,000 livres, and Jeanne set about finding the money. The Comte du Barry, however disappointed he was with his own pickings, could not but be delighted with the good fortune of his son.

The Dauphine and Dauphin expressed their horror at the marriage, but were obliged to join in the celebrations and add their signatures to those on the marriage document. Adelaide and her sisters also added their signatures. This was a great defeat for Jeanne's enemies.

They were not downcast however because they were certain that the power of this woman whom they had determined to hate could not endure. Louis was growing fat and his doctors said that he must live quietly, for there was a danger of apoplexy.

One evening when Louis had taken supper with Jeanne, they were playing cards with a few intimate friends, among whom was the Marquis de Chauvelin who was a great friend of the King and Jeanne. When a game of whist was started the King asked Chauvelin to join his party, but Chauvelin declared that he felt so unwell that he could not concentrate on the game.

Louis looked at him intently. "You are a little pale, my friend," he said. "Sit quietly for a while and watch the play instead of joining in."

Chauvelin obeyed, and after the game the King went to

his chair and asked how he felt. Chauvelin stood up and Louis saw his face twitch suddenly; he opened his mouth to speak and collapsed at the feet of the King.

Louis, who was fond of the man, was very upset; he called for doctors to come at once.

Jeanne knelt down by the side of the fallen man, and when she felt his heart looked up in horror at the King.

"Doctors can do poor Chauvelin no good," she said.

The King was horrified. He retired to his apartments immediately, and for some days he could not be comforted.

The friends of the Dauphine said: "It is not that he mourns the end of poor Chauvelin, but that he broods on his own."

They smiled well pleased. If the King felt his end to be near he would wish to repent in time; and repentance meant an end to the sinful life he led with Madame du Barry.

But Jeanne was at hand, with her glorious youth to scoff at death; and after a while Louis ceased to brood on his encroaching old age. The present was delightful while it contained Jeanne.

Dazzling with jewels she appeared at his side and it was clear that he was more infatuated than ever. The King indulged in little gestures which he thought would amuse and please her; and when he was staying at her château of Louveciennes, he was so amused by the tricks of young Zamor that he made him Governor of the Château and Pavilion of Louveciennes at a salary of 600 francs a year.

This amused both Louis and Jeanne; first it delighted Zamor, and then he began to show his self-importance. He strutted about the place, and because Jeanne had taught him to read and write he thought he was a very fine fellow. It had pleased Jeanne to dress him in scarlet and gold, and he would preen himself, thinking himself too grand for menial tasks.

All this seemed very amusing, but Zamor, having had so much, began to ask himself why it was that some, such as his mistress, should receive a great deal more.

Abusive lampoons continued to come from Chanteloup. Choiseul had lost none of his venom. Anybody who was ready to speak or write disparagingly of Jeanne du Barry was welcome in his house. He was very angry with Voltaire who had once been so anxious to ingratiate himself with the great Duke, but had now transferred his talents to be used by Jeanne. She had admired his work and done much good to him, and when the King's chief *valet de chambre*, de la Borde, was passing near Fernay, where Voltaire, who was eighty, was living in retirement, Jeanne asked him to call on the writer and kiss him on either cheek on her behalf.

Voltaire, whose pen was accustomed to drip vinegar, was so enchanted at the gesture that he became her devoted slave.

He looked at the portrait which de la Borde had taken to him, and appears to have become quite infatuated, for the vitriolic pen changed its character completely in his reply to her in which he told her how flattered he was, how enchanted that she should send him two kisses, and begged her to accept the respect of an old recluse who sent her his deepest gratitude.

He sent her verses which were made public and it was not long before they reached Chanteloup. There was fury throughout that household. Voltaire—the great writer—had set himself on her side. He had sullied his pen in his old age!

There were other matters to trouble the Choiseuls. They had been living in the utmost extravagance and debts were mounting. The Duke took no account of the fact that, having been dismissed from his posts, the salaries which accompanied them had ceased. He was determined that the hospitality of Chanteloup should vie with that of Versailles. Because of his repeated attacks on Jeanne, Louis had taken from him his colonelcy in the Swiss Guards, which meant a loss of 100,000 francs a year; and Choiseul in desperation saw no alternative but to ask help from the King.

He wrote a letter to Louis and as he could not deliver it himself he asked the Duc de Châtelet to do so. Châtelet did not approach the King direct but asked the help of Aiguillon in bringing the matter to the King's notice. Aiguillon was, somewhat naturally, disinclined to help his old enemy; and Châtelet then turned to the only other person who he believed could—and would: Jeanne herself.

He told her of the state of affairs at Chanteloup.

"He is a foolish man," said Jeanne. "He has brought all his troubles upon himself."

And, to Châtelet's surprise, she spoke of the Duke as though he were a wayward child rather than the man who had done everything in his power to bring about her downfall. She seemed to have forgotten those insulting songs which he had caused to be sung in the streets of Paris; she no longer remembered the many efforts he had made to bring beautiful young women to the King's attention in order to displace her.

"It will not be easy," she said, "to win the King's sympathy. He has been very angry with Monsieur de Choiseul—more so since he has been living in retirement than he was while he was at Court. However, it must be sad to be exiled from the Court, and I will do my best." She laughed suddenly. "I must keep this from the Duc d'Aiguillon. He will be angry with me if he knows that I speak to the King on behalf of Monsieur de Choiseul. He hates the man."

It had not been easy for Jeanne to interest the King in Choiseul's case but, after a great deal of pleading for him, Choiseul was granted a pension; and although he owed this in a very large measure to Jeanne's intercession for him he was completely without gratitude. He declared that the King had given him the favour in a manner which was far from gracious, and therefore he would say no thanks for it; as for thanking Madame du Barry, he had referred to her when he was at Court as a "*catin*", and he saw no reason to reverse the opinion he had once held. A nobleman of such high rank as himself could not stoop to express his gratitude to such a person.

Jeanne laughed at him; she was sure that she extracted a great deal more fun from life at Versailles, Petit Trianon, and Louveciennes than poor old Choiseul possibly could in exile at Chanteloup.

The behaviour of Marie Antoinette could not be lightly dismissed. The young Dauphine, under the influence of the aunts, ignored her so pointedly that Jeanne, for all her tolerance, could not help but suffer embarrassment. The rule of the Court was that a woman might not speak when she was in the company of one of a higher rank than herself until the latter addressed some remark to her.

Marie Antoinette, as Dauphine and future Queen of France, held the highest rank at Court and, as she herself had often chafed under the rigid etiquette of Versailles, she now decided to make use of it.

Whenever she and Jeanne were in the same company, the Dauphine ignored the King's mistress, thus making it impossible for Jeanne to speak. Jeanne, who wished to please the King and had been warned many times by Chon that it was advisable to bow to etiquette, found that even her mild temper was ruffled by these continual snubs.

She approached the King, who sent for the Dauphine's

gouvernante, Madame de Noailles, and complained to her.

"Our little Dauphine is charming," said Louis. "But she talks too freely and is sometimes ungracious to honoured members of my Court; such behaviour I cannot tolerate, for it has a distressing effect on my family life."

Madame de Noailles, herself a stickler for etiquette, immediately understood the King's meaning and humbly assured His Majesty that she would speak to the Dauphine, and she was sure that when the King's wishes had been made clear to her he would have no further cause for complaint.

Marie Antoinette was mutinous; but her mother, the diplomatic Maria Theresa, when warned by Marie Antoinette's adviser, the Comte de Mercy-Argenteau, of what was happening, reminded her daughter that the King's command was law at Versailles and that she must subdue her private feelings and obey him.

Marie Antoinette went to the aunts and told them what she had been commanded to do. They shook their heads and clucked together. "Disgraceful!" cried Adelaide, and Victoire and Sophie nodded and echoed the word.

The whole Court was interested in the battle between the Dauphine and the Mistress. It was considered that the Dauphine had won that which had taken place over the Comtesse de Gramont and the theatre seats; wagers were staked on the outcome of this quarrel.

Will she speak? Will she not speak? Those were the questions; and the betting was high. The Dauphine was young and dainty and the King was very fond of young girls. But consider how he admired the du Barry; and the usually careless Jeanne did seem determined on this occasion to have her way.

There came the night when both the Dauphine and the Mistress would be in the card-room. "It must be tonight," was whispered throughout the Court. "Those are the King's orders, and the Dauphine dares not disobey the King, her mother and old Mercy. She will speak tonight."

Jeanne too expected her to speak that night.

"Once she has spoken," she said to Chon, "I shall try to do her some little service to show her that I think this enmity she bears me is a little silly."

"You will have to learn," warned Chon, "that you cannot vanquish your enemies by ignoring their enmity."

They went to the card-room, where Marie Antoinette was ready, telling herself that she must speak to that odious creature. It was a matter of policy, her mother had written. She was afraid that there might be war over the partition of Poland, and if the Dauphine disobeyed the King's orders he might be very angry. Austria could not afford war at this moment. Marie Antoinette must learn that out of such trifles great events could spring.

Therefore she must obey the King and speak to Madame du Barry.

Jeanne had reached her; she was ready. But Adelaide had sidled up to the Dauphine. "My dear," she whispered, "the King is waiting to receive you." She took Marie Antoinette's arm and drew her away, leaving Jeanne, deeply mortified, looking after her.

A faint rippling titter ran through the room; and those who had laid wagers that the Dauphine would not speak began to collect their winnings.

When Jeanne told Louis what had happened he was very angry. He did not send for Madame de Noailles this time but for the Comte de Mercy-Argenteau.

"The Dauphine," he said coldly, "seems determined not to meet my wishes. If the Empress desires to preserve the friendship between our countries she must inform her daughter that it is not possible for France to be treated as a vassal."

The relations between two countries were being shaken by the foolish conduct of a young girl. It could not be allowed to continue.

There was only one way of dealing with the stubborn child; that was to write even more sternly than before to her mother. The Empress, fearful of what her country's position might be with regard to the Polish problem, wrote firmly to her daughter.

"You follow the aunts," she wrote, "who, although they are no doubt worthy Princesses, are neither respected by the King nor by the Court. What a fuss about speaking to people to whom you are asked to speak!"

It was difficult for the strictly moral Maria Theresa to command her daughter to show friendship towards one whom she considered highly immoral; but with Maria Theresa the good of her country was put before her principles. Therefore she commanded her daughter to say some word, make some ordinary remark, not to please the lady in question, but because the King, her grandfather and benefactor, had demanded that she should.

When she read that letter the Dauphine knew she must humiliate herself in the eyes of the Court and do that which she had sworn not to do.

On New Year's Day the Court assembled to watch the little pantomime. Because there was no Queen of France it was the duty of the Dauphine to receive the ladies as they came to offer New Year greetings.

Jeanne arrived with the Duchesse d'Aiguillon and when her turn came to stand before the Dauphine, there was a silence of a few seconds. Marie Antoinette swallowed and said in a high, cold tone: "*Il y a bien du monde aujourd' hui d Versailles.*"

That was all. Then she passed on.

The Court was almost hysterical with merriment. All that

fuss . . . diplomatic relations about to break down between France and Austria—and all the little Dauphine could or would say was that Versailles was crowded on that day.

The sentence became a catch-phrase throughout the Court, and to murmur it never failed to produce a smile or chuckle.

Jeanne was sorry that it had been necessary to humiliate the Dauphine publicly, but she had to agree with Chon that there had been no help for it.

She explained the situation to the King and gave such an amusing imitation of Marie Antoinette that Louis laughed aloud. He too took up the phrase and was seen to smile when he heard it whispered about the Court.

"She is a spoilt little creature," said Jeanne. "Ah well, no doubt that domineering mother of hers thought the world of her. And then she comes here and everyone pampers her. I hope she will decide to be friendly with me. I hate this enmity."

"If all the world had your nature, my dear, it would be a happier place for many of us," said Louis.

That made Jeanne laugh. "What, would you have all women *catins*—as Monsieur de Choiseul calls me?"

The King showed an unusual anger. "My dear," he said, "do not talk thus. If you have been less virtuous than the Dauphine, let us not blame you but first the circumstances in which you were placed, and secondly your incomparable beauty which must attract all who behold it."

She kissed his hand in an access of affection.

"It's true," she said, "that Madame la Dauphine did not have to learn hairdressing or read to a bad-tempered old lady, nor earn a living at Labille's. Therefore how can we expect her to be other than she is! Louis, she loves diamonds, and there is a magnificent pair of earrings which old Böhmer is trying to sell. They are valued at 700,000 livres. Could I

213

persuade you to give them to her as a present and . . . let her know that I have done the persuading?"

Louis smiled fondly.

"It is a good plan and worthy of my dearest love. Do as you wish in this matter. And Jeanne, speaking of Böhmer, I have been looking at those drawings of his. Do you remember . . . the necklace?"

"Oh, that necklace, yes. Böhmer is always talking of it. He says it will take years to complete it because he is determined that it shall be made with none but the best stones in the world."

"Tell Böhmer that when he has completed the necklace I would like to see it."

"For Marie Antoinette?"

"Indeed no, my dear. I fancy *you* have a fondness for diamonds to equal our Dauphine's. There is only one for whom I would buy Böhmer's diamond necklace. Surely you know who she is."

"It will be very costly," said Jeanne, kissing him.

She was delighted. Marie Antoinette was to have her peace offering; and she was to have the most exquisite and most valuable diamond necklace that had ever been made.

Jeanne lost no time in sending one of her women to the Dauphine to tell her that she thought she could persuade the King to give her the earrings she so much admired.

The Dauphine hesitated. She was very attracted by diamonds and the earrings were the finest she had ever seen. But to accept them from that woman, to whom she had sworn never to speak again, was out of the question.

She haughtily replied that she did not need courtesans to persuade their lovers to give her presents.

When this remark was reported to Jeanne, she shrugged aside the incident.

It was clear that the Dauphine was determined to be her enemy. Chon and Madame de Mirepoix might shake their heads with apprehension, but Jeanne was undisturbed. She believed that in any future battle she would know how to triumph over the haughty little girl who happened to be Dauphine of France.

13

THE PASSING OF LOUIS

Louis was feeling his age. He was sixty-four and as he
grew fatter he was subject to breathlessness. He could
no longer move with agility and had to be helped on to his
horse and into his carriage.

The hunt still delighted him and nothing could make him
give it up.

One April day in 1774 while he was out hunting he met a
funeral cortège. When Jeanne was not with him he frequently
thought of death and he could never resist the morbid, so
he stopped the cortége and asked: "Who has died?"

"Sire," he was told, "it was a young girl. She was no
more than sixteen."

"I am very sorry," said the King. "That is a great
tragedy. Sixteen . . . it is so young to die. What was the
cause of this child's death?"

"It was the smallpox, Sire."

The King returned to the hunt, but everyone noticed how
melancholy he was, and they declared that meeting the
funeral procession had spoiled the day's hunting.

The King, who had gone to Petit Trianon in the company
of Jeanne, continued to hunt each day, but on Tuesday
evening, the 26th April, he returned early.

Jeanne was alarmed at the sight of him, for he was flushed
and appeared to be extremely tired. He could not entertain
the thought of food and Jeanne insisted on his going to bed
at once.

She and his valet Laborde sat with him all night and in the morning she sent for Lemoine, his physician.

Lemoine lulled Jeanne's fears.

"His Majesty suffers from a fever," he said. "Keep him quiet and he will be well in a few days."

Jeanne's relief was great, but Lemoine had sent for the surgeon La Martinière, and when the latter had examined the King he was less hopeful than his fellow doctor.

"It would be advisable," he said, "for the King to leave at once for Versailles."

Jeanne felt fear grip her at those words. If the King was slightly ill there could be no objection to his remaining at Petit Trianon, but etiquette must be observed at the French Court no matter what the occasion, and it was unthinkable that a King of France should die anywhere but at Versailles.

The King protested: "I wish to stay at Petit Trianon."

"Sire," insisted La Martinière, "here it is not possible to give you the nursing you will require."

"I have Madame du Barry."

"Indeed you have, Sire, but you need to be in your own bedchamber. These low-ceilinged rooms are not good for you."

Louis felt exhausted, and he believed he understood. His condition was serious. Wearily he prepared to leave Petit Trianon for Versailles, since even he could not flout the formality of his Court.

So a cloak was put over his bedrobe, and a carriage took him across the park to the château. There in his bedchamber the doctors clustered about his bed and he was bled many times.

By evening it was discovered that the King was suffering from smallpox.

Should he be told?

Jeanne said earnestly: "No, no, he should not be told.

Let him believe that he has a slight indisposition through which we shall nurse him in a few days."

But already her position was changing, and she saw that her desires were no longer considered of such importance as they had been a few days previously. The King was sixty-four; and when the life he had lived was considered, the opinion must be reached that he could not be expected to recover from smallpox.

Adelaide, her sisters at her heels, came bustling into action.

"I have already sent for the Archbishop of Paris," she declared. "Considering the evil life my father has led it is necessary that he begin his repentance at once."

Jeanne protested. "But this will make him feel that his end is near."

Adelaide smiled at her triumphantly. Her sisters, watching her, nodded understanding. Your power came through him, they implied; and now he is laid low; he has smallpox and he is sixty-four and, considering the life he has led how can he recover? His days are numbered, Madame *Putain*—and so are yours!

Jeanne was too distracted to heed them. She only was thinking of Louis, the man; no one had ever been so kind to her as the King of France; and she, who had never faced that which was unpleasant, had refused to consider the possibility of his death. Now it was being forced upon her and she could not ignore it.

When the Archbishop arrived he followed Jeanne's wishes and kept from the King the fact that he had been sent for because it was believed he was near to death. The Church party supported the mistress because she had been the enemy of Choiseul, and Choiseul had been responsible for the expulsion of the Jesuits. Thus the coming of the Archbishop did much good to the King for, far from obeying the wishes of Adelaide, he made no mention of confession. Louis was therefore convinced that his illness could only be a slight one and his soaring spirits caused a remarkable change for the better.

He called Jeanne to him; he caressed her with pleasure; and they laughed together. Never for one moment did Jeanne betray that she knew herself to be in deadly danger from the highly contagious disease from which Louis was suffering.

And when Jeanne was not with him, Adelaide, Victoire and Sophie would be in the sick-room; they too did not spare themselves, and they washed him themselves and made his bed, saying that at such a time it was his family who should care for him. Louis tolerated them, but was very glad when Jeanne arrived, for then the three would nod their heads and march from the room determined not to share the task of nursing with a woman of whom they so heartily disapproved.

But the truth as to the nature of his illness could not be kept for ever from the King, and, glancing at his hands, he noticed the spots on them.

Then fear possessed him. He called his doctors to him and said: "Why do you tell me that I am not very ill and will soon recover? Look! I have the smallpox. I am dying. A man of my age cannot recover from that."

From that moment there was a change for the worse. All the melancholy fears which had beset Louis during the last years returned to him. Jeanne hurried to his bedside, but he was so ill that he could only just recognise her.

"You must go away," he said. "It is no place for you here."

She knelt by the bed. "I will stay. I will nurse you. You know you would rather I did it than anyone else."

The King closed his eyes.

"It is no place for one so young . . . so beautiful . . . the death-bed of an old man."

"It is no death-bed."

"I am past deceiving," he told her.

He was thinking of her and of himself; and he believed he knew what was the best for both of them. When he died there would be no one to protect her; all her enemies would descend upon her. She should leave Court before that happened; she should be in some safe place. As for himself he had urgent need of repentance. The thought of death with all his sins upon him terrified him; and how could he ask for the forgiveness of his sins when he was living an immoral life?

"You must leave me, Jeanne," he said. "I have to make my peace with God now. I have to think of the people. If I should recover, my love, the first thing I shall do is to recall you. Now I wish you to go and send the Duc d'Aiguillon to me, that I may tell him what I wish him to do for you."

Jeanne shook her head; the tears were running down her cheeks. Louis could scarcely see them but he knew that she was weeping.

She—and she alone in this great château—loves me truly, he thought.

There was no time for sentiment, scarcely time for tenderness; he was afraid of the hereafter and his fear insisted that he rid himself of this woman whom he loved.

"It distresses me," murmured Louis, "to see you. I pray you . . . go. I would make my peace . . . and yours. Go, my love. Know this: you have made my last years happy. I do not forget."

Jeanne rose from her knees, took his hand and kissed it, then slowly she went from the sick-room.

When the Duc d'Aiguillon arrived Louis was almost too ill to speak to him; but he made his wishes known that Madame du Barry was to leave at once and that she should stay for a while at Aiguillon's place at Rueil.

"Let there be no delay," said Louis, "for when the cry goes up '*Le Roi est mort; vive le Roi!*' she will not be safe at Rueil. Let her then be taken to the convent of the Pont-aux-Dames not far from Meaux. She will be safe there. Pray see to it."

The Duc d'Aiguillon assured the King that his commands would be carried out; and Louis lay back on his pillows calling out that holy water should be sprinkled on his bed and the saving of his soul begun.

He had forgotten that he had dismissed her. He called to his servants. "Where is Madame du Barry? Why does she not come to me?"

"Sire," was the answer, "she has left for Rueil on your orders."

"She has gone already?" asked Louis.

"Yes, Sire, she has gone."

Then Louis turned his face away from the servants, and his lips framed the words: "Gone. She has gone." And there were tears on his cheeks.

In the sick-room Adelaide, Victoire and Sophie reigned. Scorning infection they nursed their father. But there was little hope. On the 7th of May drums were heard in the Cour de Marbre and the Viaticum was carried in procession, in which marched the Swiss Guards, from the chapel to the King's bedchamber. All the members of the royal family walked in the procession carrying candles; but the Dauphin and Dauphine were not allowed to enter the room.

There was no doubt throughout the Court that the King was dying. The crucifix was held to his lips and the Grand Almoner, after having listened to Louis' responses, went to the door of the bedchamber and announced in a loud voice to all those waiting that the King had asked God to pardon him for the scandalous life he had led and the bad example he had set to his people, that if his life were spared he would give himself up to penitence and relieving the sufferings of his people.

The King was a little better that day, and those who had hastened to pay court to the Dauphin and Dauphine were bewildered, not knowing which way to turn. If the King recovered, Madame du Barry would be back once more at Court. This was a matter which had to be considered, and all those place-seekers who abounded in the higher circles of the Court were uncertain how to act.

They need not have worried; the King's recovery was but brief. Crowds had gathered outside the Palace; the cafés were crowded with people who seemed to be rather in a festive mood than one of mourning.

The King's repentance had been announced on Saturday the 7th May, and by Sunday evening his condition worsened. Extreme Unction was given him on Monday; and soon after three o'clock on Tuesday it was clear that the end was near.

That afternoon the Grand Chamberlain, the Duc de Bouillon, stood by Louis XV's bedside and, having satisfied himself that the King was dead, he left the bedchamber for the *Oeil de Boeuf*; there he put on his black plumed hat and called:

"*Le Roi est mort! Vive le Roi!*"

14

THE PONT-AUX-DAMES AND
SAINT VRAIN

HER eyes swollen with weeping, Jeanne sat in the carriage
which was taking her to the Pont-aux-Dames. Louis
was dead and she had lost her kindly protector. Chon had
returned to Lévignac. It was the only thing for her to do,
but she had declared that as soon as it was possible she would
return to Jeanne, and she would not know another moment's
peace until their reunion.

The Comte du Barry hastily left Paris, knowing that anyone who bore his name would very soon be exiled from
Court. Vicomte Adolphe and his wife had also left the
country. Jean du Barry's second brother who had made a
good marriage in Paris when the family fortunes were rising,
thanks to Jeanne, asked leave of the new King to drop his
own name and adopt that of his wife.

The Dauphin and the Daupine were now King and
Queen and they had never pretended to be fond of the
du Barrys, so little sympathy could be expected from them;
indeed it was clear that if the du Barrys were wise they
must remove themselves from the royal orbit as soon as
possible.

It is for that reason, thought Jeanne as her carriage bore
her onwards, that Louis arranged for me to go to the Pont-
aux-Dames.

The carriage drew up at the ancient building. Its Gothic
architecture, its ancient aspect, seemed very gloomy indeed.
Nothing could be more different from the splendour of

Versailles, from the exquisite charm of Petit Trianon, from the luxury of her beloved Louveciennes.

Here she was to live her life for who could say how long? Here she was to mourn and pray and dream of the old days. Here she was to live in solitude, the life of a nun—she, Jeanne du Barry, who had loved the world and all its glitter more than most women. As Jeanne entered the gloomy building the Mother Superior came forward to receive her. Madame de la Roche de Fontenille had heard much of this woman, and was anxiously wondering what effect her presence would have in the convent. She knew that, since it had been discovered that the King had ordered her to come here, there had been a changed atmosphere in the place, a lack of calm. Not one of her thirty canonesses and her twenty sisters had not heard of this woman; not one of them could entirely suppress her curiosity to see her.

"Come," said the Abbess, "we are ready to receive you."

Jeanne shivered. The place struck her as very cold; but the dignity of this woman was even more chilling.

"Louis!" she murmured to herself. "How could you have sent me here! How shall I live within these gloomy walls, among women such as this one?"

She was taken into an apartment which appeared to be a reception-room. There was even a mirror on the wall.

"I shall introduce you formally to the canonesses and sisters," said the Abbess; "after that you will live as one of us."

There was a tense silence as the nuns filed in. Jeanne stood waiting to receive them. She had been placed by the Abbess in such a position that she was facing the mirror and could see her own reflection looking so incongruously bright, in spite of her grief, in this gloomy place.

Then she noticed that the nuns did not look at her. They looked fearfully at her reflection in the mirror.

She could not help smiling. She knew that to them she represented the worst sort of sin to be met with in the outside world and that they dared not look at her before they assured themselves by her reflection in the mirror that she was not some monster of evil.

Smiling, she was so beautiful to these nuns that she seemed more like an angel than a sinner. Her hood had fallen back and her brilliant golden hair was visible.

They turned and looked at her; and she continued to smile.

It was impossible for the nuns to dislike her, she was so charming, and she tried so hard to fit into their ways, that even the stern old Abbess was enchanted in spite of herself. If they had expected a weeping, wailing creature, they were mistaken. She adapted herself with ease to the new life; and very soon the nuns were thinking how dull the convent had been before her coming.

They vied for the pleasure of walking with her in the grounds; sometimes she walked alone; then she would sit under the chestnut trees dreaming of the past. Sometimes the nuns would ask her to tell them of life at Court; then they would gather about her—she like a bird of paradise in the midst of a rookery—and she would tell them of the balls and banquets and splendours of Versailles.

The Abbess found herself relaxing rules for the sake of the newcomer. She delighted to receive Jeanne's confidences, and when Jeanne told her that she had been deeply in debt at the time of the King's death and wished to sell some of her jewels to pay her creditors, the Abbess promised to see what could be done about it.

It seemed harsh that she should be allowed no visitors. The Abbess knew that the King and Queen—and particularly the Queen—were eager that Jeanne du Barry should suffer the restrictions of the Pont-aux-Dames; but the

Comtesse was so charming and the Abbess did so long to help her.

She did not see why certain visitors should not be allowed. She did not see why the Comtesse's sister-in-law should not join her.

What a glorious day it was for Jeanne when Chon arrived! They embraced, and Chon could not prevent herself from smiling.

"You are as beautiful at Pont-aux-Dames as you were at Versailles. And you are not so discontented as I had expected to find you."

"Everyone here," said Jeanne, "is so good to me. But I do not feel that the convent life is the life for me. I have my debts. I wish to pay them. I have affairs to settle."

Chon nodded. "If you could receive visitors . . . visitors from the Court . . . I doubt not you might quickly find someone to intercede for you. There were many men of the Court who were eager to serve you and would have expressed their eagerness very readily, had they not feared to offend the King." Chon began ticking them off on her fingers. "There was the Prince de Ligne, the Comte de Maurepas, the Duc de Brissac; and I do not think that Richelieu and d'Aiguillon were entirely without regard for you. Why yes," continued Chon, "the first step is to arrange that you shall have visitors from Court."

At Chanteloup there was great rejoicing. Choiseul, with his sister and his wife, prepared themselves to return to Court.

"And when I am there," said Choiseul, "I shall set myself at the head of affairs once more. Have no doubt of it. We are on our way up to the pinnacle of success once more."

"And when we are there," said the Duchesse de Gramont, "we shall see that Madame du Barry remains shut up in her convent for the rest of her life. That gives me as much pleasure as anything . . . to imagine her there. Not one man on whom to turn her seductive airs. Ha! What a joke!"

"The Queen always favoured me," said Choiseul. "And the Queen commands the King. Make no mistake, it is Marie Antoinette whom we must consider, not poor fat Louis."

But he was wrong, for when the long-awaited summons came for him to return to Court, Choiseul found the King could on occasions assert himself. The Queen might wish to reinstate him, but Louis XVI remembered the enmity which his father, the Dauphin, had felt towards Choiseul, and he was determined, in spite of his wife whom he so much liked to please, that Choiseul had been sent into retirement for ever.

So, all Louis had to say to the expectant ex-minister was: "How you have changed since you went into retirement! You have grown fat and bald."

Choiseul had no alternative but to return to Chanteloup, which he did, there to live in as wildly extravagant a manner as ever.

Chon had arranged it. Now visitors were calling at the Pont-aux-Dames. Magnificent carriages rolled up and from them emerged some of the most eminent gentlemen of the Court. The Duc de Brissac was one of the first to arrive. He had always been a good friend, and he told Jeanne that he was delighted to see the affection she had aroused in the stern nuns.

"But how could they do anything but love you?" he asked. "Knowing you, it would be impossible not to do so. It is so natural to love one who is so beautiful, so kind, so good."

Jeanne laughed aloud. "It is pleasant to hear the words of a courtier once more," she told him.

It was the Prince de Ligne who, after visiting her, took up

her case at Court. The Queen reproved him, but he continued to work for her release. Maurepas' aid was sought and he was very ready to give it.

At length their efforts were successful, and, when she had spent a year in the convent, permission was given for her to leave it. But she was not to think that she could return to the old life. She would not be allowed to live in her beloved château of Louveciennes. However, she was free; and she bought the château and estate of Saint Vrain and thither she went accompanied by Chon.

They sent for Bischi to join them, and eventually Jeanne had gathered together many of her old servants, Zamor among them. He had changed, Jeanne thought. There was an enigmatic expression on his face; he was not so spontaneously gay as he used to be. Poor Zamor! thought Jeanne, he has suffered like the rest of us.

Those who lived on the estate of Saint Vrain had great cause to bless the coming of the Comtesse du Barry. Never had she forgotten what it was like to be poor.

It was true of Saint Vrain that "*Dans le château il y a toujours du pain*". Jeanne made the troubles of those who lived on her estate her own. She would drive about visiting the people, and her free and easy manners endeared her to them all. Any woman in childbirth would be provided with broth and clothes for the baby. No one was allowed to go hungry. The only time she was seen to be angry was when her servants neglected the needs of the poor on her estate.

Naturally she was greatly beloved at Saint Vrain; and she was certainly not forgotten at Versailles. Carriages arrived continually and the Queen once more began to grow jealous of the attention which was paid her.

Her good friends at Court continued to work for her; and it was the influential Maurepas who with his constant pleading had all her property returned to her.

She had spent one year in the Pont-aux-Dames and one-and-a-half in Saint Vrain when she received news from her nephew, the Vicomte Adolphe who had now returned to Paris, that very soon her beloved Louveciennes was to be returned to her. He suggested that she come to stay with him until everything was settled and she could return to her old home.

Louveciennes! She longed to be there again. Versailles was no longer for her, nor was the Petit Trianon. At both these places Marie Antoinette reigned, and where the Queen of France was there was no place for Madame du Barry.

But Louveciennes! She felt a great uplifting of her heart to contemplate her return there.

15

LOUVECIENNES

Aᴺᴰ so she returned. The house was full of memories which she treasured. She was no longer unhappy; it was not in Jeanne's nature to remain unhappy long. Fortune, which had given her her outstanding beauty and her serene and kindly nature, would never hide its face from her for long, she was sure. She had lost her protector—the most powerful man in the kingdom—but she had discovered that there would always be men greatly desirous of filling that role.

She was wise enough to know—and Chon was at her side to advise her—that her position was still precarious. Louveciennes was near Versailles; people from the Court visited her; she must take the greatest care not to intrude herself into Court life. That was more than the Queen would tolerate.

Although she did not leave Louveciennes, she was not living a solitary existence. More and more people came from Versailles to see her and when the Emperor Joseph came to France to visit his sister, Marie Antoinette, he insisted, much to her disgust, on calling on Madame du Barry at Louveciennes.

This created a great deal of gossip at Versailles, and when it was reported that the Emperor had insisted on Madame du Barry's taking his arm while they walked in the park about her house and that he had shown himself greatly impressed by her beauty, the old Empress Maria Theresa was roused to bitter comment.

But the Emperor's gesture was significant; it meant that Jeanne's exile was over and that, although she could not expect to be received at Court, at least she would not be lonely at Louveciennes.

Attention was further attracted to Jeanne when, shortly after the Emperor had left France, the great Voltaire came to Paris to see one of his plays performed.

Voltaire was treated with great respect by the Parisians, and as he was very old he found it impossible to receive all the people who called on him. Jeanne came to Paris to see him and when she was announced he would not at first see her, for he was vain and well aware of the contrast he must make to this dazzling beauty; and when she called he had not washed and dressed although it was the middle of the day.

However he could not turn her away and at last he overcame his embarrassment, reminding himself that he was after all the great Voltaire and he had not won his fame on account of his beauty and elegance.

Accordingly she was shown into his presence and he found her as charming as he had been led to believe; he was enchanted not only by the beautiful features and exquisite colouring but by the kindliness which he read in her face.

It was on that occasion that Jeanne's kindness resulted in a characteristic action. As she was leaving Voltaire's apartment she met a young man on the stairs. He was very nervous, and under his arm he carried a sheaf of papers.

Their eyes met as she passed him and because of the kindliness he saw in her face he stammered: "You have just left the great Voltaire?"

Jeanne said that she had.

"I have been trying to see him for a long time," said the young man. "Alas, he will not see me. If I could only show him my work . . . if he could only be persuaded to read it. . . . I know he would help me."

"Why will he not see you?" asked Jeanne.

"He is France's greatest writer. I am France's most unknown writer. There must be hundreds like me begging his help. Why should he give it to me . . . except that I know my work is good. If he could only be persuaded to glance at it, he would realise it."

Jeanne smiled at the young man. "Wait here a moment," she said, and she turned and ran back to Voltaire's apartments.

It was impossible for the old man to deny the charming young woman anything she asked, and in a few moments Jeanne returned to the young man on the staircase.

"You may go up," she said. "I have made him promise to look at your work."

"Madame," said the young man, kissing her hand, "you are an angel."

"I have been called by other names," said Jeanne lightly, and went down to her carriage, while the young man went up the stairs to Voltaire's apartment.

The book he carried under his arm was *Théorie des Lois criminelles* and his name was Jean Pierre Brissot. It was a great day in his life for, when Voltaire, true to his promise, read the first few pages he went on reading and a great excitement possessed the old man because he saw great merit in the young man's manuscript.

Jean Pierre Brissot's name was made, and he never forgot, even at that last moment when the knife of the guillotine was about to fall upon his neck, the great good fortune which had come to him when he had met a beautiful woman on the stairs.

Voltaire lived only three months after that encounter, and Jeanne mourned his passing; but an even greater grief was to fall upon her shortly afterwards.

She had looked upon Vicomte Adolphe as her son, and it had greatly grieved her that she must be separated from

232

him. His marriage had been far from happy and she knew that after the death of Louis XV the proud Hélène had deeply regretted her connection with the du Barry family. Instead of all the honours she had expected as wife of the favourite's nephew she found herself in exile from the Court because she bore the hated name.

Adolphe however was deeply in love with her; she was very beautiful and had been said to be second only to Jeanne. She could not forget that she was a member of the Soubise family and connected with the haughty Rohans, and she began to hate Adolphe, blaming him for the loss of the Versailles society.

They travelled in England and while there made the acquaintance of a certain Irish Count named Rice. He journeyed about the country with them and, when Adolphe discovered that Rice had become his wife's lover, his anguish and fury compelled him to challenge the Irishman to a duel.

The result of this duel was the death of Adolphe. Count Rice was tried at Taunton in April 1779, and, claiming that he had acted in self-defence, was acquitted.

Hélène returned to France where, rid of her du Barry encumbrance, she was received at Court in her maiden name. She married her cousin, but after three years her husband died as she herself did soon afterwards.

Meanwhile Jeanne, Chon and Bischi mourned this handsome nephew whom they had all loved.

Jeanne was more deeply unhappy than she had ever been since the death of the King, and she looked about her for some consolation.

She was to find it in an unexpected quarter. Living near Louveciennes was an Englishman named Henry Seymour. He was a man of fifty and a nephew of the Duke of Somerset. His first wife had died and he had recently married a Frenchwoman, Louise, Comtesse de Ponthou. Because she wished to spend a part of the year in France, Seymour bought the small château at Prunay, so that he was a not very distant neighbour of Jeanne's.

He was fond of his wife whom he had married four years before in 1775, but the beauty and charm of Jeanne were irresistible.

Jeanne formed a friendship with his daughters, Caroline and Georgiana, seeking, in her friendship for the two girls, some emotion to fill that void which had been left by the death of Adolphe.

Between Seymour and Jeanne there flared a sudden passion. Jeanne accepted it eagerly for, having lost both Louis and Adolphe, the two men for whom she cared so much, she felt the need of such a relationship to help her through the difficult months ahead.

The Duc de Brissac, who had been one of her most faithful friends from the very moment of her exile, visiting her at Louveciennes, was quick to notice the change in her; and when he saw her with Seymour he knew that they were lovers.

It was then that the Duke declared his own passion for her, the extent of which he had not realised until he saw that another man was her favoured lover. Jeanne consoled him.

"If I were not in love with Henry Seymour, my dear friend," she said, "I should be in love with you."

Henry Seymour called upon her one day. His face was white and stern.

"I am returning to England," he said.

She could only look blankly at him.

"It is the only way," he told her. "Brissac has discovered the relationship between us. If one does, others may. I could not risk Louise's discovering it. There is the family. It would break up my marriage."

Jeanne bowed her head. There was a coldness about her

lover which was in striking contrast to her own nature. Perhaps it was that strangeness in him which she had found exciting. He was so different from Louis . . . from Brissac.

And he was right, of course. That love between them had been a sudden flame destined to burn out quickly.

They were not really of a kind. He must return to England, to his country estates, to his quiet family life. And she? She was now thirty-seven, yet she seemed younger, always having enjoyed radiant health. She knew that there were many years left to her and that there would be other lovers.

She said good-bye to him with regretful tears. She felt that she had lost so many whom she had loved, and that there might well be others who could bring joy into her life.

There was Louis Hercule Timoléon de Brissac waiting to comfort her. Their friendship continued; she knew that he loved her with a tender devotion and it was not in Jeanne's nature to deny to one who gave her so much, that which he asked in return.

It was Brissac who helped her to forget Seymour, and there then began for her a happy period which extended over many years. She entertained lavishly at Louveciennes and was entertained lavishly in turn at the Duc de Brissac's house in the Rue de Grenelle.

Many visitors came to see her. She had friends at the Court although she did not go to Court. Madame le Brun, the artist, was a great friend and stayed often with her at Louveciennes, bringing with her all the news of the Court, of the splendour of the performance of *Le Mariage de Figaro* at the *Théâtre Français*, of the growing discontent of the people, of the pamphlets which found their way into the Palace of Versailles itself, of the performance of *Le Barbier de Seville* at the Trianon theatre, of the scandalous affair of the diamond necklace.

This last reminded Jeanne that the necklace had first been destined for her and that, had the King lived long enough to give it to her, much trouble might have been saved Marie Antoinette, the poor Queen of France, who had suffered greatly because of it.

Driving through Paris it was impossible to avoid seeing those caricatures of the Queen, her hair piled ridiculously high, and always about her neck the diamond necklace.

Nothing, thought Jeanne in the years that followed, has been quite the same since the affair of the necklace—and if the King had lived and that necklace had been mine, it would have been merely another trinket.

So the years passed—those most dangerous years—yet Jeanne did not realise their danger.

The year 1788 was not memorable to her because the King had decided, as was the custom only on occasions of dire emergency, to call the States-General; it was the year in which she lost three old friends. The first to die was Richelieu; he was ninety-four and people had begun to say that he was immortal. He had been prominent at Court till the end, a grotesque figure, firmly corsetted, his face painted, his calves padded, his eyes ogling in the same manner as they had ogled in the days of Louis XIV.

Little more than a month after Richelieu's passing the Duc d'Aiguillon died, but he had been ill for a long time so that his death was not unexpected.

And in the same year Jeanne's mother died at the age of seventy-five. Jeanne could console herself that since she had been able to look after her Anne had lacked nothing. More than ten years ago, when she could ill afford it, Jeanne had found the money to buy her and Nicolas a house at Villiers-sur-Orge, and had paid 53,000 francs for it.

She could smile tenderly now to recall their pride in it; and how Anne had loved to ride out in her own carriage, and had boasted about her plate.

So life went on and even after the 14th July of the year 1789, when the people rose in the *faubourgs* and marched through the streets of Paris to the Bastille, life at Louveciennes did not immediately change for Jeanne.

In October of that year there occurred the march of the people from Paris to Versailles, and the terrifying and humiliating procession which accompanied the royal family on their enforced drive back to the capital.

Jeanne had forgotten that Marie Antoinette had been far from friendly to her; her pity went out to the proud woman whose extravagances and follies had so incensed the people that there were many who now declared it was her conduct which had led to the present disaster.

It was during this October that certain soldiers, who had been wounded when attempting to protect the King and Queen from the mob, escaped and found their way to Louveciennes.

Jeanne immediately offered hospitality to the fainting men. She ordered her servants to make beds ready for them and prepare food.

In her house the guards were nursed back to health.

When the Queen—a somewhat different woman from the giddy creature who had remarked on the number of people at Versailles to Madame du Barry in the card-room—heard how Jeanne du Barry had cared for the guards, she was touched.

She remembered how unkind she had always been to Louis' mistress and she saw too that Jeanne, in helping the soldiers, had placed herself in danger.

Jeanne was of the people, she had distinguished herself by her kindness to the poor; therefore in this fearful tragedy she had a very good chance of being left in peace. Yet she had endangered that peace in order to save the lives of members of the King's guards.

Marie Antoinette therefore could not allow the gesture to go unnoticed. She sent a message in which she expressed her gratitude.

When Jeanne read the message she wept a little.

"It is so sad," she said to Chon. "You see we can be friends now. Life is so full of sorrow at this time for the Queen. How much pleasanter it would have been if we could have been friends then, when we could all have been so happy."

Acting on impulse she wrote to the Queen. It was a letter in which she expressed her pleasure in hearing from Her Majesty. She declared that it was a delight to her to help those men because their actions had saved the lives of the King and Queen. She placed Louveciennes at the Queen's disposal if she should at any time desire it. She reminded her that before his death, the King had showered gifts upon her as though some presentiment warned him that he would not be long with her. She knew how hard-pressed the Queen was at this time, and she sent her deepest regrets that it should be so. She wished Her Majesty to know, however, that all her wealth was at the Queen's disposal. Gladly would she render to her anything she asked. She, Jeanne du Barry, was Her Majesty's most faithful servant and subject.

Chon read the letter and laughed scornfully at her; and then oddly enough—and perhaps because Chon realised more than did Jeanne how very tragic were these times in which they lived—she broke down suddenly and began to weep.

Jeanne looked at her in surprise, and Chon said: "I am weeping for the Queen and for France, and perhaps for you. May you have all the happiness you deserve, for that is a great deal." Then Chon laughed through her tears. "I laugh because you, my foolish Jeanne, were treated so churlishly by her when she was in a position to treat you so; now when she is brought low and you could abuse her

238

as she has abused you, what do you do: Tell her you are her humble servant, and place all your possessions at her disposal!"

"And that is foolish?" mused Jeanne.

"Perhaps. Who can say? All I know is that it is Jeanne du Barry."

16

THE PLACE DE LA RÉVOLUTION

THE country was seething with revolution but these events did not seem to touch the châtelaine of Louveciennes. Her kindness to the poor of her neighbourhood was often talked of with gratitude. "There was always bread at the *château*." Madame du Barry was rich but she was of the people and she had never forgotten what it was to be poor.

In January of that fateful year 1791 de Brissac gave a fête at his house in the Rue de Grenelle, and Jeanne was invited. The Duke had always kept Jeanne's apartments ready for her in the Rue de Grenelle whenever she should need them, and Jeanne set off in anticipation of a happy stay in the house of her lover.

Chon and Bischi accompanied her, and Chon was aware of the almost desperate attempt of all the guests to enjoy themselves; it was as though they were conscious that there would not be many more opportunities. The King and Queen were now virtually prisoners in the Tuileries whither they had been brought after the terrible and humiliating October drive from Versailles.

It was small wonder that all these people, thought Chon, were determined to enjoy the few hours of pleasure; for who, in these dark days, could be sure that they would not be the last?

Jeanne was very gay that night. Her devoted and dearly beloved de Brissac had been her lover for more than ten years. It was a long time—a period of serene joy to put a bridge between the present and the past which held sad memories.

Jeanne was approaching fifty—although she only confessed to being in her early forties. Even so, people were astonished that one could look so young, for her hair was as fair and abundant as ever, her eyes as lively; she was more restrained than she had been as a young girl and her manners would have caused no complaint at the Versailles of Louis XV. She had spent so many years with the nobility as her friends and constant companions that she had become as one of them.

It was the morning after the fête in the Rue de Grenelle that a messenger came riding there.

He asked to be taken immediately to Madame du Barry; and when he was in Jeanne's presence he cried: "Madame, thieves have broken into Louveciennes during your absence. I fear a great deal has been stolen."

Jeanne, in alarm, hurried back to Louveciennes, where, to her dismay, she found that much of her valuable jewellery had disappeared.

She went into immediate consultation with her jeweller and her notary. These people seemed to have no understanding of the mood of the country for they arranged that notices should be posted in the streets of Paris offering a reward of 2,000 louis for a return of the missing jewellery. The list of jewels was printed below the reward. There were necklaces, rings, bracelets, brooches, set with emeralds, sapphires, rubies and diamonds. Anyone discovering the whereabouts of any of these jewels was to report at once to the jeweller, to the notary or to Madame du Barry at Louveciennes.

About the notices the hungry people of Paris clustered. The extravagance of royalty was recalled. This Madame du Barry had received these valuable jewels, the price of which would have kept many a family in food for the whole of their lives, from Louis XV who had lived in luxury while the people starved.

Those who were most bitter were the women, their crying children clutching at their skirts, their own bodies wasted through lack of food, their once youthful freshness gone for ever in the dreadful fight against poverty.

After that when people talked of the aristocrats Madame du Barry's name was often mentioned.

The thieves were discovered in London, and in the company of the Chevalier d'Escourt, who was adjutant to the Duc de Brissac, and several servants, Jeanne set out for that city in order to recover them.

This she failed to do during a three months' stay; but she was not disheartened, as she was sure that eventually the jewels would be in her possession once more, and in the meantime she was well received in London society. Many *émigrés* were already settled there and she joined their company; on account of her beauty, charm, wealth and interesting history she was a welcome guest in the highest society.

She was seen at Ranelagh; her portrait was painted by Cosway; and when she rode about the streets of London and saw the poverty of certain of its inhabitants she gave alms in such a generous manner that she became the talk of the back streets as well as of the Court.

Proceedings against the robbers were long drawn-out and Jeanne grew homesick for France and her lover; therefore she returned to Louveciennes in April.

But no sooner had she returned than she was told that her presence was needed once more in London, and back to London she went. There she remained only for a few days, but when she returned to France she was again recalled to London.

She was not in France during the tragic flight of the King

and Queen to Varennes; she saw nothing of the journey of the royal family from Varennes to Paris. She was un-aware that the temper of the revolutionaries was grow-ing more and more dangerous, and that her name was often mentioned in the papers. When orators were urging the people to greater revolutionary efforts in the Palais Royal, her name was frequently mentioned. Jeanne du Barry had ceased to be the friend of the people; she had consorted with the aristocrats; she was rich, as the recent robbery showed; she was fast becoming an enemy of the people.

The robbers were acquitted in the English courts since the theft had been committed in France and therefore the affair was outside English jurisdiction. The jewels were recovered but there were many formalities to be gone through before they could be restored to Jeanne, and she must prove that they were hers.

In August she returned once more to France, still without the jewels.

Events in France were moving rapidly towards a climax. Louis XVI was still called King but he was the prisoner of the State, and the Legislative Assembly insisted that a Con-stitutional Guard should be appointed. He was allowed to select a certain number of those who made up the guard, and naturally he chose his old friend de Brissac as com-mander of the household brigade.

The revolutionary leaders had long marked de Brissac as an aristocrat; his participation in the affair of the robbery had not made the people love him any more. The guillotine was hungry and it was men such as the Duc de Brissac who the revolutionaries had decided should give it the blood it needed.

It was so easy to trump up charges against him. His enemies complained that he did not act as guard of the King;

that he was a friend of the King and the friends of Kings were enemies of the people.

De Brissac, who was so much more aware of danger than Jeanne, knew that at any moment he would be seized.

It was Chon who brought her the news.

She was walking across the park at Louveciennes and thinking, as she sometimes did, of the days when it had been merely a pavilion, a place in which she and the King entertained their friends; now it had become home to her. She had made the spacious reception-rooms more cosy, and if she had not been conscious of the sense of impending doom which seemed to hang over everyone and everything, she could have looked upon Louveciennes as the home in which she would live out a peaceful old age.

Chon hurried across the grass to her and Chon's face was ashen.

Chon said: "He has been arrested and taken to Orléans."

"Arrested! But . . . on what grounds?"

"Treason."

"It is impossible. He is no traitor."

"He is an aristocrat, my sister; and that, in these terrible days, is tantamount to being a traitor."

She was determined to save him.

"We will leave at once for Orléans," she told Chon. "I will find some way to help him. I will arrange his escape, and then we shall go to London. There I have many friends and so has he."

Chon shook her head. "Do you not see, sister, that you should have taken him to London months ago? And you should never have come back."

"You are right," said Jeanne. "But it is not too late. I will get him out of prison, I assure you I will."

"How?"

"With money," said Jeanne. "All these stout revolutionaries, who love liberty, equality and fraternity so much, love money even more. You will see."

Jeanne was right. Money brought an interview with her lover.

He took her into his arms when he saw her, but she was impatient. She had plans. There must be no delay. They would leave at once for London, she told him.

He looked at her sadly. "Do you think there is escape for me, Jeanne? No. I should never get out of France. I have to stand my trial."

"Then you will be proved innocent. What have you done to be called a traitor?"

"I have served the King. I am a member of one of those families which they have determined to destroy."

"But we waste time," said Jeanne. "We can leave. I have bribed the jailor. I am rich, as you know. We will go to London. We will stay with Grenier at his hotel in Jermyn Street where there are many such as we are."

But de Brissac shook his head. "We should be caught. You know the punishment for those who try to run away. They would take you, Jeanne, too. I would not risk that."

"There are always risks in life."

"There were never such risks as there are now in France. I belong here, Jeanne. I belong to the old *régime*. You . . . are different. There are many years left to you. It is for you to go to London. It is for you to make a new life there."

"I shall take you with me. When you have stood your trial they will free you. They must. For what have you done to be called a traitor?"

"After my trial," he said gently, "perhaps, my love, we shall be together."

And so she was forced to leave him.

.   .   .   .   .

Excitement at this time in Paris was growing to fever pitch. It was June and the first storming of the Tuileries had taken place.

A few prisoners had escaped from the jail in which de Brissac was being held in Orléans, and it was decided to take him to Paris.

De Brissac knew that his end was near. He had heard that the mobs which were roaming the streets of the capital were composed not of Parisians but largely of ruffians from the south who had come into Paris to loot and murder.

He was aware that the old *régime* was passing; and on his last night in Orléans he wrote to Jeanne.

". . . I kiss you a thousand times. My last thoughts will be of you. . . . Why cannot I be with you in a desert? Since I am only able to be in Orléans where it is very uncomfortable to be, I kiss you a thousand times. Adieu, dear heart. . . ."

The next morning he was put into a cart with other prisoners and so began his journey to Paris. All along the route the rabble threatened the prisoners, and shouts of "Death to the aristocrats" were hurled at them. The journey took four days, and on the arrival in Paris the furious mob declared that they would not wait for trials and orderly executions.

They picked him out from the prisoners. He was so tall and he had an air of aloof dignity—the hall-mark of the aristocrat—which never failed to infuriate.

"There is de Brissac," they cried. "We will have him." And as the people fell upon the prisoners de Brissac heard his name repeated again and again in accents of fury.

He sought to defend himself; but what use was that against so many?

Chon saw the mob marching towards the house. They

seemed orderly; they were singing one of the songs of the Revolution.

Jeanne had run to the window.

"What do they want?" she said. Then she saw it. It was held aloft for her to see. There on a pike was the head of her lover.

"Chon!" cried Jeanne; and the faithful arms of her sister-in-law were waiting to catch her as she fell.

The Revolution had come to Louveciennes.

She was heartbroken. Life, which had always seemed so full of promise to her, was drear and full of foreboding.

Events were moving to a climax of which no one could see the outcome. For the second time the Tuileries had been stormed and the royal family imprisoned in the Temple. The terrible September massacres had occurred in which had perished so horribly the Queen's friend, the Princesse de Lamballe.

There was apprehension too terrible to be examined all about her. At last she could no longer believe in the good fortune life had to offer. She had seen the mutilated head of her lover, and she confessed to herself that the world was a cruel place.

She was writing a letter to one of her friends.

"I am in a state of suffering that you will easily understand. The ghastly crime has made me thus. It has left me with an eternal sorrow and I feel my grief at every moment. . . ."

She looked up and saw a figure coming across the lawn. She had never seen the man before. When he had come close to the window and looked in at her, she started to her feet in horror. Every stranger nowadays might be a murderer.

He bowed.

Oh God, she thought, he has an evil face, this man.

She went to the window and spoke to him.

"Your business, monsieur?"

"I am a neighbour of yours, Madame. I called to pay my respects."

She felt relieved. "Then pray come in."

Her servants brought him to her and she offered him refreshment. He talked easily and pleasantly in fluent French although he had a slight foreign accent.

"You are English," she said. "It is scarcely noticeable. You speak our tongue so well."

He admitted that he was English. He was engaged in literary work. He had translated Franklin, Washington and Priestley into French.

"That must be very interesting," she told him. "But what do you do in France during these sad times, monsieur?"

"France is the most interesting of countries at this time," he answered her.

She discovered his name was George Greive and that he was lodging at a near-by inn.

"I trust," he said, "that you will forgive my calling on you thus informally, but these are informal times, are they not?"

"Alas," she answered.

"Knowing that I was so near the famous Madame du Barry I could not resist calling."

"That was kind of you," she said.

When he took his leave, she was glad.

Zamor came into her room, and she said to him in her impulsive way: "Ugh! I am glad he has gone. I did not like him."

"Did you not, Madame?" said Zamor. *He* had liked the gentleman very well, as he had been generously tipped by him. Zamor's lips curled a little. Madame thought herself too grand to receive those who were less than dukes. But times were changing; Madame would understand that one day.

George Greive called often and Jeanne began to understand why. Chon and Bischi knew too.

"That man imagines he will become your lover," said Chon.

"He will only be that in his imagination," retorted Jeanne sharply.

"There is something sinister about him," said Bischi; "when he looks my way he sends shivers down my spine."

"One of these days," Jeanne said, "I shall ask him not to call."

"Have a care," cried Chon quickly. "One cannot make enemies at such times as these."

But when George Greive came the next time Jeanne did not heed her sister-in-law's warning.

And when he tried to make love to her she pushed him away, unable to hide her revulsion.

"Madame is proud," said the man with a sneer.

"She is not," answered Jeanne. "She merely has no love for you."

"Having squandered so much of it on kings and dukes?" asked the man.

"Monsieur Greive, I must ask you to go away."

"Do not imagine that you can dismiss me like that. You are not the favoured mistress of a king now, you know; nor of a duke."

"I understand that perfectly. Will you go and never come here again. If you attempt to, I shall have you forcibly removed from my house."

He laughed bitterly and cruelly. "I see," he said, "that I am not handsome, nor royal enough, to aspire to your bed. But—have you forgotten something, my fine lady? Have you forgotten that the times are changing?"

He left her then. Chon and Bischi, when they heard what had happened, were worried. But Jeanne refused to allow the man to disturb her, and shortly afterwards she forgot him, for there was more news from London. The reward for the recovery of the jewels had been claimed by a Jewish jeweller of London to whom the jewels had been offered; he it was who had denounced the thieves. The jeweller was asking more than the reward of 2,000 louis offered and therefore Jeanne's presence in London was urgently needed.

She was glad to leave France which, since the death of her lover, had become a melancholy place to her, so she decided to go to England at once.

How different was this stay in London from the last! Now she had no heart for gaiety. There were no more happy days spent at Ranelagh; no more dinner-parties. Her days were passed in visiting *émigrés* and discussing the terrible happenings in their country.

Several months passed in this way while the news from France grew more and more alarming. October, November, had come and gone, and in December Louis XVI, King of France, was brought to trial.

In England Jeanne, with her friends, waited eagerly for news, and on that day in January when Louis made his last journey through the streets of his capital and finally came to rest in the Place de la Révolution she shed many tears, remembering him—that *gros enfant mal élevé* who had so disliked her when she had been the beloved mistress of his grandfather.

She went to the funeral service at the Spanish Embassy Chapel, for such services were held at every Catholic church in London in honour of France's martyr.

Had Chon been with her she would have commented on her folly, for there were many spies in England, in the very heart of that little colony of *émigrés*.

Her friends warned: "Do not go back to France. It would be folly to return."

"You are right," she said.

But she knew she would go back. She had known when she had first seen Paris that she would never wish to be far from it. It was a different Paris now; but it was still her home.

And so she returned to France, to Louveciennes where the sinister George Greive was her neighbour and where there were spies in her own household.

"You were a fool to come," Chon told her angrily. "Do you not realise that people, such as you, are doing all in their power to escape from France? Yet you, safe in England, return to . . . God knows what."

"This is my home," said Jeanne. "I could never be happy away from it."

"Pray God," said Chon earnestly, "that you will be allowed to be happy in it."

She stood at her window, looking out over the lawns where once she had walked with Louis, and when she saw them coming she knew why they came.

From the moment she had seen the man she had sensed that he was evil; he had sought to be her lover and, because she had repulsed him, he had determined to bring her to this end.

In vain had he tried to stir the people of Louveciennes to rise against her. That was impossible; they remembered the hundred kindnesses they had received; but in Paris it was a different matter. There was a mob in Paris which asked to be inflamed.

So to Paris George Greive had gone demanding: "Death to the courtesan of Louveciennes, the friend of kings and aristocrats!"

He was at the head of those who now came to arrest her. He kicked open the door of her room and came striding to her, the evil smile on the face which he now put close to hers.

She stood unflinching.

"You do not ask what I want now, Citizeness," he said.

"I think," said Jeanne, "that I know."

Her beauty inflamed him suddenly; he seized her in a furious embrace. Angrily she fought him off, and exultantly he matched his strength with hers.

He threw her on to a couch; she tore at his hair and his coat. "Not this!" she panted. "I would rather die. . . ."

She cried out with relief and pleasure as the gendarmes whom Greive had brought with him came into the room. Shamefacedly Greive drew away from the couch, and with dignity which she had acquired during her years at Versailles Jeanne rose to her feet.

Greive shouted in a sudden burst of frustrated fury: "Take the woman to the prisoners' cart. Take her to Paris and put her with her fellow prisoners in Sainte-Pélagie."

So this was the end of the beautiful Jeanne du Barry. They had tried her and found her to be "an enemy of the people".

They cut off the luxuriant curls and put about her the coarse robe which those condemned to die must wear on the way to the guillotine.

She, who had so loved life, could not believe even at this late hour that her life was nearly over. She was relieved to think that Chon and Bischi would be able to go back to Lévignac. It was with great sorrow that she remembered Zamor whom she had once petted and whom she had taught to read and write, for he it was who had added his voice to that of Greive and assured the tribunal that she was the friend of aristocrats, that she helped the *émigrés* and plotted against the Revolution. Ungrateful Zamor!

But all those about her now believed she had but a few hours left. She thought over that spectacular journey of hers from Labille's to Versailles, and from Versailles to the guillotine. Jean, the Comte du Barry, who had been the first to lead her there, had laid his head on the guillotine only this year. She had wept for him; he had died with a nonchalance that won the grudging admiration of the crowd; he died like the aristocrat he had always striven to be.

In October, but two months earlier, proud Marie Antoinette had laid her head under the knife.

So many deaths, and still the people clamoured for more. It was tragic to think of her lost friends; yet it was incredible that she herself should die.

But now that they were ready for her, now that the tumbril was waiting and she must take her last journey through the streets of Paris, a terrible fear came to her. She could no longer turn away from the truth.

As she rode through the familiar streets a voice in the crowd shouted: "There she goes! A king's courtesan! To the death! To the guillotine!"

But not Jeanne du Barry! She wanted to cry: What harm have I done? I have loved the people. Ask those of Saint Vrain. Ask those of Louveciennes.

But they would ask no one; they would believe no one. The hungry guillotine was waiting and it could not have enough of the blood of aristocrats.

But I am of the people, she wanted to cry. I belong to the people. I always did. I always shall.

Ah, she answered herself, but you lived among them; you learned their ways; they made you one of them. This is the price you must pay, Jeanne du Barry, for the life of luxury and ease that has been yours.

But for her beauty it would never have happened to her. She had been raised to a position of power by a King on account of her beauty; and she had been brought to the guillotine by an informer on account of her beauty.

She looked at the faces of women in the crowd, women who watched her with atavistic hate, women who had once envied her and now demanded she should pay for the splendour which had been hers.

There was Labille's. The girls were standing on the balcony, their faces pinched by the biting December wind.

"There she goes," they told each other, "the fabulous du Barry who was once one of us!"

She called to them as she passed: "I have done no harm. Save me! Give me my life and I will give up all else."

"That which you once had is no longer yours to give up," jeered a voice in the crowd. "It has gone where it rightly belongs . . . to the nation."

Even at that time her beauty had retained its appeal, for suddenly a man in the crowd drove his fist into the face of the man who had said those words.

But the tumbril rattled on.

She mounted the steps; the great knife was above her head. She looked across the square; and because the trees were bare she could see the grey stones of the Louvre.

She must now say her farewell to her beloved city, and she remembered fleetingly those days when her mother had taken her out in the early mornings to the markets.

Paris! The teeming life of that city had touched something which was essentially vital in herself. She wanted to go on living. Here under the shadow of the great knife she wanted to hold off death.

"Give me one moment," she whispered. "One more moment to be alive . . . in Paris."

But the tumbrils would continue to roll through the streets of Paris and the guillotine was waiting.

She struggled. She was no aristocrat to die as though she

cared nothing for death. She wanted to live . . . passionately she wanted to live.

"Messieurs . . ." she began. "Help me . . . Messieurs. . . ."

But there was no help. The knife descended, severing the beautiful head from that body which had once enchanted a King of France.

THE END

THE REGENT'S DAUGHTER (Princess Charlotte)
GODDESS OF THE GREEN ROOM (Dorothy Jordan and William IV)
VICTORIA IN THE WINGS (End of the Georgian Era)

The Queen Victoria Series
THE CAPTIVE OF KENSINGTON PALACE (Early days of Victoria)
THE QUEEN AND LORD M (Victoria and Lord Melbourne)
THE QUEEN'S HUSBAND (Victoria and Albert)
THE WIDOW OF WINDSOR (Last years of Victoria's Reign)

The Ferdinand and Isabella Trilogy
CASTILE FOR ISABELLA
SPAIN FOR THE SOVEREIGNS   } Also available in one volume:
DAUGHTER OF SPAIN   ISABELLA AND FERDINAND

The Lucrezia Borgia Series
MADONNA OF THE SEVEN HILLS } Also available in one volume:
LIGHT ON LUCREZIA   LUCREZIA BORGIA

The Medici Trilogy
MADAME SERPENT
THE ITALIAN WOMAN   } Also available in one volume:
QUEEN JEZEBEL   CATHERINE DE'MEDICI

Henri of Navarre
EVERGREEN GALLANT

The French Revolution Series
LOUIS THE WELL-BELOVED
THE ROAD TO COMPIEGNE
FLAUNTING, EXTRAVAGANT QUEEN

The Queens of England Series
MYSELF MY ENEMY (Henrietta Maria)
QUEEN OF THIS REALM (Elizabeth I)
VICTORIA VICTORIOUS (Victoria)
THE LADY IN THE TOWER (Anne Boleyn)
THE COURTS OF LOVE (Eleanor of Aquitaine)
IN THE SHADOW OF THE CROWN (Mary Tudor)
THE QUEEN'S SECRET (Katherine of Valois)
THE RELUCTANT QUEEN (Anne Neville)
THE PLEASURES OF LOVE (Catherine Braganza)
WILLIAM'S WIFE (William & Mary)
ROSE WITHOUT A THORN (Katherine Howard)

General historical novels
BEYOND THE BLUE MOUNTAINS
THE GOLDSMITH'S WIFE
THE SCARLET CLOAK
DEFENDERS OF THE FAITH
DAUGHTER OF SATAN

Stories of Victorian England
IT BEGAN IN VAUXHALL GARDENS
LILITH

Non-Fiction
MARY QUEEN OF SCOTS: *The Fair Devil of Scotland*
A TRIPTYCH OF POISONERS
(Cesare Borgia, Madame de Brinvilliers and Dr Pritchard)
THE RISE OF THE SPANISH INQUISITION
THE GROWTH OF THE SPANISH INQUISITION
THE END OF THE SPANISH INQUISITION